P9-DBT-218

THE
REDEEMED

TIM PEARS

THE REDEEMED

BLOOMSBURY PUBLISHING

NEW YORK · LONDON · OXFORD · NEW DELHI · SYDNEY

BLOOMSBURY PUBLISHING
Bloomsbury Publishing Inc.
1385 Broadway, New York, NY 10018, USA

BLOOMSBURY, BLOOMSBURY PUBLISHING, and the Diana logo
are trademarks of Bloomsbury Publishing Plc

First published in 2019 in Great Britain
First published in the United States 2019

Bloomsbury Publishing Plc does not have any control over, or responsibility for,
any third-party websites referred to or in this book. All internet addresses given
in this book were correct at the time of going to press. The author and publisher
regret any inconvenience caused if addresses have changed or sites have ceased to
exist, but can accept no responsibility for any such changes.

ISBN: HB: 978-1-63557-382-4; EBOOK: 978-1-63557-383-1

Library of Congress Cataloging-in-Publication Data is available

2 4 6 8 10 9 7 5 3 1

Typeset by Integra Software Services Pvt. Ltd.
Printed and bound in the U.S.A. by Berryville Graphics Inc., Berryville, Virginia

To find out more about our authors and books visit www.bloomsbury.com and sign
up for our newsletters.

Bloomsbury books may be purchased for business or promotional use.
For information on bulk purchases please contact Macmillan Corporate and
Premium Sales Department at specialmarkets@macmillan.com.

Gladys Whittle, née Sercombe, cousin of Leo, housekeeper at
the big house
Sidney Sercombe, Leo's brother, head keeper on the estate
Gracie, Sid's wife, and their children Stanley and Elsie
Levi Hicks, gypsy horse dealer

Principal Characters

Leopold (Leo) Sercombe
Charlotte (Lottie) Prideaux

The Battle:
Willy Burd, stoker
Jimmy White, boy seaman
Lieutenant Pyne, 'Y' Turret officer
Petty Officer Jeffers
Sergeant Nutley

The Vet:
Patrick Jago, veterinary surgeon
Herb Shattock, Lord Prideaux's head groom
Arthur, Lord Prideaux, Lottie's father, owner of the estate
Alice, Lady Prideaux, Arthur's second wife
Duncan, Lord Grenvil, Arthur Prideaux's friend, Alice's father
Maud, Lady Grenvil, Duncan's wife

The Scuttle:
Able Seaman Victor Harris
Jamie Watt, Orcadian boy horseman

The Salvage:
Ernest Cox, entrepreneur
Tom McKenzie, Bill Peterson, Sinclair MacKenzie, divers

The Grey Thoroughbred:
Muriel Furst, Lottie's fellow student

The Return:
Wally Luscombe, farmer
Agnes, Ethel and Myrtle, his daughters
William Carew, ex-estate manager, war veteran
Helena Carew, William's sister

For Hania

'Fear not, for I have redeemed you;
I have called you by name, you are mine.
When you pass through the waters, I will be with you;
and through the rivers, they shall not overwhelm you;
when you walk through fire you shall not be burned,
and the flame shall not consume you'

Isaiah, 43: 1–2

Part One

THE BATTLE
1916

I

6 a.m., Monday 29 May 1916

His Majesty's Ship *Queen Mary* was a coal-firing battlecruiser. When, every few months, she ran low on coal, she required a delivery of three thousand tons. Today was such a day. The crew were woken early. Leo Sercombe and the other boys smeared their eyelids and eyelashes with margarine or Vaseline, and poked it up their nostrils.

When Leo was a child he thought his father a hard taskmaster. Albert Sercombe ruled the stables with a rod of iron and the men who worked the horses bent to his will. But there were only four of them. On this battlecruiser well over a thousand men and boys were crowded. There were endless rules, discipline was rigid and strictly enforced. It was unbearably oppressive until you accepted it.

Yet coaling days were different. It was like no other drill or job. All hands were piped 'clean into coaling rig' and could wear what they liked. Men attired themselves in overalls, dinner jackets, plus fours. One officer was kitted out in his red hunting jacket, jodhpurs and riding boots. What had ever made him consider these worth bringing on board, Leo could not fathom. Perhaps he wanted to be reminded of horses. One old seaman wore a dress. On their heads perched equally odd coverings: a topper, a turban, berets, bandanas, three-cornered tricornes. Everyone on board took part, excepting only the captain, the medics and the paymaster. Even the schoolies and the chaplain had to join in. It was like a party. Except the participants did not dance. They worked.

The collier ship was made secure alongside. Four gangs from HMS *Queen Mary* were allocated to each hold. A gang was made up of four men and one boy, one gang to each corner. They scrambled down onto the collier. As a boy seaman, Leo did not shovel coal. He was not yet strong enough. Instead he held a bag for the men, who in their haste to fill it thwacked his knuckles. Each bag when full weighed two hundredweight. Ten bags thus made up a one-ton hoist. The hoists were swung to the decks of the *Queen Mary* by derricks.

On the decks of the ship each bag was transferred from the hoist to a barrow, wheeled to a chute and emptied. At the bottom of the chute Willy Burd and the other stokers loaded coal into the bunkers.

As the derrick came back round to the hold of the collier, if the next ten bags were not ready for the hoist the other gangs let that corner have it.

It was back-breaking work with barely a pause, for the gangs were in competition with each other. A fanny or jug of lime juice was passed around. Leo blew the coal-dust scum away from the surface and drank. There was a thirty-minute break for lunch: two slabs of bread

4

with bacon or cheese washed down with a basin of tea. Then the men lay down on the decks, eyes closed, till they were piped back to work.

Every hour, signal flags were hoisted at the yard arms, indicating how many tons of coal had been stowed during the previous hour. Today, the whole squadron was coaling together, across the Firth of Forth, so that competition was all the more intense, between as well as within ships. Vast clouds of filthy black powder rose from the holds and from the ship's bunkers, settling everywhere. The Royal Marine Band, perched precariously on top of the centre gun turret, played 'The Sailor's Hornpipe', 'Drunken Sailor' and other sea shanties, with soot rising around them and their instruments, until they all resembled coloured minstrels from the music halls.

The air was thick with suffocating dust. Leo could not imagine what it was like for Willy down in the bunkers. By six o'clock in the evening these were filled. All hands now turned to washing down the ship from truck to keel. A tug steamed slowly around the vessel, washing down the upper works with high-pressure hoses.

When the *Queen Mary* was clean the hands could go below to wash themselves and their clothes. There were no showers. Boys were given one bucket of cold water between four of them. Afterwards coal dust stuck for days to those who'd smeared their eyebrows and eyelashes with Vaseline, and they looked to Leo like some odd species of owl.

2

9 a.m., Tuesday 30 May

The ship lay at anchor in the Firth of Forth. On the day following the coaling, after morning division, HMS *Queen Mary* was prepared for gymnastics. Older men, those over thirty-five, were excused, and instead kept busy rigging different sets of apparatus across the upper deck of the battlecruiser for their younger colleagues. All the other hands fell out and made their way, by divisions, to different exercise stations. The bugler played a G note, and gymnastics began. Leo Sercombe's division climbed onto the roof of the casemate for the four-inch guns, on the forecastle deck. On its port side a horizontal climbing rope had been erected, from hooks screwed into metal stanchions. The boys took turns wriggling along it.

The night had been cool but the sun was rising bright and burned off the last of the mist that clung to the water. Battlecruisers and other ships lay at anchor all up and down the Firth, placid as rocky outcrops in the unruffled tide. When the bugler played a G note again the boys' division climbed down to the deck and, one after another, jumped over the horse. Then they moved round the bows to the tug-of-war, and on to the trapeze, to parallel bars, to Swedish drill, shifting around the ship each time the bugler played the note.

Leo spent the afternoon on a wooden platform slung by ropes over the side, painting the upper hull. Seawater corrosion meant that hands were continually redecorating their ship. Chipping away flaking grey paint, sanding the surface, applying a fresh coat. One part or another always stank of fresh linseed and turpentine.

Now and again Leo glanced behind him at the leisurely pace of activity across the estuary. A collier cast off from a destroyer depot-ship. Picket boats traced overlapping lines between cruisers and shore as if weaving some intricate watery thread. A tug chugged upstream towing a line of barges, only the smoke belching from its squat funnel indicating the strain it was under. An oiler berthed beside one of the new battleships that had oil-fired engines. Long tubes connected the two vessels. Pumps began to inject the fuel into the great ship as if with a fresh infusion of blood.

It was almost 6 p.m. Some of the officers were yet to return from an afternoon ashore, in Rosyth or Edinburgh. Leo cleaned his paintbrushes in white spirit. Jimmy White was polishing brasses. His hands were black and his face too for he was forever scratching a tickle or wiping off sweat. Leo gazed periodically out over the starboard side, to Queensferry, and beyond, where the vague bluish shapes of the Pentland Hills rose in the far distance. Jimmy must have noticed for he said, 'Ain't you never goin to get used to bein a seaman?

You looks like a maid peekin at the land like 'er lover boy's over there.'

Leo smiled and turned back to his brushes. 'I like the lie of it,' he said. 'Can you not imagine ridin up into they hills?'

Jimmy did not reply to this but said instead, 'Aye, aye. Here we go.' The boy turned and looked up and watched as a long string of flags was hoisted from the masthead of the *Lion*. Activity around him on the lower deck ceased as others noticed too. When the string settled, Jimmy said, '*Raise steam for twenty-two knots. Bank fires at half an hour's notice*. Looks like we're off on another bloody exercise, mate.'

A bugle call augmented the flags. It was played aboard the *Queen Mary*. With ships anchored beyond Rosyth up as far as Charlestown, Leo now heard the faint echoing notes of their bugles, like Canada geese calling to each other across the estuary.

Leo and the other painters stowed their equipment. The crew formed in divisions on deck. Leo's job while raising steam was in the team weighing anchor. Other seamen in his division hoisted a boat inboard. There was no frantic commotion. Each officer and hand knew his role, having performed it many times. Watertight compartments were closed, gangways raised. Men uncovered the guns and the searchlights. Jimmy's job was passing slip-wires at the buoys.

Down below, the stokers got busy at the boilers. Smoke rose from the funnels. Leo's pal Willy Burd was a stoker. He was two years older than Leo, four inches shorter but twice as strong, all muscle. One of five hundred stokers to power the battlecruiser's coal-fired engines, Willy had trained in the Portsmouth Naval Barracks, shovelling stones instead of coal into disused boilers. Leo himself had undergone basic drills in the bunkers and stokehold, as every boy had to do, and he had no intention of going down there when he was fully grown.

Yet his friend, inexplicably, loved the arduous labour. There were two classes of stoker. Willy was second class and a trimmer, or lumper, running the coal in a wheelbarrow from the bunkers to the boiler rooms. The first-class stokers were firemen, who either hurled coal into the furnace or, wielding nine-foot-long pokers, shook and broke up the mass of clinker while a colleague held a shovel in front of the furnace door to protect the fireman's face from the heat. The temperature in the boiler room, furnaces roaring, reached a hundred and fifty degrees. The firemen sprayed fuel oil on the coal to increase its burn rate. The fire bed flamed to a white heat. They wore blue-tinted glasses, and were scalded frequently.

The ship had forty-two boilers, arranged in seven boiler rooms, to drive her huge steam turbines. Willy was proud of these engines and informed Leo that they were capable of seventy-five thousand horsepower, to overcome the vast inertia of their massive battlecruiser and then to drive her through the water. 'That means the strength of seventy-five thousand horses. Not little ponies either,' he'd told Leo. 'Your gurt big carthorses, boy.'

Leo was in the starboard anchor team. Each huge anchor weighed ten tons, and was winched into the anchor bay by a capstan engine, the great chain links clinking together and crunching tight.

Three hours after the flags had been hoisted, the fleet moved through the Firth of Forth at dusk: six battle-cruisers and four of the mighty dreadnoughts. Leo had never been aboard one but Jimmy White told him they carried crews of three thousand men. It was hard to imagine.

There was one seaplane carrier, and all the light cruisers and destroyers. Four thousand yards' distance was kept between the rear ship of one squadron and the leading ship of the next. They sailed under the bridge and past Edinburgh and Leith on their starboard beam. Though the engines hummed and throbbed, Leo had grown so used to the sound that it was as if the fleets sailed silently out onto the ocean with the only noise the swish of the waves. He could feel the churning of the screws, a vibration all through the ship's thirty thousand tons as she gathered way. Ahead of them the minesweepers cleared a safe passage, as they set off on this the latest of their customary sweeps of the North Sea.

Willy would be sweating down below but Leo was still in the anchor bay shivering with cold, for in case of emergency the anchors had to be kept ready for letting go until the ship was clear of harbour. Finally, the order was given and they cranked the anchor home into its hawse-pipe. The chain was hove taut and secured, and Leo and the rest of his crew climbed up from the bay.

3

1 a.m., Wednesday 31 May

The mess-decks never lost the odour of unappetising food slowly cooking. The ventilation system, from whose fan motors came a faint perpetual hum, issued forth stale air. On winter nights coal stoves were lit and the crew slung their hammocks, hung snugly together. Men learned to sleep on their backs. The atmosphere became dense and suffocating, thick with condensation, which sweated on the casings and dripped onto the bodies of the snoring men.

Summer was now upon them. Leo was one of the first to request to sleep outside, in the open air. Hooks had been inserted all over the casings for this purpose. There were two cats on board the ship. The older one, a big black beast they called Billy Bones, ignored Leo, but the younger one, Jane Hawkins, sought him out. She sprang into his hammock and curled up on his belly. Leo scratched her behind the ears, and she purred her approval.

Leo had kept a space beside him, and when Willy's night shift was done his friend climbed up from below and came outside.

'Still awake?' he whispered.

'Aye,' Leo said. The cat raised itself up, annoyed at this intrusion, and jumped down from the hammock.

'Off to catch herself a rat,' Leo said. He asked Willy whether he had noticed anything different down below.

'Coal's the same colour as it usually is, if that's what you're askin,' Willy said.

Leo said he thought he'd detected a certain nervousness in one or two officers. Like they had been told something the men had not, and were trying to hide it. Willy said this was wishful thinking. Leo was an optimist and a dreamer. This voyage was just another flap. Another stunt. Down in the lower holds where the likes of Leo never went it felt the same as ever. Leo should not get his hopes up.

'I don't hope for nothin.'

'Don't you want action? All you gunners do. Everyone up above does.'

'I ain't everyone.'

They lay in their hammocks. There were a few others sleeping out, scattered across the deck, some snoring. After a while Willy, speaking quietly so as not to disturb them, asked Leo what his friend did want.

'I've got a mind to apply to be a diver,' Leo said. 'I liked goin underwater when I was a boy, and I reckon I could work down there.'

Willy did not reply at first. Perhaps he was trying to imagine what it was like beneath the surface of the ocean. Then he said, 'Not for me, mate. Down in the bunkers we're already workin below the waterline. A single torpedo in the wrong spot'll do for us. We're close enough to water where we are. I don't want to get no closer.'

They lay in their hammocks, the sky open above them, black and sparkling with pinpricks of light.

'I was speculatin,' Leo said. 'There's lads in the trenches a northern France lookin up at these same stars tonight. My brother Sid, a gamekeeper on the estate I grew up on … if he ain't been called up he might be out trampin the woods, and pausin to contemplate 'em too.' He studied the stars himself. 'There's a girl back there who could be standin on the roof of her house right now, gazin on the same sky.'

Willy said his mother's latest letter informed him that two more lads from their street in Bristol had gone missing in action in Flanders, presumed dead. She wrote of how glad she was that he'd joined the Royal Navy.

Leo agreed they'd made a wise choice. The only worry he had was about once their service was over – how they'd adjust to life on dry land.

'We'll relish it,' Willy said, yawning. 'Don't you worry about that, mate. We'll relish it for the rest of our lives.'

Leo pondered this welcome prospect. But another misgiving arose. 'I fears I'll have forgot which end of a horse is which,' he said.

'You're the oddest mixture of a man I've come across,' Willy told him. 'Tomorrow you're not bothered about, but you worry over what might come to pass in ten years' time.'

Leo smiled to himself. 'And you, Willy,' he said. 'What'll you be good for? A stoker on a train?'

Leo waited for a reply, but when it came it was not in words but snores instead. He closed his eyes. Even soothed by the motion of the big ship, he found it difficult to get to sleep. He could not say why he was nervous. He was sixteen years old, and he was one of thirty-four boy seamen on HMS *Queen Mary*. The full crew of officers, men and boys numbered one thousand two hundred and eighty-six. Numbers placated his unsettled nerves. He ran the other ranks on board through his mind. There were thirteen midshipmen. Three surgeons. Thirty-three petty officers. One chaplain, the loneliest man on board. One sailmaker, a remnant, in this age of steam. Five signal boys. One plumber and two plumber's mates. Leo's anxiety eased. The numbers made him drowsy. One cooper. Two blacksmiths. But no horses. Two blacksmith's mates. This ship was no place for horses. Only for cooks and stewards. And musicians. There were a dozen band members, plus the two buglers ...

The boy slept.

4

7 a.m., Wednesday 31 May

On the huge vessel pounding across the sea the day dawned grey and cold. After Leo had lashed and stowed his hammock, the boy made his way to the upper deck, trousers turned up to the knees, bare-chested. Jostling with other boys, he washed at one of the large water butts, then presented himself for inspection. The petty officer passed him and Leo went down to the mess-deck and poured himself a basin of thick hot cocoa from the kettle and took a biscuit. He consumed these while standing.

Back up, Leo joined a line of boys strung across a deck, armed with long-handled scrubbers. Water was hosed over the boards and the leading seaman yelled, 'Scrub forward. Scrub aft,' and so they worked in rhythm. Then they mopped up the water and dried the deck and finally went down to breakfast. Leo was hungry, as they all were, the more so now that they were at sea. The others wolfed their food, but Leo ate his porridge methodically, and drank sweet tea. As his fellow eaters rose from the table, others squeezed into their places on the bench. They smelled of damp serge and mothballs. Leo spread his cube of margarine on a half loaf, and ate it patiently.

'Come on, bumpkin boy,' someone said. 'You goin to chew the cud all fuckin day?'

Leo swallowed his last mouthful of tea. He rose and, with one hand on the shoulder of the boy to either side of him, levered himself up and swung his legs out behind the bench. There were clocks all over the ship, a recent innovation older hands insisted there was no need for. Leo changed into his duck suit, pulled a jersey over it, and at 8 a.m. fell in on deck. He was sent back to the mess with Jimmy White to scrub out and prepare breakfast for the next batch of seamen. At 9 a.m. he fell in at divisions on the upper deck amongst the men of his turret. They stood facing inward. Between funnels and casings Leo glimpsed divisions of stokers on the starboard side, and caught sight of Willy Burd amongst them.

Lieutenant Pyne inspected Leo's division for cleanliness in dress and person. The drum and fife band were on the far side of the turrets amidships, between the funnels. The brass band were on the near side and they struck up. All the men, the entire crew, turned to their left and began to trot around the ship. Leo skipped over hatches, slid down ladders. If you forgot how big your ship was, the exercise reminded you. It was like running around a one-and-a-half-acre field, strewn with obstacles. The band played with quickening tempo, and the runners increased their speed, leaping over obstacles ever faster until they were sprinting and knocking into each other and the music reached a crescendo. Then it ceased abruptly. All crew fell in, panting and sweating.

Petty Officer Jeffers called his turret crew to attention, then ordered them to stand at ease, and they were able to get their breath back. The PO stood with his legs apart, shining boots planted on the deck, and in his deep booming voice detailed hands for instruction or for work. Rifle drill signals, rope-splicing practice. Messenger and call boy duties. Leo was the last named.

'Sercombe, accompany me to inspect the turret.'

Theirs was 'Y' Turret, towards the stern of the ship, and they made their way there. PO Jeffers strode straight-backed across the swaying deck as if marching on a solid, flat parade ground. Leo tried to match his regular stride and could not for with each step he had to compensate for the motion of the vessel. Yet on dry land Petty Officer Jeffers was one of those seamen who walked with a rolling gait. None of the boys imagined they would ever do likewise, but if they stayed in the Navy long enough most surely would.

They inspected the turret from bottom to top. Down in the shell room they counted the ammunition stocks. They made sure the ready-racks had been refilled. Up in the gun room the PO studied the log to make sure the guns had been sponged out and greased. He enumerated each object he assessed, whether reminding himself or to educate the boy Leo was not sure. Perhaps both. Leo listened anyhow and nodded. 'Spare lengths of flexible piping,' the PO said, his basso voice resounding around the gun room. 'Urinal buckets. First-aid dressings, plenty of 'em. Biscuits and corned beef … good. Drinking tank.'

When they had finished, Leo requested permission to speak. He asked the PO if he thought this was just another exercise.

Petty Officer Jeffers frowned. Planting his feet apart he said, 'Who do you think I am, boy? The captain? They'll tell us when they reckon we need to know.'

The sun came out and shone across the wide, deep sea. Hands were given a make and mend. Leo went to the dry canteen and bought cigarettes for Willy Burd and climbed up and dossed down on the quarterdeck. There Willy found him, after he had been released from the stoking rota. Leo gave him the cigarettes. Willy handed over the money, and thanked Leo for saving him time, and lit one. Leo did not join him. He did not imagine the pleasure derived from smoking would merit the punishment should a boy not yet eighteen be caught. Cells for three days on low diet, bread and water.

They looked out from the quarterdeck. The wind beat on the grey metal around them as the ship ploughed through the leaden-tinted ocean.

'What do you reckon?' Leo asked. 'Twenty knots?'

'Nineteen,' Willy said.

They could see the *Lion* and the *Princess Royal*, other battlecruisers, ahead of them. Behind were the *Tiger* and *New Zealand*, and further back the four battleships.

'You know, p'raps you was right,' Willy said. 'One a the lads below reckons he overheard an officer say the Grand Fleet itself is a few miles right behind us, steamin out a Scapa.' He took a final drag of his cigarette and threw the dog-end in the spit-kid.

The *Queen Mary* was as steady as a log in a placid stream as she forged on in *Princess Royal*'s broad, white wake. Willy said that it was a lovely old day, a fine day for a battle, perhaps today would be *Der Tag* after all. Jimmy White joined them at that moment, having just done the dog watch. He told Willy that there was no chance. This was just another sweep and they would find nothing, for the Huns were like rabbits in their warrens inside the port of Wilhelmshaven.

'The only craft they've guts enough to send out's them fuckin U-boats,' he said. 'Or they sneak out for a quick raid on our coast, chuck a few shells at Hartlepool or Scarborough, maim a poor civilian. The only thing they're bold enough to meet us with is mines.'

Leo watched the two battlecruisers ahead, and light cruisers and destroyers that steamed ahead and either side of them like eager guard dogs around a flock of regal sheep. You grew up in a crooked valley in the West Country, nestled between the moor and the Quantock Hills, and you could not imagine how vast the sea was. How bare. That you could look all around these broad vistas and see only an empty horizon. Yet a battlecruiser steamed across the ocean with over a thousand men on board, confined in a kind of floating hotel, indeed, as Rufus Devereaux, the hermit tramp who'd shared his woodland glade with Leo, had called it.

Leo looked up. Occasionally, he saw gannets fly over, in one direction or another, no land in sight. And there were smaller birds, too, with black heads like plastered-down wigs, and red beaks. Arctic terns. Willy called them sea swallows and it was true they swooped through the air with great elegance. Their migration was a phenomenon. Not just their infallible compass, but their single-minded intention.

A rumour was passed along that someone had spotted a Zeppelin, high up in the sky above them, but Leo and Willy and Jimmy all peered and could not see it.

'I been on polishin all this week,' Jimmy said. 'You can ask Leo. I've polished portholes. Fire-hose nozzles. Brass dogs and bollards ... and don't even get me started on the fuckin ward rooms. Can you smell the ammonia on me? I can smell it. Can't get it out a my nostrils.'

Now that he mentioned it, Willy said, grimacing, he too could detect Jimmy's perfume, and he shifted himself away.

Leo smiled. He and Jimmy White had trained together at Devonport. Months learning how to heave the lead, steer a boat, knot ropes. Explosives, fire control, heavy gun drill. Most of their cohort were now scattered across the fleets. They were Boy Seamen Second Class.

Jimmy said that last night's stewed corned beef was coated with cinders. 'Just my luck to be on one a the last coal-fired ships. I bet the oil-fired engines don't coat every fuckin thing with cinders.'

Willy asked Jimmy if he was trying to put him out of a job. Leo suspected that Willy had first attached himself to them because he found Jimmy's endless grizzle of complaint amusing, before he became Leo's best pal. 'Just because the stokers beat your gunners at the miniature rifle shootin,' Willy said. 'I heard the captain's considerin swappin us round. Get your lot down in the coal bunkers and us lot up in them lovely clean turrets, seein as we're better bloody shots.'

Jimmy scowled, lost for words for a moment. Then he said, 'Somethin wrong with the bloody rifles, there was, everyone knows that. Anyways, at least a gunnery crew won the cricket.'

Willy laughed out loud, so trivial was the boast.

Not all the upper-deck recreations were competitive. Leo's favourite was roller skating, up on the fore-deck. Neither Willy nor Jimmy could see the point in it. Some men liked to skate in pairs. Leo preferred skating alone. Places were also told off for boxing and wrestling. Two weeks earlier they'd had an inter-ship assault-at-arms with the *Princess Royal*. All of *Queen Mary*'s weight classes were represented by stokers.

Willy Burd asked Jimmy White if he knew that Leo was of a mind to train as a diver. Jimmy said, 'He's got a screw loose, don't he? Goin down in the drink when he don't have to?'

Willy admitted that in this case Jimmy had a point, he was obliged to agree.

They lay in the sun and dozed. The bosun's mate came out and called, 'Hands to tea.' The trio rose from the deck and joined the crowd making their way below. 'You know, I thought I might see summat a the world if I joined the Navy,' Jimmy said. 'And all I've seen is the North fuckin Sea.'

'You shouldn't have joined just before a war,' Willy said. He went further aft to find a less busy ladder.

'I'll see you later,' Leo called after him.

'Not if I see you first, mate,' Willy yelled back. He ducked through a hatch and disappeared.

Jimmy said, 'He's been comin out with that line ever since we come aboard and he still thinks it's funny.'

Leo smiled. 'It is.'

'How do you figure that then?'

'The more times he says it, the funnier it gets,' Leo told him. 'Don't ask me how.'

Jimmy White shook his head, with an expression upon his face meant perhaps to convey that it was his misfortune to have to indulge these immature lads, though he was one himself. Just then the bugles sounded off, with the call for 'Action Stations'.

'Bollocks,' Jimmy said. 'We've been lyin around all afternoon and they call an exercise action at teatime.' He cast around him for a clock, and shook his head. 'See? Bang on three-thirty.'

Leo did not have time to tell Jimmy that a further note had sounded while he nattered. The extra note signified 'At the Double'. Leo was already running. If Jimmy had not heard it himself he would realise soon enough that this was not an exercise. The ship was like an ants' nest, suddenly, men dashing this way and that, some yanking jumpers on. They ran down to their shell rooms, or up to controls. Hands struck down mess stools and tables, and bedding in officers' cabins, and other inflammable objects. Leo took the first hatchway back up from the mess-deck. Stokers were closing bulkheads and shutting watertight doors, and rigging hoses that could be left running on the upper deck to keep it wet. Above, extra white ensigns were hoisted at the mast and yards.

Leo climbed a ladder to the fo'c'sle deck and came up the starboard side, and sprinted aft past the funnels, the lashed-down cutters and whalers and pinnaces, past the captain's gig and the sixteen-foot dinghy below the torpedo control tower. There he shot down the ladder using his hands to slide.

Hammocks were being put up. On some ships they were struck down as a fire precaution, but on HMS *Queen Mary* the captain preferred them slung, to check flying metal. Damage control and fire parties stood back out of the rush as they assembled at their meeting points, and were cursed whenever they got in someone's way.

Leo raced along the deck towards the stern, to 'Y' Turret. He swung himself up and inside through the hatch. Petty Officer Jeffers climbed in shortly behind him and shouted, 'Turret's crew, number!'

Jeffers watched the men take their positions in the gun room. Gun layers, trainers and sight-setters stood at their stations by one or other of the two guns. Number ones stood at the loading-cage levers, facing the breeches. Number twos in line with their breeches, facing the muzzles. Number threes in front of number twos. Number fours at the sides, facing inwards to the breeches. The spare gun layer also had the job of recording the number of rounds fired.

Boy Seaman Leo Sercombe was the only hand in the turret without a specific task. The boy was a general dogsbody. He would pass food or drink as required, bring the urinal bucket, empty it when necessary. He might be ordered to fetch something or, if the wireless packed up, run with a message. Now he stuck close to Petty Officer Jeffers.

The second captain of turret and numbers five and six were beneath the gun room, in the working chamber. Further below were another petty officer and eighteen men in the magazine, and a similar number in the shell room right down at the bottom of the turret. The men there wore masks with goggles, respirators and anti-gas apparatus. The first time Leo had seen them, in the din of iron doors banging and machinery clanging, he was startled. They looked like demons. Fallen angels kept in chains under gloomy darkness.

All were correct from top to bottom. PO Jeffers pulled the hatch shut and the crew was closed up. He went to the cabinet at the rear of the turret. Leo followed. It was sound-proofed so that the turret officer, Lieutenant Pyne, could hear as he spoke over his Navy phones to the control top and to the transmitting station below.

Lieutenant Pyne had an air of simultaneous impatience and calm. He gave the impression that he resented being stuck in the cabinet and would much rather be in the gun room with his men. Leo saw that they liked him. He knew every one of their names and would ask a question out of the blue about their family, or say something that was peculiarly apt. The only words he had so far addressed directly to Leo were that what he missed most about being in the Navy was hunting. As if he knew of this boy seaman's love of horses, the officer had described his favourite mount, a white hunter that he prayed had not been purloined for the French campaign but was still in its stable at home awaiting his return. Leo asked him what their countryside was like for riding and the lieutenant told him his home was in the Midlands, which was neither flat enough nor hilly enough. Which he supposed was also its saving grace.

'Very good, PO,' he said now. Behind Lieutenant Pyne stood his snotty, or midshipman, assistant. 'Better get the hands to test the loading gear.'

Once this was passed, men had a moment of peace in the gun room. Some had practices or superstitions of their own to be observed. The lieutenant unstrapped his watch and emptied his pockets. He reckoned that any unnecessary articles, that might complicate wounds, should be removed. One of the sight-setters placed his tobacco tin in the biscuit box. Sergeant Nutley wore a thin shirt whose arms he'd torn off at the shoulders, to allow him greater freedom of movement. He also had a hunting knife hanging by a lanyard from his neck, which he used for cutting the rope grommets that protected the driving bands on the projectiles.

Leo could feel the increase in speed, the engines working harder far below them. Now and then the ship seemed to shiver or tremble. He did not imagine any of the others, busy with their tasks, noticed.

Lieutenant Pyne stepped out of the cabinet and announced that he wished to say a word. The men in the gun room turned their attention towards him. The lieutenant said that they could expect to meet anything from a light cruiser to the biggest battleship of the High Seas Fleet, and that 'Y' Turret's foremost duty was to get off the maximum number of rounds.

'Let us hope that we shall imminently be permitted to do what we have trained to do, and hoped to do, for many months now,' he said. His voice did not carry like the PO's, so he shouted, that all the hands could hear him. 'Every man on every battlecruiser in this fleet knows that the crack gunnery ship is this one. The *Queen Mary*. And the finest turret on the *Queen Mary* is this one. "Y". I trust you will not miss a single salvo, gentlemen.' He looked around the room, and smiled. 'Not a single bloody one.'

The men roared their approval and said they would waste no opportunity to welcome the enemy to the party. All Huns were invited. They described exactly what any German ship that came within range could expect. A bomb shoved down its gob. A shell rammed up its arse. Leo looked around at the other fourteen seamen inside this steel box. The atmosphere today was different from on any of their many drills. He inhaled a peculiar smell. Musky, rank. It came from the men, sweating from deeper pores, primitive glands, some true authentic depth of their being, preparing them for battle, turning them into warriors.

Altogether one turret held across its four floors almost a hundred men, each allotted his own task. The order came to load the guns with common shell. Down in the shell room the projectile for the left gun was clamped and guided onto the tray in the cage. Each projectile weighed over half a ton. The cage rose hydraulically to the magazine room. There, four quarter charges were manhandled into compartments of the steel box above the projectile. Each quarter charge weighed a little over fifty pounds, the weight of a bushel of barley. Leo's father had carried sacks of four bushels. Few men could. The cage rose again, into the gun room.

When the cage reached the open mouth of the gun a rammer shot out, butting the tail of the projectile and propelling it into the breech. Then the rammer flicked back, and as soon as it was clear of the tray the flap door of the cage sprang open and the two lower quarter charges of cordite dropped down into the tray. These were rammed in, then the upper quarter charges dropped likewise and they too were rammed into the gun. The rammer withdrew, the cage dropped, the breech door slammed shut, and one of the sight-setters unlocked a bolt that had been holding the left gun steady. The crew stood down. Then the right gun was loaded likewise.

Leo had no idea what was going on outside the confines of their turret. There were no windows in the gun room. The guns were loaded there but fired by the gunnery officer from his position on high, up above the bridge. His crew had rangefinders and trigonometrical calculating machines to assess the trajectory of the shells, bearing in mind the distance, course and speed of the target. They passed directions to the turrets, via a transmitting station deep down in the ship, of the guns' required elevation and angles.

The order came through on Lieutenant Pyne's headphones and he said, 'Bring the guns to the ready.'

The trainer moved the whole barbette or upper part of the turret with a single handwheel that operated hydraulic controls. The gun layers and the sight-setters inside the gun room aligned the guns. They followed a system of electrically controlled pointers on dials, and when each gun was in the correct position, electric circuits were closed and Leo knew that the 'gun ready' light would come on in the director tower. The gunnery officer there could now press a trigger and fire when he wished.

In the gun room the crews waited. Sergeant Nutley broke a small piece of cotton wool off a wad and rolled it into a tight ball and stuffed it in his left ear, then did likewise for his right. He saw Leo watching him and offered the wad to the boy, but Leo shook his head. PO Jeffers and one or two of the older men accepted. The two five-man crews stood by. Lieutenant Pyne and PO Jeffers watched and waited.

The lieutenant's eyes were wide in concentration and excitement, lids drawn back, like a horse's. 'I do believe, PO,' he said, catching Leo's eye as he did so, 'we're about to blood our guns.'

5

3.50 p.m., Wednesday 31 May

The guns were once more brought to the half-cock. Each hand was concentrated, like men at a shoot, though they could see nothing of what the big guns were aiming at. Leo observed the sweat breaking out on their faces. Already half the crew had removed their upper garments. The gun room smelled of grease and oil and men. Then it seemed to Leo as if not only himself but everyone else around him held his breath, as if all knew that the gunnery officer far above them had decided to fire. Sound ceased, movement stilled, time stopped. Then Leo heard or thought he heard the warning bell in the transmitting station ring in the distance, and both guns fired together with a great crashing concussive explosion.

Leo flinched. When he opened his eyes the men were already working. Now the routine began, with new shells and charges sent up and the guns loaded, and reset as necessary, and fired. The sweet smell of cordite was added to the stink of men in the steel room. The PO told the guns' crews to go steady, for he thought them a little too swift, as if each crew was trying to outdo the other, and they settled to a concerted, synchronous rhythm.

Leo watched the men. They performed their tasks with mesmeric repetition. They got off each round in under a minute, sending the projectiles, each a thousand pounds in weight, at a muzzle velocity of over two thousand feet per second, pounding into the midst of German ships up to ten miles away. Amid the din of guns and smoke there was much yelling of information and orders. The crews were like tiny models of men, serving the huge guns of this ship that was a great monster of war. Leo heard a scattering percussion and realised it was the rattle of a hail of shell splinters on the ship's side. So the enemy were straddling them too. He had forgotten they might do so. But the day had come at last and Leo knew, as all did, one thing with certainty. We will win, because our ships are better, our guns bigger, our crews more skilled.

How fortunate he was to be in a turret. His mate Willy Burd was down below, barrowing coal to the boilers. When the big guns went off, Willy had said, he could feel the ship sink down and rise up in a shudder. Dust was shaken out of crevices. The air was filled with black dust. It was surely Hades, the worst place to be.

It was true that you could not see out of a turret except through the periscopes, to which only Lieutenant Pyne, PO Jeffers and the turret-trainer had access. Some said gunners were moles just not underground, but still, it was good to know you were close to the open air. Outside, the barbette was protected by thick armoured plating. PO Jeffers sat watching his sweating men at their gleaming oiled machinery. He had told Leo he'd marked him down as a gunnery lad; the boy had only to watch and listen and his chance would soon come to join a crew.

The PO took a look through his periscope, and stepping closer Leo heard him say quietly to himself, 'Good God above.' Then he leaned away from the periscope. He blinked and looked around, and seeing the boy right there beside him said, 'Take a look, lad.'

Leo peered through the periscope, amazed at the privilege. It took him some seconds to make sense of what he was seeing. At first he thought it was a kind of optical illusion, like some naval version of a what-the-butler-saw machine. He could see in the smoky distance enemy ships, the red flashes of their guns firing. And lying becalmed between the *Queen Mary* and the far-off German line, both sides' shells hurled over her, salvo after salvo, lay a three-masted barque with full sail. Leo recalled once as a small child seeing such a ship; it must have been in Watchet Harbour. But this one was bigger and more beautiful. The poor merchant seamen aboard her were trapped in the middle of this modern conflagration, their ship somehow sailing into the battle from another century.

6

4.10 p.m., Wednesday 31 May

Ashout went up that something was wrong. The regular sounds of loading ceased. The left gun rammer wasn't working. One of the crew had opened the breech too soon after the gun had gone off. The PO took a lever to the rammer and twisted and shifted then rushed it back and forth until it ran true once more, and they resumed firing the guns.

They fired constantly for many minutes, one deafening twin salvo after another from their thirteen-and-a-half-inch guns, and with each salvo the ship shook. 'Right gun?' 'Ready!' 'Left gun?' 'Ready!' Leo watched the clock above the cabinet. Almost two salvoes a minute. He could not believe how much more intensity the crews attained than during training. Shells came up from the shell room with messages chalked upon their sides. *This one for Kaiser Bill*, read one. *Sink the bastards*, another. The noise of each explosion inside the turret was so loud it gave those close to it a percussive shock and resounded with a great ringing boom. Leo saw that some of the gun crew had blood trickling out of their ears. He fingered his own and although they felt dry he now regretted not taking the cotton wool Sergeant Nutley had offered him.

A request came up from the magazine. The quarter charges were filled with cordite, a blend of nitroglycerine and nitrocellulose, gelatinised with petroleum jelly to lubricate the bore of the gun. Men in the magazine had to remove the charges' sealed lids, and the fumes of the cordite, acrid and sweet, like putrefying meat, were released into the room. The petty officer in charge down there asked for permission for his men to go out on deck. Lieutenant Pyne said they could come up as long as the firing rate was not affected. They ascended in pairs and Leo watched them climb out of the hatch. As soon as they reached the fresh air they threw up their lunch on the deck. Then they came back in and went down to make way for the next pair.

Leo felt a sudden unsteadiness in his feet. He flexed his knees to keep upright. Above the crash of the turret guns, and the roar of the smaller four-inch guns being fired in between, he wondered if he had heard, faintly in the distance, a sound like a dresser full of crockery falling over and all smashing at once. He looked around. No one else seemed to have noticed anything. Then he caught the eye of one of the sight-setters, who was frowning at him, and said or perhaps mouthed the words, 'Ship's been hit.'

There seemed to be a fault in one of the air blasts, for when the crew opened the gun, smoke was still in the barrel. It hung in the already stuffy air of the gun room, the smell strong and unpleasant. The PO ordered the breech-blocks open, to let the smoke out. Now they could hear enemy shells hitting the water close to the ship, with a crashing that jarred Leo's eardrums.

Suddenly Lieutenant Pyne came rushing through from the cabinet and announced that the control top reported their target, the third ship of the German line, was dropping out. All the men in the turret cheered.

PO Jeffers had a look through of the periscope. 'She's goin down by the bows,' he called out.

They resumed firing, presumably at a new target. Then all of a sudden the whole turret seemed to tremble and the ship beneath them shook. The roof of the turret was pulverised with all manner and size of metal. Leo choked with dust that blew into the gun room. The turret-trainer reported the front glass of his periscope fouled or blocked up.

Another explosion shook the turret. Someone yelled that the bastards had found their bloody range. Leo went over to the pressure gauge and saw that the pressure had failed. At that moment came another explosion, far larger than the ones before. Leo was thrown off his feet and tossed around the gun room. It was like being thrown from a horse but worse, for it was as if the earth had tossed the horse. He felt at any second his head or limbs would be smashed. By some miracle they were not. Leo came to rest, winded, dazed. His breath came back slowly, and he climbed carefully to his feet. The PO and a few others were dangling in the air on bowlines. The left gun appeared to have fallen through its trunnions and smashed up the crew members behind it. The floor of the gun room was bulged and warped. There was utter silence, an incongruent atmosphere of peace that did not make sense. Then sounds returned and Leo realised it had been not silence after all but his own temporary deafness.

Petty Officer Jeffers unhooked himself and went back to the cabinet. Leo followed him. The PO asked, 'What do you think has happened, sir?'

Lieutenant Pyne said he had no idea. The PO said the guns were useless and they might as well get to the four-inch guns outside and offer any help they could. It was better than staying and being sitting ducks.

'We don't know what's out there,' said Lieutenant Pyne.

Leo volunteered to take a look. The PO said, 'Go on, lad.' Leo climbed up and put his head out of the roof of the turret. The four-inch battery below him was all smashed up. A shell landed in the water and sent a great spout of liquid into the air, which fell into where the battery had been. Then, as the ship tilted, the water flowed back out, freshly red.

There was fire all around. A cloud of smoke blew past, leaving a stink of high explosive. He turned and looked amidships and saw dead men being laid out on deck, side by side. He saw burned men with their heads and hands wrapped in cotton wool, and bandages with slits for their eyes, wandering about the deck like ghosts. Then the ship lurched and these walking cases and other men on deck fell over, all ten or twenty of them, and rolled and skittled down to the port side.

Leo climbed down and reported that the small guns were no good. 'The ship's got herself a terrible list to port, sir,' he said. He realised now that a number of men were groaning. Either Leo could not hear them before or they were too shocked by their injuries at first to cry out. Lieutenant Pyne told PO Jeffers to clear the turret, the PO yelled the order, and those men who could climbed out. Leo waited. He watched the PO go across and give a hand to a seaman coming up from below. Jeffers asked the man why there were no more coming up behind him from the magazine or the shell room and the man said it was no use, the water was right up, and Leo saw then that the man's clothes were sodden and he understood that the ship's hull was breached beneath them and all the men in the magazine and the shell room were drowned.

And if water was flooding into the engine rooms then stokers were surely drowning. Willy Burd was down there.

The PO told Leo to go on up through the cabinet and out through the top. He and Lieutenant Pyne would follow. Leo climbed out of the turret and as he descended the ladder at the back the ship listed further to port. He gripped the rungs tightly and hung on. The man before him, the drenched seaman who had climbed up from below, stepped off the ladder and slid down the deck to the port side, smashing against a hawser and bouncing off it. Leo froze, clutching the ladder. He had no idea what to do.

'Here, lad.'

He looked up and saw Sergeant Nutley, holding on to the rail on the starboard side. Next to him was the sight-setter who had told Leo the ship was hit. The setter looked from the sergeant to the boy and took hold of

Sergeant Nutley's hand and let go of the rail. Sergeant Nutley held the rail with his right hand and clasped the sight-setter's hand with his left, at full stretch.

'You can do it, lad,' the sergeant yelled.

Leo dropped from the ladder and kicked off it and caught the sight-setter's leg. He scrambled up his body. Then he clambered up and across Sergeant Nutley too, clutching his trousers, grip slipping on his sweaty torso, till he reached the rail. The sight-setter followed likewise and the three of them clung to the rail together. Leo saw that many others were doing so too, all along the starboard side.

There was another explosion at the far end of the ship, forward. Smoke billowed from fierce flames. Above the smoke, a boat – a dinghy or pinnace – soared, spinning like a little toy.

Leo held tight to the rail. Men were coming out of hatchways and slipping and sliding down the steeply inclined deck to the port side, where they slammed into a scrum of bodies pressed against the rail or toppled over them and flipped into the water. The sight was grotesque and the boy felt something like laughter lift from his stomach; it rose in his throat and came out of his mouth as vomit. He saw a man stagger out of the smoke, his clothes and face and hands as black as a chimney sweep's. Then he too lost his balance and fell. Leo prayed that he would see Jimmy White or Willy Burd, then he prayed that he would not. Blood pooled and swilled across the deck. The decks were all warped from the heat beneath them, and where they were still dry the resin under the corticene linoleum crackled with a noise like burning holly. One of the cats, Leo could not tell which one, flew out of a smoking doorway and disappeared behind a lifeboat. A man limped into view, and Leo saw that his right foot was hanging off his leg by no more than a single tendon or muscle. He looked up at the man's bespattered face and recognised the chaplain. The horsemen who had been foretold had come. Fire and smoke and sulphur would issue from the horses' mouths. The second angel would pour his bowl into the sea, and it would be like blood, and every living thing in the sea would die. Seven angels with seven bowls of the wrath of God.

More men emerged from the smoke. Some had managed to put on respirators, but it would not save them. They clung to whatever they could on the listing decks. Most fell and tumbled as the others had before them.

'The bow's going into the drink,' someone said.

When he heard this, the boy understood that their great ship was sinking. What he could not understand was why the enemy was still firing. Heavy shells landed in the sea alongside, raising enormous spouts so close that tons of stinking water crashed onto the ship, a wet stench like spent fireworks, soaking and suffocating all the men there. Or he heard shells shrieking and tearing the air like ripping canvas as they passed overhead. Could the German gunnery range-finders not see that their target was doomed, their mission completed? Why fire at dead men? Why bomb the drowned? Leo cowered, trying to shield himself even as he hung on to the rail. His comrades flinched as shells landed and splinters careened all over the ship. The air was full of them. When they flew close the boy heard their ominous hum. He caught glimpses of polished steel as it flashed past. Men let go of the rail as they were hit and fell abruptly backwards into the water or down across the deck.

Still more of the crew crawled out of turrets and hatches, coming out of the fires as the ship burned. The boy could hear her now, roaring, crackling, new flames sprouting here and there and joining the one great conflagration. She still pounded forward, her very speed fanning the flames that devoured her. The sound was like the roaring from an open furnace door. Perhaps the boilers down below were all out of control and powering the inferno, gutting their ship with fire. The boy remembered stories of Viking funerals. The bodies of warriors put to sea on their burning ships. Perhaps he and all his fellow crew had been already dead when they launched. There was a new smell in the noxious fumes. Like meat roasting.

Then Leo saw paper blowing out of the after hatch on the quarterdeck. Reams of white paper streamed out, spare rolls of chart paper from the gunnery office. Like pennants or bunting wildly celebrating freedom, they went trailing away over the side of the ship into the bubbling sea.

Petty Officer Jeffers was suddenly there beside them, clutching the starboard-side rail. 'Come on, you lads,' he yelled. 'She's going under. Into the drink.'

'She'll float for a long time yet,' Sergeant Nutley called back. Leo wanted to believe him, for no seaman wished to leave his ship for the great grey waves of the North Sea. But he could not. Someone had shouted that the bow was sinking but he must have been wrong for Leo could see it now sticking up in the air. And looking the other way the stern, too, many of its metal plates red hot, was lifting up off the surface of the sea. HMS *Queen Mary* was broken amidships.

The PO did not pause to persuade anyone further but clambered over the rail and slid over the slimy bilge keel and dropped into the water. One or two men followed. Leo did likewise. The boy entered the cold water and began to swim hard away from the ship. He was vaguely aware of others around him doing the same. He did not know how long he swam for or how far he got, twenty-five or thirty yards perhaps, when there was suddenly a huge explosion behind him, greater than any of those that had blown already.

The boy took a deep breath and dived under the water but then he was sucked down anyway by the shock waves of the explosion. He looked up and saw through the water a distorted vision of a storm of debris flying through the air, pieces of the ship large and small, great chunks of metal and fragments of wood, but he could see less and less as he was pulled deeper into the sea by the suction or backwash from the huge bulk of the great ship sinking and Leo knew now that this was it. He gave up, for had he not been told that to fall into the drink and drown was not the worst way to die so long as you did not fight it? No, he need not struggle. The boy relaxed and sank. Death did not have to be the horror Leo had just seen. This was easy enough. But then it occurred to him that there was something he still had to do in his life, though he could not at this very moment quite remember what it was. And so he fought against the suction. And he found that it was growing weaker, if he kicked and paddled hard he could prevail against it, and so Leo Sercombe rose and in time broke the surface of the water and gulped air.

The boy felt sick, and spewed and retched. He had swallowed not only saltwater but also oil. The filthy taste of it was in his mouth and throat. He could see a thick black layer all over the surface around him. He saw wreckage, and men's heads bobbing in the foul water. Were they alive or dead men floating? There were great numbers of fish lying on the surface, different kinds of them, stunned by the detonation. The water rose and fell. Whether this was further reverberation from the sinking ship or the natural swell of the sea Leo did not know. Something floated close by. He reached out and grabbed it. It was a large hammock, or part of one, with a big timber spar, and he was able to grasp the rope that fanned out from the spar along its length. He wished to pull himself up onto the timber but doubted whether he had the strength to do so. But then the swell of the sea lifted him and with a little effort Leo reached over the timber and hung on.

Smoke wafted through the air. There was mist too, more in the distance. Amongst the debris all around him were floating brass cylinders, by which a smoke-screen was made, for it was easier to aim at an enemy out of smoke than into it. Perhaps there was mist or fog to the south and so in terms of weather the German gunners had the advantage. That would explain the inexplicable.

Gradually Leo became aware of ships moving by, and he turned to watch the dreadnoughts of the Fifth Battle Squadron steaming past, firing their huge guns. So Willy Burd was right, they had all come out behind the *Queen Mary*, out of Scapa Flow. Too late! The enemies' shells landed in the water around him. The battleships ploughed on. In their wake the water rose and fell more strongly. Now the Huns were in trouble. In the added turbulence, Leo hung on, until the ocean calmed again somewhat, and he clung on more. He would hold on until help came. He could do that. He must do that.

It seemed a long time before destroyers came. They zigzagged to and fro, dodged oncoming shells, slashing and churning the water. They did not stop for the survivors but sped on into the battle, flinging themselves from tack to tack. Perhaps their crews could not see the men floating there in the water. Their swell, too, roughed up the sea. Leo held tight to the timber.

Then he saw that one destroyer had slowed. Though it was under fire it turned to port and lowered its whaler. His hopes rose. But he watched and saw that the whaler could not be forced through the wreckage of parts of the *Queen Mary*, the debris was too thick on the surface. So then the guns' crews and the upper-deck hands of the destroyer hung over the side on fenders and lines and nets trying to haul any survivors that they could reach aboard, even as they began to steam ahead once more. Enemy shells still fell about them. The men of the destroyer struggled to pull survivors out but these men in the water were covered in oil and so the crew were unable to hold onto them. Leo could not tell how many they saved, a few, but he saw they would not save him for the boat veered away. He thought it would have been a help if they had left the whaler, perhaps he could have made his way to it. But they had hauled it back on board.

When the sea was calm once more, and empty of vessels, the boy looked about. He saw fewer heads bobbing above the surface now. Dusk was falling. The green-black water was bitterly cold. The smell of the fuel oil was almost as horrible as its taste. Leo saw something moving slowly towards him. He could not work out what it was, nosing its way through wreckage just beneath the surface. Then he understood. A torpedo. It slowed down and floated past no more than twenty feet away, and came to undetonated rest.

How much time passed then? Around the boy, men went under. Whether they lost consciousness and sank or let themselves go deliberately Leo could not tell. To see the destroyer stop to help then leave had been a cruel blow. He clung to the hammock spar. His eyes felt a new sensation and Leo could not work out what caused it. Then he realised he was weeping, or trying to. 'My God,' he cried out. 'My God, why hast thou forsaken me?' Darkness fell over all the sea. Leo cried out again with a loud voice and yielded up his spirit. He fell asleep.

7

When the boy awoke he was halfway off the spar of the hammock. With a great effort he managed to haul himself back. He felt very sick, full of fuel oil, his stomach, his innards, clogged with it. His eyes were blocked up and he could barely see. He felt his jersey and found it thick with oil but rolled back one arm and wiped his eyes with the sleeve of his flannel shirt. He got rid of enough of the thick oil to be able to see again but his eyes ached badly. Which was worse, the pain in his eyes or the cold? He shivered and his teeth chattered and he felt the chill deep and resident down in his thin bones. *'He casts forth his ice like morsels,'* a voice said. *'Who can stand before His cold?'*

But just as he began to understand that there were many stations on the way to death, you did not choose which one would be the last, before he could contemplate the matter in his exhaustion, so just then more destroyers appeared, all lit up on the horizon, and came closer, and one slowed. Leo rose up on the spar of the hammock and waved. In doing so he lost his grip and fell back in the cold water. He hardly knew whether he was alive or not, conscious or unconscious. Perhaps now he was dreaming, and the boats were part of his delirium. But then the destroyer was there, huge above him, and he saw that a line had been thrown. He caught it and held on with his cold weak hands and would not let go even if he lost consciousness, no, he would not, and they hauled the skinny boy in his oil-sodden clothes up onto the decks of the destroyer.

Leo did not know who they were. A man spoke English but perhaps he was an educated German. Or a spy. Leo could not speak. He could not see, or hear, or think.

When he came to, he was lying on some kind of settee or bunk. Someone told him he was all right, another that he should not struggle so. He could not see who spoke and concluded that he was blind, but it did not matter much. The Lord had smote him with madness and blindness and confusion of mind. He would grope at noonday, as the blind grope in darkness. He was given brandy or whisky or other spirit to drink, and fell back asleep. He dreamed of a white hunter standing in a stable somewhere in England, waiting for his master.

When Leo woke again it was to find a surgeon bathing his face. His eyes caused him awful agony and the surgeon cleaned what he could of the oil away. Leo asked where they were going and someone said, 'The lad can speak and is one of ours, I was right.'

The surgeon said they were steaming at reduced speed back to Rosyth, for they themselves had been badly hit after they had picked him up. Despite the pain,

Leo slept again. They reached the Forth in darkness. He woke and heard someone tell the surgeon that as they passed under the bridge just now railwaymen had thrown lumps of coal at them, yelling that they were cowards who'd run away from the enemy.

A hospital boat came over. The boy joined half a dozen wounded men. They were taken to Queensferry Hospital. There he was made comfortable in bed and fell asleep. He woke to find a doctor waiting to clean his eyes. He said he had not wished to disturb the boy before. When he had finished he applied a bandage. He told Leo that they would change this daily for a week. He said that he hoped the boy's eyes would be all right again in time.

Leo asked the doctor for news of survivors of his ship. HMS *Queen Mary*. For names. The doctor paused. Leo could not see him but he sensed the man look away, then he turned back and said there were plenty of other survivors, he did not know how many for certain, he could not say. Leo was unsure whether or not he believed him.

Part Two

THE VET
1916–1917

I

The veterinary surgeon Patrick Jago lifted the pony's foot and examined it. A stable lad held the halter. The girl watched.

'I suppose I am too big for Blaze, poor boy,' Lottie said. 'Or he is too small for me.'

Herb Shattock, her father's head groom, told Jago that he had considered corns, quitter and canker, and did not believe the problem was any of those.

'Perhaps the likeliest explanation is the simplest,' said the vet. 'When was he last shod?'

'Four days ago,' Herb Shattock said. 'But yon Crocker won't be at fault, I'll guarantee that. I don't say as he's never drove a nail into the sensitive parts a the hoof, but he don't hide it when he does. Then we deals with it. And his son, he's learned as good as Crocker himself.'

'But that's the son who's gone, Mister Shattock,' Lottie said.

The vet walked across the loose box to where he'd laid his bag of tools.

The groom frowned. 'Aye,' he said. 'Jacob's back on the farrier work. The other son's not much good.'

'The cripple?' Patrick Jago asked. He returned to the side of the pony. 'How old is Crocker now?'

'Can't be no more'n a year older'n me,' Herb Shattock told him. He nodded in the general direction of the village. 'We was in the same class at school.'

The veterinary surgeon tapped Blaze's hoof with his hammer. 'Remove the shoe, please,' he said.

Herb Shattock told the stable lad to fetch pliers and clippers. Lottie held her pony's halter and spoke to him, reassuring him that he was in good hands. The best. The lad returned and took the halter once again, while Herb Shattock set to removing the shoe.

'We've always struggled with their feet, of course,' Patrick Jago said. '"Then were the horsehoofs broken, by the means of their prancings." Judges.'

Lottie understood that it was she who was being addressed.

'Entire Roman armies had to be disbanded in consequence of their horses' hoofs wearing out.' The vet laughed. 'I blame those endless stone roads of theirs.'

Herb Shattock stood with the pony's leg between his like a smith and clipped all the turned-over ends of the nails, then he levered the shoe off. Lottie could see that Blaze was discomfited by his doing so. Another lad meanwhile brought a bucket of warm water.

'William the Conqueror is generally credited with introducing the art of shoeing into this country,' the vet continued. 'Though I've not heard any evidence for that. On the farms of your father's estate the horses are generally reshod every four to six weeks, I'm glad to say.'

The lad holding Blaze's halter said, 'No foot, no horse, sir.'

Herb Shattock lowered the pony's foot and stepped away. Patrick Jago took his place. The vet lifted Blaze's foot and with the knife that he called a searcher cut the horn of the hoof, explaining that he was looking for a bruised area. Then he passed the knife to the groom and asked for his pincers. Herb Shattock handed these to him and he pressed them into the foot, until the animal flinched. He asked for the water bucket and cleaned the foot. Then he dressed away the sole of the hoof, following the black spot with the point of his knife. Out of the bottom of one nail-hole came a dirty, thin, dark-coloured fluid.

Lottie asked what this was. Herb Shattock said it was gravel, and the vet declared this to be an obscure local name for a kind of pus or feculence. Once this dark matter had escaped, the vet told Herb Shattock to prepare a cold bran-poultice with a tablespoonful of carbolic acid or phenyl or indeed any good antiseptic if he had some other preference.

'When the inflammation has subsided,' Patrick Jago said, 'dress it with a tow and tar ointment. Protect the hoof with a leather sole, and put the shoe back on.'

Lottie asked what tow and tar consisted of. The vet explained that it was a mixture of one part of green tar and three parts hard fat, melted together. Herb Shattock said that he would prefer to use palm oil if the vet did not object. Patrick Jago said that he did not, palm oil would surely work just as well. Such an ointment was useful in general to counteract the brittle nature of a horse's hoof. He had seen it used often for sand crack, while a student at the Royal Veterinary College in London.

'I've hardly ever seen the condition here,' he said. 'Sand crack appears to be a lot less common in the countryside.'

Herb Shattock agreed with this observation. Patrick Jago collected his tools and walked out of the loose box. The groom accompanied him. The girl followed. Herb Shattock asked the vet what he thought of stopping the feet of a horse. Lottie had never heard this expression. The groom explained that it referred to the practice of stuffing the bottom of the feet with matter of a moist constitution.

'Numerous authorities are against it,' Patrick Jago said. 'I myself am undecided.' He asked Herb Shattock for his opinion. Lottie looked from one man to the other. She thought that she could listen to them talk of horses all day.

'In my experience,' the groom said, 'there's two kinds a weather where it may be useful – a long hard frost or a hot spell, when a horse is workin every day on a hard dry road. The moisture of the horn's liable to become exhausted. Then I am in favour of stoppin the feet. Keep 'em moist and pliable. The horse don't half appreciate it.'

The vet nodded. He asked what Mister Shattock used for the purpose.

'I've not yet found nothin to beat equal parts a cow-dung and clay,' he said. 'Applied alternate nights.'

Patrick Jago considered this potion. 'Ideal,' he said. He shook hands with the groom. He told Lottie that her pony would be ready to bear weight again within a week but that she was probably right. She was a full-grown woman now, if slender yet, but she had likely reached her full height and could ride a much larger horse. If neither of her father's remaining hunters appealed perhaps Lord Prideaux should look out for a new one for her, though he conceded it would not be easy to find one in wartime. He walked across the yard towards his own horse tethered to a ring.

Lottie told Herb Shattock that she would be back. He said that he and the lad would attend to the horse. She trotted after Patrick Jago. When she reached him he was putting his tools into a saddlebag.

'Mr Jago,' Lottie said. He turned. 'Would you take me on your rounds as your assistant?'

The vet frowned. He asked what her father would think of the idea.

Lottie said they had already discussed it. 'Father believes it would be good for me,' she said. 'He thinks I am in need of a useful role. If I were older he would not discourage me from joining the Ambulance Service.' She was intent, serious, then her eyes widened suddenly, and she said, 'It was practically his idea, actually.'

Patrick Jago tightened the strap of the saddlebag. 'It is often hard physical labour,' he said. He looked her up and down, in her trousers and waistcoat. 'I'm not sure you would be up to it.'

Lottie said that she was strong. With her left hand she rolled up the right sleeve of her white shirt and flexed her bicep muscle and said that she could ride or fight as well as any boy her size, he had only to ask her cousins, and she had no fear of hard work. The vet said he had no doubt that Lottie told the truth.

She said that she would cut her hair. 'None need even know that I am a girl.'

Patrick Jago smiled, raising his eyebrows, and said that he thought that would be a fine trick for such a pretty girl to pull off. He put his foot in the stirrup and mounted the horse. 'Both my assistants have been conscripted,' he said. 'Let us try it, Lottie.'

She watched the vet surgeon ride away, then she ran to the house. She found her father in his study and told him that Patrick Jago had just asked, practically begged, her to help him in his work. He was desperate, she said, for his assistants had gone to the trenches.

Arthur Prideaux took off his spectacles and rubbed the bridge of his nose. His estate manager William Carew had long gone, with a cavalry regiment, and Lord Prideaux was once again managing the estate himself. He peered at the papers on his desk. Perhaps they absorbed him such that it took him some moments to turn his attention from them to his daughter.

'Jago', he said, 'does all kinds of veterinary work, does he not? From lapdogs in Bampton town to bulls on the moorland farms.'

Lottie agreed.

'You could help him with the small animals,' Arthur Prideaux said. 'A girl could do that. Why not?' He nodded to himself, frowning. 'You could assist with his evening surgery. We'll need to find you somewhere to stay, at least during the week.'

Lottie rushed around her father's desk and embraced him.

'Thank you, Papa,' she said. 'Thank you, thank you, thank you.'

She skipped out of the study and climbed the stairs. On the landing she passed a large portrait of an ancient Prideaux, which one she could not remember, astride his horse.

'Silly Papa,' Lottie said to this unknown ancestor. 'Does he think that horses are small animals?'

2

They rode the buggy in darkness onto the farm, near Withiel Florey. Patrick Jago had not been here before and did not know the occupants. A lad met them and led the way to the stables. There they found a shire mare standing huge and forlorn in her loose box. Around her and outside the box, looking on, were a number of men, grim and exhausted.

'We never needed a vet before,' the farmer said, by way of introduction.

Patrick Jago ignored him. He addressed instead a man who stood in his shirtsleeves, with a hand upon the rump of the great horse. 'Are you the carter?' he asked.

The man nodded. 'I can't figure it,' he said.

The box smelled of shit and straw, urine and blood. Lottie saw that the litter on the ground around the horse was soaked. She watched the vet examine the mare's hindquarters. The two tiny forelegs of the foetus were presented.

'We been pullin and pullin but it don't come,' the carter said. ''Tis as if it's caught up with another one, but I don't believe there's twins in there.'

'We've not needed a vet before,' the farmer repeated.

'How long has she been in labour?' Patrick Jago asked. No one answered. He looked around but all kept their heads down.

'We've great hopes for this foal,' the farmer said. 'The sire's—'

'The foal is dead,' Patrick Jago told him. 'Let us try to save your mare.' He turned to the carter. 'Ten quarts of linseed jelly.' The carter motioned to his lads and they trotted out of the stable. 'And strain it through a cloth,' the vet called after them. He asked Lottie to fetch the enema syringe from the boot of the buggy. When she returned he explained to her that all the mare's waters had been expelled, there was no more. Her uterine contractions were surely exhausted, the uterus most likely tight as a steel band around the foetus.

While the potion was being prepared, Lottie Prideaux laid out the vet's parturition instruments upon a bench brought into the box. The finger knife, with its ring to slip over the middle finger. The hand knife, with a cord for the wrist. The short, three-and-a-half-inch hook, with four and a half feet of cord attached. The long hook knife, with its two-and-a-half-foot wooden handle. The crutch, of equal length. They looked like instruments of torture, not aids to birth, yet Lottie knew a foetus could be stillborn and stuck, and have to be dealt with savagely.

When the lad returned, Lottie drew the jelly into the enema syringe while the vet stripped to the waist. He took the syringe and inserted its nozzle into the mare's vagina, past the forelegs of her dead foal, and pumped the jelly into her womb. He told Lottie, who stood close by him, that the linseed jelly would distend the womb and float the foetus. 'I hope it will also act as a lubricant,' he said, 'in place of the natural water.'

The syringe had to be refilled a number of times. The vet demanded more light. The farmer barked orders and lads scuttled away and returned with hurricane lamps, which they hung from rafters. Patrick Jago requested the long hook. Lottie brought it over to him. He said that the head of the dead foal must be bent back in one way or another. With its nose pointing forward behind the elbow, or with its nose pointing back towards the flank, or with its head turned over onto its back, if she could imagine those fatal configurations. He slowly inserted the long hook. 'I will try to put it into the eye-socket,' he said. 'We need to press the foetus back into the womb and then manipulate the head into its correct position.'

Patrick Jago fished around with the hook. He could not see into the darkness of the womb. Lottie watched his face. Though his eyes were open it was clear that he saw nothing of the stable but rather what was in his mind's eye as he attempted to interpret or decipher what he discovered with the hook. He continued for a long time, adjusting and readjusting the handle. Occasionally he took a deep breath, as if to signify his hope that he had a catch, and began to tug the hook slowly out, only to sigh with disappointment as it slid too easily free.

The great shire mare stood calm all this time, suffering the pain and the indignities that had been wrought upon her and continued to be. Did she know that her foal was lost, that its heart beat no more inside her? That these human beings were intent upon saving her life? Lottie did not believe so. No one spoke to her, or stroked her. Not on this farm. She wished to do so herself but did not. She glanced around and saw that one or two more people had gathered, including a woman of the same age as the farmer. They looked to her with their stern faces in the yellow light like macabre spectators at some morbid entertainment. As if they could not help themselves, though they wished to save their prize mare, from taking pleasure in watching her suffer.

Patrick Jago withdrew the long hook and gave it to his assistant and asked her for a length of cord. Although so little had been achieved so far, the vet's bare chest was already marked by spots of the linseed jelly and blood and other matter. He looped the cord around one of the dead foal's pastern joints and twisted it tight and told the carter to hold it taut.

'Pull it when I tell you to, not before,' he said. He asked Lottie to fetch the long embryotomy knife. This he introduced carefully into the mare as he had the hook, and pushed it in half as far.

'We need to get on to the shoulder,' he said. He manipulated the knife, telling Lottie that he was now cutting the skin, and dividing it down the limb. He then withdrew the knife and asked her to use her fingers to detach the skin from the shank-bone, and pull it loose.

Lottie removed her jacket and rolled up her sleeves, and felt along the limb for where the skin had been cut.

'Ain't the lad gonna take off his shirt?' the farmer's wife called out. Perhaps this was meant as a joke to lighten the morose proceedings, but none laughed. Patrick Jago ignored her. He asked the carter to tug gently but steadily on the cord. Lottie found the loose skin and separated a little of it from the limb. She tied a piece of thin cord to the flap of skin and extracted her hands from the mare and pulled the cord. At first it would not give but when she applied all her strength she could feel the skin tearing off the flesh beneath.

The vet reintroduced the long knife and cut the muscles between the shoulder and the body. The carter kept pulling on the cord fixed around the dead foal's pastern until, with a grotesque watery sound of snapping bone or gristle, and rent flesh, the foreleg came away.

Jago wasted not a moment to celebrate this revolting success but exchanged the long knife for the hook as before and tried once more to secure the head and turn it around to a normal presentation. He was not able to but this time did not spend so long, but set to repeating his operation to remove the other foreleg of the foetus. Again Lottie pulled loose the skin. Again the vet cut the pectoral muscles and the carter tugged with all his force, and the foreleg was yanked and ripped off the body of the dead foal so abruptly that it came slithering out of the vagina of the mare and the carter staggered backwards across the wet straw of the loose box with the severed limb, like a man astounded by what he'd been given, struggling to retain his balance.

Lottie looked up and saw that a girl now stood at the head of the mare. She had not seen her enter the stable. The girl stroked the horse's neck. She was looking at

Lottie, and when their eyes met did not look away but kept staring directly at her.

The vet now inserted the long crutch and pushed against the foetus. Robbed of its support, it slid easily back into the bottom of the womb. Once again Patrick Jago did not waste time but with both the long hook and the short hook, with four or five feet of cord attached and a wooden handle at the other end, he got the head round and was able with the carter's assistance to pull the mutilated body of the dead foal out from the mare, a messy bundle of flesh and jelly and blood. As she felt her offspring's delivery, the exhausted mare appeared to stumble, her knees buckling at the relief or the disappointment, Lottie could not tell which. Recumbent, on her side, the big horse breathed softly, her flanks trembling.

As the carter's lads took away the foetus of the foal, Patrick Jago told Lottie that if they had called him earlier he might have saved it. His bare torso was now covered in bloody gore and filth. He told the carter to water the mare immediately, and to mix a simple powder of four drachms of nitrate of potash and two of carbonate of iron in her mash each night for one week.

'And either move her to a different box or stall or change this straw immediately,' he said. The girl knelt beside the mare, still stroking her neck, still staring at Lottie.

The farmer's mood was changed. He seemed to have forgotten the prize foal and was grateful to have his mare alive. He insisted that the vet and his assistant come to the farmhouse to clean up and enjoy the breakfast they deserved.

They returned the instruments and ropes to the cart, stumbling through the darkness. Patrick Jago told Lottie that he was glad to see someone had thought to take it upon himself to stable their cob, and no doubt give it some hay. Lottie thought of the girl with the wide eyes.

Though it was warm in the farmhouse kitchen Lottie kept her jacket on, covering as it did her blood-spattered white shirt. The farmer's wife served them porridge with cream and honey. Lottie was sure that after what she had witnessed she would have no appetite at all, and would sit mute and unfed while the vet and the farmer ate and talked, but to her surprise her hunger was great. She had little idea what time it was. The farmer's wife put plates with three eggs each and four rashers of bacon before them, and cut slices of bread from which steam rose. Lottie spread a slice with yellow butter.

The farmer proclaimed that he had never called a veterinary surgeon before, he thought he might have said so already but wished to repeat it. 'I'll never have that quack horse doctor again,' he said. 'With his blocks and his pulleys. Near as dammit killed my best mare. But you saved her, Mister Jago. With your young lad there. You saved her with all your fine tools.'

They drank sweet creamy coffee, then Patrick Jago said they must be on their way. When they stepped outside Lottie was surprised to find the sky pale grey and the barns and hayricks discernible in the pre-dawn light.

As they drove the cob slowly back to the surgery in Bampton, Lottie asked if there were further abnormal positions a foetus could be aligned in beyond those Mr Jago had outlined. He said there were. Many. She must study the plates in Thompson's book.

'There are times one is forced to do what we have just done, or similar butchery, to a live foetus, and kill it in order to save the mare. There are other times when a foal or calf is of more value than its mother, and we must perform a Caesarean section to save the offspring, and run the risk of losing the mother.'

The vet handed the reins to Lottie and while she drove, he filled his pipe and lit it. 'When I say risk, I should add that of the half-dozen Caesareans I have performed on mares, I have lost the mother every time.' Patrick Jago sucked on his pipe. 'It can be a savage business, Lottie. Reproduction is the most extraordinary miracle in the whole of nature, yet it can go wrong in so many ways. A paradox of obstetrics I imagine one will never fully comprehend.'

3

The surgery had belonged to Patrick Jago's father, who was awarded his diploma from the Royal College of Veterinary Surgeons in the early sixties and then surprised his contemporaries by retreating at his wife's request to set up practice in her small home town in Devon, close to the Somerset border, below the moor. Patrick was their only child, and followed his father's calling. When his father died, from the infectious disease of glanders, picked up from a horse, Patrick took over the practice. His mother still lived in her home beside the surgery, and Lottie now lodged with her while Patrick and his wife lived across town.

What had once been a two-stall stable up against the house, Patrick Jago's father had converted into a surgery. In the gloomy loft above the stable and adjoining coach house were dusty glass cases in which were mounted obstetrical monstrosities the old man had collected. Lottie climbed the steps and wiped the dust off the glass. She studied calves with two heads and three eyes. Lambs with supernumerary limbs sprouting from their backbones.

New stables and kennels had been built in the garden. At the back of the surgery was a dispensary or

pharmacy. Patrick Jago had inherited his father's facto-
tum, Edgar Riddell, who stood for hours every day at
a granite mortar, grinding vegetable roots and barks
to powder, for incorporation into tonics and cough
mixtures, with a heavy marble pestle.

Today Lottie was not with Jago on his rounds, and
there were no visitors to the surgery, so she assisted
Edgar compounding ginger and aloes with black treacle
into physic or horse balls. They pounded hard lumps
of carbonite of ammonia, mixing the powder with
gentian and fenugreek, aniseed and ginger, and pushed
the mixture into four-ounce parcels wrapped in brown
paper and sealed with wax.

They prepared pint-and-a-half bottles of cattle
drench containing many ingredients infused over a
gas-ring in a large cauldron, filling the dispensary with
herbal odours. Edgar Riddell made black draughts
for the relief of colic and permitted Lottie to cut their
corks level with the neck of the bottle and to seal them
by dipping each one, upside down, into a saucepan
containing an inch of boiling pitch.

Edgar did not talk much. At the end of his working
day he shooed Lottie out of the dispensary so that he
could tidy up on his own. His last task was to polish the
mahogany benches, blackened by age, with a beeswax
and turpentine concoction he had prepared himself.

While Edgar cleaned his territory, Lottie stepped into
the surgery. She told Jago sitting at his desk that she
found the preparation of these powders and electuaries
strangely enthralling.

The vet laughed. 'It's terribly out of date,' he said. 'All these ingredients, painstakingly prepared. Wholesale firms can sell us stock medicines ready for dispensing. But how can I let Edgar go? And the thing is, they trust him, you see, Lottie. When a farmer or horse-owner calls to settle his bill, he invariably looks around the dispensary and is tempted by those shelves of drenches to take a dozen or two away with him, to replenish the harness-room first-aid cupboard.'

Lottie asked the vet to tell her of his studies to become a surgeon, at the Royal Veterinary College in Camden Town in London.

'We lived in diggings,' he said. 'We were mostly the sons of veterinary surgeons or registered practitioners. One, of a quack. The others of yeomen farmers. None of us great scholars, it must be admitted. I was the only one I knew who'd been to any kind of public school. An extremely minor one, I should add.'

He told her how in their second year they were admitted to the dissecting room, a dank and evil-smelling place. A supply of aged ponies was kept in readiness in the college stables. Two or three at a time were shot, and prepared by an injection into their arteries of red wax, and into their veins one of blue.

'The carcases were laid out on trestle tables. Each of us was allotted a portion. As our dissections proceeded, quantities of flesh were discarded upon the concrete floor around us. After a day or two this meat rotted and stank. You could see the pieces undulating under the influence of blowfly larvae. I had the advantage over some, as the son of a vet, of being somewhat inured to

the sight of corpses and the smell of putridity, but most of my fellows would no sooner enter the dissecting room than have to rush out and be wonderfully sick. Until they learned not to have breakfast on dissecting days.' He shook his head. 'I'm sure by the time you go, Lottie, it will be very different.'

'Me?' she asked, astonished. 'Surely I cannot hope to maintain this lad's disguise forever. Neither do I wish to.'

'No,' Patrick said. 'I mean that a woman will be admitted to the College one day. Why should the first one not be you?'

4

Lottie rode home three days before Christmas. She stabled the horse she'd inherited from Jago's old assistant, and spoke with Herb Shattock. A lad carried her saddlebags to the house. Lottie walked to the back of the house and entered by the kitchen. The cook fussed over her and would not let her go until the girl had tried her new sponge.

'You can't wait for lunch, my lovely,' she said. 'Not after a long ride like that.'

That was where Alice found her. As they embraced, Alice caught sight of the recipe on the kitchen table. She told Cook that it was not right to use so many eggs in the Christmas pudding, when in London and no doubt other towns and cities eggs were in short supply and people had to do without. She said there was a more suitable recipe in yesterday's newspaper and she would find it. She smiled at Lottie and walked out of the kitchen.

Cook did not understand. 'The hens is still layin,' she told Lottie. 'If a lot a the men is gone, there must be more eggs for the rest of us, like it or not.'

'I suppose Alice ...' Lottie began '... Lady Prideaux, I mean, would say that eggs can be boiled and dried and powdered, and sent to the troops.' Lottie was not sure she would ever be able to conceive of Alice as her stepmother. Her widowed father's young second wife, not five years older than Lottie herself.

Cook said she did not think that dried and powdered eggs sounded very tasty, for soldiers or anyone else. Alice returned with the recipe, which she had torn from the newspaper, and placed it on the table. Cook leaned over it.

'Look, you see,' Alice said, 'it uses no eggs, and only one large spoon of sugar.'

Cook squinted and read aloud, 'Six spoonfuls a flour. Half a pound a beef suet. Half a pound a currants. The sugar. One large carrot.'

'The secret,' Alice told her, 'is in the boiling. The longer a Christmas pudding is permitted to boil, the richer it will become.'

'One large carrot,' Cook repeated.

'Precisely,' Alice said. 'One assumes that is what will give it sweetness, and moisture. And there is no shortage of carrots, you see.'

Cook frowned. She shook her head. 'I don't know, your ladyship,' she said. 'I never heard a that before.'

Lottie said quietly that she had better get washed and changed into more appropriate attire, though she was not sure whether either of them heard her, for they remained engrossed in their discussion of ingredients.

Lottie climbed the stairs to the nursery. As she approached she smelled paint. Linseed, turpentine. She opened the door and walked in and for a moment thought that she had entered the wrong room or the wrong floor. As if the configuration of the house had been altered in her absence. She had only been lodging in Bampton for a few months but it was the longest she had ever been away and perhaps that was all it took to forget what you thought you knew so well. Then she understood.

The long attic room was empty, save for dust sheets on the floor and one paint-spattered stepladder, and tins, brushes and other decorating paraphernalia. All the old furniture was gone. In the middle of the room was a single object, covered in a white sheet. Then she saw that a number of crates stood at the far end. Lottie walked down the long room, her footsteps muffled by the sheets on the wooden boards. The heavy rain of 20 December had been followed by these cold bright days, and sunlight glared into the bare attic through the dormer windows and skylights.

Lottie raised the lid of the first crate, disclosing items covered in layers of newspaper. She lifted one out and carefully unwrapped it. A fragile skeleton, that of a hare, one of those Leo Sercombe had given her. She had brought him up here after one such skeleton was crushed when she attacked him. Had sneaked him up here, in fact, surreptitiously.

Lottie rewrapped the hare's skeleton and put it carefully back in the crate and replaced the lid. She turned and walked to the centre of the room. Lottie took hold of the white sheet and dragged it off the object beneath. She had assumed it was a piece of furniture or some such solid mass, but as she pulled the sheet over it the object moved. Lottie let go of the sheet and took a step back. Whatever it was remained in the same place yet in motion. Perhaps it was a clockwork mechanism of some kind. The girl took courage and slid the sheet off entirely. There before her was a rocking horse, brand new, brightly painted. It shifted on its rockers then came to rest. Lottie stepped around in front of the wooden horse. It looked past her with oddly lifelike painted eyes.

Lottie wished to protest but how could she? To complain, at the age of seventeen, that her nursery was being taken over?

She fetched the stepladder and carried it across the room. One of the skylights possessed a concealed pair of hinges that opened it wide and allowed access to the roof. She pushed open the skylight, and rose up through the opening until she was standing on the top step of the ladder. She put her hands on the window ledge and sprang up, lifting one hand and at the same time twisting so that she came to rest sitting on the ledge. She swung her legs up and walked across the roof.

A walkway ran along the centre between a chimney stack at each end, and in the middle was a raised wooden platform. Lottie did not know its function or provenance. She had never seen anyone else use it. Her father said he had been told that his great-grandfather liked to shoot birds from an armchair brought up here, but this sounded like a family fable. His grandfather was a keen astronomer, so perhaps there had once been a telescope mounted there through which to view the cosmos overhead.

The platform was rickety. It always had been. Lottie was not confident it would bear her weight, but she climbed it tentatively and stood upon it. The air was still as it had been for days and she was grateful. The platform tottered, swaying as she moved. A sudden breeze could have carried it off.

Lottie looked around. The height afforded her a panoramic view of the estate and the land surrounding it. The horse-ploughed furrows, the grazing pastures, the woods. Moor rising away on one side, hills on the other. She did not believe her ancestor was either a hunter or a stargazer, but rather like her he had loved his home and simply wished to contemplate it. Its beauty and its bounty.

For dinner they had ox-tail soup followed by a soufflé with oysters, which Alice's mother Lady Grenvil had brought down from London. The servants cleared the plates. The Christmas crackers were decorated with pictures of the dreadnoughts of the Royal Navy. Duncan Grenvil had bought them in Hamleys. They pulled the crackers. Lottie's father Arthur and his wife Alice. Alice's parents Lord and Lady Grenvil. Lottie. And Doctor Pollard, a widower from Taunton. Each tiny explosion left an odour of saltpetre in the air.

Lottie looked at the smaller end of a cracker with which she had been left. 'You'd better make a wish then,' she told the doctor.

'I imagine we all have the same one,' Doctor Pollard said. 'That the war will be over soon.'

'Over by Christmas,' said Duncan Grenvil. 'Yet again.'

Alice asked her father not to be morose. He apologised, and said that he had spotted a rather wonderful board game, called *Kill Kiel*, based on sinking German submarines. His wife exclaimed that Duncan was as brilliant as ever. Had he already forgotten that the game was under the tree, all wrapped up, and ready to be Arthur's present? Her husband had just spoiled the surprise.

'Not at all,' Arthur said. 'Now I shall look forward to opening it all the more. And playing the game this afternoon.'

'Observe what is going on, Alice,' Maud Grenvil told her daughter. 'I trust you are taking note. This is a reflex action for them, they stick together.'

The men made sighs and gestures of demurral. Lottie watched them. Duncan Grenvil was her father's best friend. Was it odd that Arthur had married his daughter? Was it odd for Maud?

Alice nodded to the butler, Mister Daw, and the main course was served. Roast turkey with chestnut stuffing. Boiled ham. Lottie concentrated hard on keeping gravy stains from the frills of her white blouse.

'No goose, Papa?' she asked.

'Apparently not,' he said.

Alice looked from Arthur to Lottie, her brow furrowed in perplexity, or suspicion.

'Papa loves goose,' Lottie explained to the guests. 'We've always had it at Christmas.'

'You never said,' Alice told her husband.

Maud Grenvil commented that it was quite a spread. She had not seen so many vegetables in London all year.

Duncan asked, 'What word from young Carew?'

'He writes far more to Lottie than to me,' Arthur said. 'You'd better ask her.'

Lottie told them that their former estate manager was now in the cavalry. William's most recent letter assured her all was well. They'd delivered the Germans a crushing blow at the Ancre river, taking so many prisoners it was a challenge to feed them.

'I hope you write back to him,' Alice said.

'Of course,' Lottie assured her.

The Grenvils had not been down to the West Country since the summer. Now Alice asked Arthur to try to persuade them not to go back to the capital. 'They can evacuate to their own home down here,' she said. 'Out of reach of those dreadful Zeppelins.'

'You mustn't worry, Alice,' her father said. 'Our plucky little aircraft mob those ugly balloons and are bringing them down now. We barely see them any more.'

'No,' Alice agreed. 'But only because the Germans are sending bomber planes now.'

'But one feels one's needed there,' Duncan Grenvil said. 'And your mother's doing wonderful work at the hospital.'

Doctor Pollard asked what work this was.

'I simply organise some volunteer nurses,' Maud Grenvil said. 'One's friends' daughters. Their friends.' She turned to Lottie. 'You could come and join us, my dear, if you're looking for something to do.'

Alice remonstrated with her mother. 'I want you to stay here, Mama, and instead you're trying to take people in the opposite direction. You can't! Anyhow, Lottie is doing her bit already, acting as an assistant to one of our local veterinary surgeons whose assistants are at the Front.'

Lottie told them a little of what she had been doing with Patrick Jago, how much she was learning. Doctor Pollard said that increasing numbers of women were becoming general practitioners, and with the casualties in France he suspected that unfortunately this may need to continue after the war was over. Presumably it would be the same for veterinary medicine. Duncan Grenvil said that with small animals perhaps that would be so, but surely there was a difference between treating humans and manhandling shire horses and bulls, with which all agreed.

After the main course they were served plum pudding and mince pies, and orange jelly. Lady Grenvil said that girls in the Voluntary Aid Detachment kept watch on the tons of hay stacked on the docksides, waiting for shipment to the horses of the Expeditionary Force. She asked Arthur Prideaux how the farms on the estate managed to bring in the harvest with so many men and lads gone.

'A number were permitted to return from the front line to help, actually,' he said. 'Many thousands came back for the harvest.'

'What if the enemy had found out?' Lottie wondered. 'They could have overrun us.'

'I imagine,' her father said, 'German farm workers went home for the same purpose, at much the same time.'

'Poor Arthur's wearing his fingers to the bone managing the estate,' Alice told her guests. 'I hardly see him.'

'The problem is one that's been forty years in the making,' Lottie's father said. 'We allowed ourselves to rely on other countries for wheat, meat, sugar. Staples. The war's simply brought the situation into stark relief. We nearly ran out of wheat this year.'

'And hasn't the price risen by an extraordinary margin?' Duncan said. 'You farmers must be raking it in.'

Doctor Pollard said it was going to get worse if, as was feared, the Germans moved to unrestricted warfare and attacked merchant convoys bringing food from across the Atlantic. Arthur Prideaux disagreed. He said that he did not believe a civilised nation would abandon the rules of war.

'The ministry wants us to plough up our grazing land,' he said.

'They want everyone to,' Maud Grenvil said. 'You should see the allotments in front of Kensington Palace. And I hear His Majesty's offered up the gardens at Buckingham Palace for vegetable production.'

'I can just picture Queen Mary out there with her fork and spade,' said Alice. 'She's game for anything, you know.'

'It's all very well for those flat counties in the east,' said Arthur. 'I mean, they're virtually prairies. The West Country here's higgledy-piggledy. It's no good for corn in any quantity. Best kept for dairy.'

'I'm sure we'll always want milk, Papa,' Lottie said.

'We can all see you're in your element, Arthur,' said Duncan Grenvil. 'You've always been a farmer at heart.'

After the food had been taken away they drank coffee and liqueurs, and nibbled at desserts, and spoke of how the wounded were brought home on night trains. How medicines were scarce in Taunton, but that people seemed to visit their GP less often with trivial aches and sprains. Lottie said little. She wondered how soon she could return to Bampton, and the veterinary practice.

5

People brought their dogs and cats to the surgery. Patrick Jago was indifferent to them. 'I know it's the way things are going,' he said. 'But at the College we saw ourselves as horse specialists, and I'm afraid I still do. I can't help it.'

After Christmas the vet left the small animals to Lottie, while remaining on hand if she needed to consult him. In the middle of January a woman brought in her spaniel. 'It has become melancholy,' she said. 'I have no idea why.'

Lottie examined the dog. It did not object but stood upon the table gazing glumly at the wall. She felt its stomach. Dogs swallowed all sorts of things. Nails, meat skewers, hat-pins. Safety pins and needles. Golf balls, tin-tacks. She wondered what this one had snapped up.

Lottie took the spaniel out to the yard, followed by the owner. She squatted and gripped the dog's mouth with her left hand, pressing down the hanging lip on either side with finger and thumb so that it covered the molar teeth of the upper jaw. It could not bite her fingers now without first biting its own lips.

It was surprising how few people knew that a dog could be made to vomit by giving it a crystal of washing soda, no bigger than a garden pea. Whippers-in of hounds knew, and always carried a lump or two with them, for hounds sometimes picked up poison that had been laid for vermin. Lottie flicked her soda grain to the back of the spaniel's tongue, and its reflex movement gulped it down. The dog looked at Lottie with a blank expression. Then it opened its mouth, retched a couple of times, then vomited easily and copiously – and there on the ground, mixed in with the animal's breakfast, was a medium-sized brooch. Lottie picked it up and held it out to the owner, whose relief was equalled by her distaste. Lottie handed her the dog's lead instead, and took the brooch to the tap.

A week later another dog, a Labrador this time, was brought to the surgery by its owner, a retired sea captain. This dog was well known in the town. The owner gave him a penny each day to take between his teeth to the bakery, where he was given a currant bun, for which he had a predilection. One day the baker met the dog's owner in the street.

'I don't mind your dog havin his bun,' he said. 'But he don't always bring his tin.'

Now the captain said his dear Lab had been taken ill with symptoms of stomach derangement. Lottie could hear a faint rattling as the Labrador walked into the room. Patrick Jago took a skiagraphy, which revealed a cluster of coins. Too many for a simple emetic. They told the captain to leave the dog at the surgery over-night. Lottie watched Jago carry out a gastrotomy, and together they extracted from the dog's stomach a total of one shilling and tuppence.

Lottie washed the money and when it was dry she gave it to Jago. He told her to keep it, she was earning every penny.

'I should be paying you,' Lottie said. 'For everything you're teaching me.'

Unless Patrick Jago knew that he would require a great deal of tackle, of instruments and stocks of medicine, he rode on horseback to his country clients, a length of cord slung around the horse's neck, saddlebags over its rump. Lottie rode his old assistant's cob beside him, over hills, through wooded valleys, up onto the moor. They rode in sunshine and darkness, in rain and hail and snow. When the roads were icy they tied sacks around the feet of their horses. Some nights Lottie fell asleep in the saddle and her pony carried her back to Bampton unprompted.

She trusted that no one knew the smooth-cheeked lad accompanying the vet was in reality a girl, still less that she was Lord Prideaux's daughter. But Bampton was more than ten miles from the estate, and few people in the town knew aught of it, while those on the farms they visited rarely ventured beyond their own valley.

They were called to a farm outside the village of Skilgate. A mare had become vicious. She would not let anyone near to groom or ride her. The farmer thought she was incurable and must be destroyed, but Patrick told him it was likely due to a cystic condition that could be cured. They needed a variety of instruments for use in this case and took the buggy. They laid straw in the yard and cast the mare, and the vet carried out the operation.

Afterwards, Lottie returned the instruments to the buggy. While Patrick talked with the farmer and his carter, giving instructions for the mare's convalescence, Lottie looked around. She heard voices coming from a cowshed and peered in. There was a cow, in poor condition, being examined by two men. One told the other that the beast had worm in the tail for sure. Lottie watched in horror as he lifted the tail and drew a razor across its end and squeezed out a thin white tendon. 'Got it,' he said. 'That'll cure it. Rub a load a salt on the cut now.'

Lottie returned to where the vet and the farmer were still in conversation. 'Do you know what your man is doing?' she interrupted. 'While the surgeon here applies his learning, acquired through the painstaking accumulation of scientific knowledge, a quack back there attacks a poor cow with his knife. It's barbaric.'

The farmer flushed, whether from anger or embarrassment it was hard to tell. And if the latter, was it that he'd allowed such quackery or did not know it took place upon his premises? Or perhaps he did not take kindly to being spoken to in such a way by a fresh-faced boy. Before the farmer could say anything, Patrick Jago said he believed the mare was in good hands and with luck would give no more trouble, and they must be on their way.

As he drove the buggy, Lottie recounted to the vet what she had seen. He shook his head and told her she must not talk to people in that manner.

'But they need to be cured of their stupidity,' she said.

'They are our clients,' he said. 'My customers. I shall lose them if you annoy them. Besides, superstitions do not die out overnight. We must be patient.' He smiled. 'Many of the older farm workers round here still carry a potato in their pocket to ward off rheumatism.'

'A lack of education is no excuse for idiocy,' Lottie said.

'But if you ask them they will show you how hard the potato has become, proof that the rheumatic poison has gone from their body to the vegetable. Hard as a stone.'

Lottie did not know what to say to that.

'If you wish one day to be a practitioner yourself,' Patrick told her, 'and not to lose all your clients, you will need to learn a little humility, Lottie.'

A vet was required to be equally expert in foaling, calving, lambing, farrowing and whelping. Patrick Jago taught his assistant that the simplest way to tell a good from a bad large-animal obstetrician was that a bad one starts by pulling, a good one by pushing. For the secret of rectifying a miscued presentation was to encourage the foetus back into the womb, in whose relative spaciousness one might manipulate disordered limbs. That spring of 1917 he bought them both rubber overalls. Lottie alternately sweated and shivered with cold. Her arms were chapped from continual rinsing. Under his guidance she found herself lying on a wet and filthy cowshed floor, up to her armpits while exploring the position of a calf. Sometimes the cow's labour pangs came when Lottie's arm was trapped between the calf's head and the cow's pelvic bone, and the girl cried out in pain. She returned to Bampton with fingers stiff and cramped, arm bruised blue from wrist to armpit.

Lottie was fed by Patrick Jago's mother's cook. The housemaid washed her clothes. The vet himself lived across town and did not speak of his wife, whether out of discretion or shame Lottie did not know. She understood that Mrs Jago was an invalid, with some illness of the mind and perhaps the body too. She was looked after by a nursemaid, overseen by her husband's sister, who acted as their housekeeper. Knowing this much, Lottie did not feel able to ask more. She did not know whether or not the Jagos had children and so one day while they were out in the buggy she emboldened herself to enquire.

'No,' he said. 'It is something one assumed would happen.' He relaxed his grip on the reins. 'And although it has been clear for many years that it will not, I must admit I am still not reconciled. To the absence, I suppose. The loss of what should have been. Of what should be.'

The cob had slowed down and the vet had not urged him on. The horse's hooves and the iron rims of the wheels on the road made little sound. Gazing ahead along the lane, it was easy to speak to the person beside you.

'You might have heard of the theory of alternative worlds,' Patrick said. 'That this life we live is but one of infinite possible lives. If we had taken that road, not this. Had met this person, not that one.'

Lottie shook her head. 'I'm sorry,' she said. 'I could not believe in that theory. Of course we can imagine other lives, but they are not real. Only this one is real. This horse, pulling this buggy, along this lane, on this cool morning.'

'Yes, of course, Lottie, you're right.'

They rolled on in silence for a while. 'And yet,' the vet said, 'we know how random the process of reproduction is. How many spermatozoa fulfil no purpose. I wonder whether somehow those souls I should have fathered exist somewhere. If only in a realm you might call potential.'

Lottie turned and looked at him. Grey hair clipped close beneath his hat. The dark moustache. His weathered skin. He was not yet old. 'You would have made a good father,' she told him. 'I'm sorry. I mean, you would make a good father.'

Patrick smiled at her. His eyes crinkled. 'Thank you,' he said. 'May I ask what makes you say that? Apart from generously offering consolation to a maudlin old fool?'

'You are kind,' she said. 'And your children would surely be curious. And, as proof that you are a good man, horses trust you.'

The vet nodded his thanks. 'Never take a horse's trust for granted,' he said. 'One kick, and ...' He raised his left hand from the reins, lifted it into the air as if it held something which he tossed away like some lost redundant soul, or spermatozoa, into the air.

6

From 20 March the vet and his assistant were to spend two days a week on a round of farms and stables. On the first day they took the buggy, for they needed to carry a great weight of rope as well as instruments. The season had arrived for the gelding of horses.

Patrick Jago told his assistant that, in his opinion, in the years before the war horse breeding had been at its zenith – both in terms of the number of foals produced and in their quality. Thoroughbreds, hunters, hackneys, hacks and cobs, shire horses, Clydesdale and Suffolk Punches. The war, of course, had only concentrated demand. In addition, there were droves of wild ponies across the moors, the Highlands of Scotland, the Welsh hills and mountains, and the New Forest.

All the wild and semi-wild unbroken colts had to be rounded up, surplus males castrated and sold. Many farmers kept one or two mares from which to breed. Even in peacetime there was a demand for geldings to act as remounts for the army. If a horse didn't look like maturing into a valuable hunter or an officer's charger, so long as he was sound he could be sold as a troop horse.

*

They came to a farm the vet knew well. He had been visiting regularly all his life, at first as a boy with his father. Lottie noticed a mound of carrots in the stable yard. Patrick said these were for pregnant mares. Foals here were sometimes born with yellowy-orange skin.

A rag of colts jostled together in a pen. Patrick had requested that they be rounded up and starved for at least twelve hours, to lessen the risk of a ruptured stomach.

While the vet spoke to the farmer, Lottie lit the coals to heat up the iron, and sharpened the vet's knives. He had explained the procedure, and warned her that it had to be performed swiftly. She understood what she had to do and hoped to remember it. He would have no time to instruct her on what he was doing. She would have to make sense of what she saw as he carried it out. There were six colts, of various size and conformation. 'They's risin one year old,' the farmer said. 'Except for that one there.' He nodded towards a chestnut with a white diamond emblazoned upon his forehead. 'He's risin two, I reckon.'

The vet asked for four men to help him. He put on his surgical coat, and a dirty old cloth cap Lottie had not seen before. He wore it back to front, the peak over the back of his neck. Lottie asked him why he donned so filthy an article when about to perform surgery.

'A lot of the colts will be infested with lice,' he said. 'It's to stop them getting into my hair.'

'You did not warn me of that danger,' she told him.

'Since you never remove your own cap I did not think it worth mentioning,' he said.

'I don't see what is humorous about that,' Lottie said.

Patrick stopped smiling. He furrowed his brow. 'Just remember,' he said, 'that these colts have not been handled or haltered. They are liable to strike out using both their fore and their hind feet. Not to mention their teeth.'

The vet made a loop at the end of a length of hemp. He spliced a wooden peg into the rope so that the knot would not slip so tight around the horse's neck as to throttle it. He walked up to the nearest colt, the two-year-old chestnut, and swung the lasso up into the air. Lottie watched it fall over the animal's head as easily as if the colt had been waiting patiently for precisely such an occurrence. It was only when it felt the rope tauten upon its skin that it struggled.

Lottie wondered why the vet had chosen this horse first. Or perhaps it was simply the first colt he came to, and when you had done this a hundred times you did not bother to make such choices. She would not have chosen the two year old herself.

Three of the four men, including the farmer, took up the hemp rope. The fourth, a lad, opened the gate and they drove the colt into the open field beyond, the men running behind. When the lad had closed the gate he ran to catch up with the others and grabbed a section of rope himself. In the middle of the field the men hung on to the rope with all their weight, and held it low to the ground. The colt planted his feet and tried to pull himself away.

While the animal raged, Lottie laid out the vet's instruments upon a board. Patrick Jago prepared another, thin rope. It was some forty feet long.

The farmer called out, 'What the hell is that made of?'

'Cotton,' Jago told him. 'It's softer than hemp, less likely to injure their limbs. Supposedly.'

'I hope for you and your lad's sake it's strong enough.'

'I'm assured it is,' Jago said. 'And I hope so too.'

The vet made a loop in the middle of the cotton rope. This loop he passed over the end of the rope held by the men, each man releasing his grip to allow the vet to slip his loop along, towards the horse. Lottie picked up a long-forked stick from where she'd laid it on the ground and took up the far end of the cotton rope, walking out to one side. Patrick walked out to the other. At a nod from him they walked up either side of the colt, Patrick on his right, Lottie on his left, sliding the loop up the hemp rope to his neck. He became aware of this further intrusion and, eyes wild with panic and anger, threw his head around. Lottie used the long stick to manipulate the loop over the colt's head.

'Watch those feet,' Patrick called out when he feared the girl was getting too close to the horse.

When she had got the cotton rope around the colt's neck, Lottie walked away backwards.

'Is your young lad up to this?' the farmer called out. 'You want one a my men to help you?'

'No, thank you,' Patrick Jago said. 'He'll do.'

The vet had explained to Lottie the procedure for casting the colts, using the simplest method he knew of, known as 'the side-lines'. They would work in tandem. Still, she scrutinised exactly what he did on his side of the horse and followed suit closely.

The vet walked up to the horse and threw his end of the cotton rope between the hind feet and walked around the back of the colt and picked it up. Lottie did likewise. The colt kicked and plunged though he was still held by the four men on the hemp rope and so constrained.

Once the animal's protests subsided, Patrick slowly approached the colt's front and passed the end of his rope between the neck-rope and the colt's shoulder. Then Lottie did the same. The four men watched in silence, their grip on the hemp rope firm. Then, at Jago's request, leaving the farmer and the lad on the hemp rope, one of the farm workers came and joined the vet, the other joining Lottie.

'We'll cast him on your side,' Patrick Jago called out. 'You two over there, pull sideways and backwards.' He turned to the man behind him and said, 'We pull forwards. Ready?'

Now the farmer and the lad let go of the hemp rope. As the other two pairs slowly pulled on the cotton rope, both of the colt's hind feet were drawn inexorably up to his elbows. His eyes were wild and he looked as if he wanted to struggle but was too surprised by what they had sprung on him to do so. He slowly toppled over and lay on the ground on his left side.

Patrick Jago used shorter ropes to secure the hind legs together at the pasterns with a double hitch, then the forelegs likewise. Lottie wondered whether he would ever trust her or anyone else to tie these particular knots. Finally he fixed the back rope to the upper hind shank and passed it under the loins to the other side, to keep the legs in the right position and give himself more room to operate.

'Keep his head well back,' Jago told the farmer. 'He'll struggle less and be less liable to injure his spine or his lumbar muscles.'

The vet washed the penis of the colt with cold water and carbolic soap, and dried it with a rough towel. He poured into the sheath a little carbolic oil and smeared some of it over the bag or scrotum. With his left hand, he pressed the closest testicle tight into the scrotum and with one quick sweep of his knife made a bold opening. The gland thus exposed, he pulled up. One or two inches up the cord he attached the clam.

Lottie passed Patrick the hot iron. He looked at it and murmured approvingly, 'Dead red-heat,' and took it and quickly cut through the vascular or hinder portion. Then he carefully seared through the spermatic cord or string. The vet handed the iron back to Lottie. By gently opening and closing the clam he checked to see that the bleeding had stopped. When satisfied it had done so he released the clam, and then applied the same procedure to the second testicle. The colt lay trussed up, on his side. Lottie saw him trembling, eyes wild with pain and anger and fear. He lay utterly still. She could feel him quivering, discerned his potential energy, waiting to be unleashed. It was apparent to her. Perhaps not to everyone.

The vet asked the men to free the ropes from around the colt's neck. He unhitched the shackles around the horse's feet in the same order in which he had tied them but in reverse. When the last hitch was undone they all stepped away. For a moment the animal lay there, unfettered but motionless, as if he did not believe he was free, and this was a trick. If he tried to move, the human beings would laugh and truss him up again. Or as if he desired a moment of repose in which to contemplate his new, emasculated state. Perhaps trying to find some good in it before entering this next, denuded stage of his life. Then he appeared to come to a decision. With an awkward kind of shrugging, stumbling movement, the gelding staggered to his feet and in a moment had cantered away to a far corner of the field.

Patrick Jago undid a button of his coat. He reached in and withdrew his pocket watch, and studied it.

'Twenty minutes,' he said. Lottie had not noticed him checking when they began. He put the watch back in his waistcoat pocket and rebuttoned his surgical coat. 'Let's try and speed it up,' he said, to no one in particular. Perhaps to all.

The farmer shook his head. 'Your old man I seen cut the horses standing up,' he said. 'Applied the twitch to their lip and that give him no more than two or three minutes.' He shook his head. 'Madness. But that's the kind a thing they could do in the old days.'

Lottie wondered if the farmer knew that Patrick Jago's father had died from an equine contagion. She put the iron back in the coals and followed the men to the yard to start in on the next colt.

The castrations proceeded. The fifth horse bled after the operation, but one of the farm workers secured him and walked him about, while another dashed a few pails of cold water under the tail and the bleeding ceased. If it resumed, the vet told the farmer, or if another of the horses were to haemorrhage, they should plug the opening with tow, well saturated with a tincture of iron and water.

When they had finished, the farmer was in a fine mood. He invited the vet to lunch but Patrick Jago said they had to get on. The farmer told his lad to run to the house and ask his dear wife to bring beer and cake. While Lottie coiled the ropes and gathered the instruments and stowed them in the buggy, the farmer told Patrick that his father had once come to castrate a large old boar pig. 'His tusks were six inches long, near as dammit,' he claimed. The pig was tied by a rope, applied around its upper jaw, to an iron rail in the cowshed. But it struggled and the rope broke. 'I never saw my pig man move so fast,' the farmer said. 'Nor your father. Nor myself, for that matter. We spent much a the day sitting up among the beams under the roof. The boar sat below us, champing his jaws, waiting for the first of us to fall off.'

The vet did not say anything but Lottie could not help herself. She came up to the men and asked the farmer what happened then.

'My dear wife come looking for us eventually,' he said. 'She saw what was going on, fetched my gun and shot the pig.'

The farmer's wife came out with a tray of provisions, which they ate and drank standing up. The fruit cake was thick and moist and buttery. The woman asked after the vet's wife. He said she was as well as could be expected, and thanked the woman for her concern.

The farmer told his wife that he had related the story of when she had shot that boar. The woman looked at

Lottie and rolled her eyes. 'If I could have been sure this old goat would be the first to fall, I'd have left the pig to it,' she said. 'But I couldn't risk poor Mister Jago being gored.' She nodded at the memory. 'That pig was a mean old bastard.' Then she turned to Patrick Jago and said, 'What a pretty lad you have. Better keep him away from our maids until he grows whiskers and turns ugly.'

The vet reminded the farmer to keep an eye on the colts. 'Check the swelling. It will drop down into the sheath, and should disappear inside a week. If the sheath is very big and pendulous you may stab or prick it with the point of a clean, a very clean, penknife, to allow the escape of the collected serum.' He said that even when the operation had been performed with skill and dexterity, complications could arise. 'Protrusion of the omentum, or net. Septicaemia or blood poisoning … '

It seemed to Lottie that the vet was precisely enumerating these dangers less for the farmer's benefit than for her own.

'… an abscess in the scrotum. If any of these occur, you should send for me at once.'

They visited two more farms. They ate lunch at the first. By the end of the afternoon a score of colts of all manner of horse had been castrated. As they rode back on the buggy, the cob ambling along the rough lanes, Lottie realised that though her eyes were open they saw nothing. She could not summon the effort to hold up the weight of her head, and let it lean against Patrick's shoulder. Then her eyes closed.

Back at the surgery, Lottie took the instruments inside and cleaned them while Patrick reversed the cart into its shed and stabled the cob. When he came inside, Lottie pointed out a note Edgar Riddell had left, saying that he had come down with a bilious attack and gone home.

'We are short of certain medicines,' she said. 'I shall make them up.' She had removed her cap and unpinned her hair, which though much shorter than it had once been still fell upon her shoulders.

'My dear Lottie,' Patrick said, 'you are admirably punctilious. By some miracle there is no one waiting in the surgery with their cat or mutt. I shall help you. Two apothecaries together.'

First they replenished the stock of tonics for horses. Patrick prepared a mixture of nitrate of potash, powdered resin, powdered digitalis, sulphate of iron and oil of juniper, while Lottie wrote labels that stated: GIVE ONE DAILY FOR FOUR TO SIX DAYS. Then she made the mixture into a ball with soft soap, while the vet prepared the next.

When they had a dozen balls, divided into two small boxes, Patrick fetched a bottle of sherry and two glasses from his office. He filled the glasses and gave one to Lottie, saying, 'You did very well today. You did as well as any assistant I have taken gelding. You have the makings of a fine surgeon, I am convinced of it.'

Lottie thanked him. She told him that she was confident when he was there, but if he went away she forgot everything he had explained or she had read.

'There is much to take in,' he said. 'But it will stick eventually, do not worry.'

Lottie drank the sherry. It was pleasantly dry. Patrick Jago was in his forties, but he was not old. It was only the fact of his invalid wife that made him sometimes appear so. He was still vigorous, though he'd dealt with the colts today as he did with all animals – with calm deliberation, using force seldom, as a last resort. It occurred to Lottie that perhaps he saw her as the child he and his wife could not have. Of course. It was so obvious. How could she not have considered that before?

It was warm in the dispensary. Lottie removed her jacket. They made embrocation. The vet dissolved two drachms of gum camphor in two ounces of turpentine, to which Lottie added five ounces of colza oil, three drachms of strong liquid ammonia and three of liquor potassae. This mixture she shook well together then sealed the bottle and wrote upon labels, EMBROCATION: APPLY EXTERNALLY.

They made up thirty bottles. Each time, the foul smell of the ammonia was subsumed by the other ingredients, leaving behind only its effect, upon inhalation, of a headiness, an aeration of the nostrils and sinuses.

'Does your right arm pain you?' Patrick asked after a while. 'I fancy you are favouring your left.'

Lottie raised her right arm in the air and rotated it. 'My shoulder,' she said.

'Let me take a look,' the vet suggested.

Lottie unbuttoned her shirt far enough to slide it off her right shoulder. Patrick Jago moved his fingers across her skin, tapping here, prodding there. 'I can see no bruising,' he said. 'But your muscles are extremely tight. Allow me to apply some of the embrocation we have freshly concocted.' He chuckled, pleased with this coincidence.

Lottie sat down and Patrick Jago stood behind her. He poured liniment into the palm of his left hand then rubbed his hands together and applied them to the girl's right shoulder. His hands were warm. He rolled the palm of his right hand over her shoulder and rubbed her skin with his fingers. Lottie closed her eyes. The vet rested his left hand on her neck, either to keep her torso in position or to assist his own balance, she wasn't sure. She understood that, though he was an animal doctor, human beings were mammals, after all, and he could surely picture her musculature and the underlying bones. She tried to do likewise, but the more relaxed she became the harder this was, and a drowsy image of upper parts of her own skeleton mingled with colours on the inside of her eyelids.

She did not notice Patrick further unbutton her shirt, but she realised he was kneading her left shoulder now as well as her right, and her neck also. He invited her to lie face down upon the carpet so that he could massage further down her back. When she stood up from the chair, she found her shirt was loose. It was pulled gently off her from behind and she let go. Then she felt his fingers take hold of the bottom of her vest. She raised her arms and let him lift it up over her head. She lay down.

The light was fading from the room. Patrick lit a single hurricane lamp. He knelt down beside the girl and poured more embrocation, rubbing it gently and deeply into her knotty back. Up and down the vertebrae of her spine. Across her shoulder blades. Down her sides, the skin rippling beneath his strong fingers.

Although the massage was deeply relaxing, it was also uncomfortable lying on the carpet. Lottie could feel its pattern pressing into her left cheek. Fortunately just then Patrick asked her to turn over and Lottie was relieved to do so, and lie on her back. He applied embrocation to her arms, down to her hands and fingers, then up and across her shoulders. His ministrations were so pleasant, she could barely tell which precise part of her skin Patrick's hands massaged. Waves of warmth pulsated and flowed through her body such as she had never felt before. Lottie sensed herself sinking into a delicious sleep. She did not want to, for insensibility would rob her of this pleasure. But it would be such a voluptuous slumber.

Patrick paused, perhaps to rest. Then Lottie realised he had unlaced her boots, and was pulling them off. When he unbuttoned her trousers and slid them down her legs she raised her hips from the floor to make it easier. He massaged her feet, her ankles. She drifted back towards sleep. The muscles of her calves softened. Patrick kneaded her knees, then moved his hands up her thighs. She heard him murmur, 'Oh, Lottie.' His voice seemed to come from far away, and for a moment she wondered whether she had imagined it. But then all of a sudden Lottie was wide awake.

She was no longer floating in a sensuous cocoon but lying almost naked on the carpet of the surgery. Patrick Jago's fingers were now clumsier than they had been. Lottie felt a surge of embarrassment. She must not be here, but she could not move. The vet had lost his air of calm deliberation. He was undoing his own attire. He lay beside her, then on top, his weight upon her, and she struggled. She pushed his face away from hers so that he could not kiss her and she grabbed his wrists and punched his face and tried to bite him.

Lottie Prideaux thought that she was strong. She thought she was equal to a man but she was not. She fought Patrick Jago but he overcame her. He twisted and throttled her in the throes of his ardour. She thought he might wring her neck like a goose or a swan, and so she yielded.

Afterwards, Patrick was overcome. With remorse. With shame. With love. He said he was so sorry, he said that he had taken advantage of her, it was unforgivable, she would never forgive him, he could not forgive himself … but he could not help himself, did she not see that? Perhaps she had enjoyed it a little? After all, they were not beasts of the field. They were homo sapiens. He rambled, and raved. He would kill himself. He would leave his wife, he would kill his wife, would Lottie marry him? He was not so old, forty-four. He would send his sister away. Could Lottie see herself as the young wife of a country vet?

She sat up and pulled on her clothes as the vet spoke. Then she rose and, carrying her boots, walked out of the dispensary and through to her lodging in his mother's house.

Part Three

THE SCUTTLE
1916–1919

I

The naval eye surgeon said it was a miracle that the boy's sight had recovered entirely.

'I've already been told 'tis a miracle I'm alive at all,' Leo said.

'Do not be despondent.'

'Two miracles do seem greedy.'

'Cheer up, lad,' the oculist told him, and sent him on his way.

After the Battle of Jutland in 1916, Boy Seaman First Class Leopold Jonas Sercombe, once his miraculous recuperation had been completed, was assigned to the battleship HMS *Benbow*. This ship had led the 4th Division of the Grand Fleet at Jutland, and afterwards was based in Scapa Flow. Even after much of the Fleet removed south to the Firth of Forth, still it was like a city of ships anchored in the Flow, and each battleship was like a floating district or suburb of that aquatic settlement.

Benbow had a crew of a thousand men. They were strangers to Leo Sercombe. Only a few became less so. She had her communities, of stokers, signalmen, engineers. A dozen football teams were put up from the wardroom and the gun room. Two teams would take a pinnace ashore to the Isle of Flotta for a game, the result of which was recorded for the ship's league. Leo did not play but was coerced into accompanying them to run the line. He watched the Orkney gales suck and blow the ball with malevolent humour, making a mockery of players' intentions, but men who had been cooped up in an ironclad with little distraction beyond cards and bingo for weeks at a time were glad of an escape.

Officers played hockey on the decks, using a piece of wood provided by one of the carpenters. A bucket of these chuckers remained on hand, for many were lost over the side.

Leo and the other boys knew themselves to be the hand-rags. Much of their time at anchor was spent on their knees, on decks that had been hosed with seawater and sprinkled with sand and coarse grit. From six in the morning the boys knelt, barefoot, trousers rolled up over the knees, with their holystone or bible, a block of sandstone, endlessly scrubbing and whitening the wooden boards.

Compared with what civilians at home were getting, according to the men with families, the food they ate was good. Each man and boy received half a pound of meat and a pound of potatoes a day. They had cheese, butter, eggs, salt fish. Haricot and butter beans. There was pea soup at supper, after which the men in their hammocks on the mess-decks would break wind in untuneful concert. Bread, though often dry, was plentiful. There were occasional vegetables, rare deliveries of fruit.

When a petty officer had the idea of seeing what might be done with seagulls, the commander told him that he couldn't have men wandering around his ship firing rifles willy-nilly, but catapults might be used. These were made by the ship's carpenters, and boys were tried out for their aptitude with them. Leo did well and became one of those sent up the mastheads. It was an envied job, preferable to holystoning the decks. It reminded him of being cartridge boy on shoots back home. He carved a monogram of his initials, LJS, on the handle of his catapult. The gulls he hit fell to the decks and were collected by a bag-boy. The cooks skinned and jointed the birds, and made a dish they called oosh, a stew that tasted like fishy chicken, firm-fleshed and not unpleasant.

The boy did not make friends as he had on HMS *Queen Mary*. His mates Willy Burd and Jimmy White had perished in the North Sea, along with all the rest. Leo was one of fewer than twenty survivors. Other hands kept their distance from him. Or perhaps Leo was aloof, though it was not his intention. He knew how fortunate he was to have survived, and so did they. Lucky too that his eyesight seemed unaffected. Others who had been rescued from hours in the oily water were half-blinded for life. He'd reached his full height, too, over six feet, as tall as his father had been. This was no advantage on board ship, where he was forever bending and stooping through low doorways.

Boys were not allowed alcohol. The daily ration of rum was not issued until a sailor was twenty-one. On his eighteenth birthday, in June 1917, Leo was rated, and was cajoled by other members of his mess to pay a visit to the wet canteen. The drifter picked them up, calling at ships on its way to Flotta. On that bare island stood a single one-roomed shack that sold beer and port wine. The men from *Benbow* drank until the canteen closed at 8.30. Then they stumbled back to the pier, half-carrying their young ordinary seaman, and with much cussing and laughter found their own drifter among the many tied up there. On the long trip back to *Benbow* they had to piss the beer they'd drunk over the side into the waters of the Flow, while leaning against a rail or getting a pal to keep hold of them. Some puked too, Leo among them.

Clambering noisily back aboard, they had to pass the officer of the watch, who on learning the initiatory nature of the excursion let them go, and they lifted the quiet Devon lad into his hammock. In the morning he said nothing, and thereafter declined to repeat the experience.

Leo did not resume his gunnery ambitions. When he entered a turret now his hands began to tremble and his teeth to chatter, and he could not control them. Yet despite his experience in the battle, he did not mind being back in the water. The first time he swam again it was with much trepidation, but as soon as he ducked his head beneath the surface he left the world behind, and any anxiety was washed away by a sense of calm.

He pursued his application to be a ship's diver and took the aptitude test. He was a strong swimmer, and was sent, on a ship bound for the south coast of England, to Portsmouth on a four-week course. The training consisted of physical fitness routines and compressed-air or open-circuit diving, going underwater in a diving suit with a tube delivering oxygen into the sealed helmet. He received instruction on searching ships' bottoms for explosives, as well as practice in the more usual labour of inspecting and repairing of ships' hulls.

Leo returned to the Orkneys by rail, on one of the so-called Jellicoes out of Euston Station. The long double-engined train was packed with soldiers and sailors. It rumbled north for seven hundred miles. Leo found a seat in the corner of a carriage. After an hour he rose to stretch his legs, but the corridors were full of men and their packs, kitbags, rifles. Sailors carried their hammocks. Men who had made the trip before did not bother to attempt a trek to the toilet but went to the window of their carriage and opened it to relieve themselves.

'Never stick your head out a Jellicoe train,' someone said.

The air in the carriage was dense with cigarette smoke. When night fell, men removed their boots and added to the fetid atmosphere the stink of their feet and socks.

The train steamed slowly north, straight through some stations, halting without warning at others. In Crewe, Leo alighted to get a cup of tea, but the queue was long and before he could reach the serving hatch the train began to pull out again and he ran to reboard.

In Carlisle, he managed to buy two meat pies from a stall on the platform. Those in the know said the stop in Perth would be longer, for they would wait there for carriages from King's Cross to join the train. Sure enough, though they reached Perth in the early hours of the morning, there in a temporary wooden building was a Forces canteen run by a Church organisation. Volunteer ladies stood behind a long counter and offered the men tea, coffee or cocoa, sandwiches and cakes, sweets, cigarettes.

Leo returned to the darkness of his carriage and slept. Dawn broke and he watched out of the window as the train rolled across a landscape of bare, undulating hills and moorland that hardly changed for hours.

Eventually they arrived at Thurso, the end of the line. Outside the station was a line of horse-driven waggons. Shouldering his pack, Leo climbed into one. Others hauled their equipment aboard. The waggons took them to Scrabster Harbour, where they boarded a steamer. One of the men who'd been in the same carriage on the train as Leo told him that the Pentland Firth, the narrow body of water which lay between them and the Orkneys, was a confined channel where the North Sea and the Atlantic Ocean met.

'It's like two hosepipes aimed at each other,' he said. 'Where they meet's is where we's crossin. Permanent turbulence. And the wind don't help.'

Leo thanked him for the warning. He said nothing more but did not believe that he would have a problem, for though so young he still had as sturdy a pair of sea legs as any old salt on *Benbow*. He noticed many of the soldiers and airmen crowded in the saloon to the fore of the main deck.

No sooner had they left the harbour than the sea rose in huge billows that came broadside on. The ship rolled like a barrel, and the soldiers came staggering out of the saloon to vomit in the scuppers, and to wallow there. Leo, along with other sailors, had remained on deck, swaying with the movement of the little steamer. But the water roiled and churned and made the boat lurch and twist, buck and bounce. He thought it similar to riding a wild unbroken colt. And that was the last thought he had, before he stumbled to the rails and pushed his way between two men already there and emptied his stomach of what remained of those welcome refreshments they'd been given in Perth. He spent the rest of the brief voyage to Stromness at a boat davit, wedged between a post and the rails.

To maintain his qualifications and his extra diver's pay, Ordinary Seaman Leo Sercombe was required to take a dip each month for a minimum of half an hour. In Scapa Flow the ocean floor was sandy, which meant that visibility was good.

Hermit crabs scuttled along the seabed. On the rocks were sea anemones of different colours, and kelp beds in which fish sheltered. Leo had never really looked at fish before, in their own habitat. Little lump suckers and flat flounders, fish considered to possess a wonderful ugliness, had their own alien beauty, he discovered. When the sun was out, it was amazing what could be seen down there. Langoustines, like small lobsters. Feather duster worms fluttering in the current. Leo caught occasional glimpses of shoals of pollock and saithe, of cod and ling, that turned shyly away when they saw him and darted off, silver bellies shimmering.

Often he forgot the time, and was interrupted in his absorption when he felt a tug on the line above him, and rose slowly, regretfully, back to the surface.

In spring the water warmed and an algal bloom spread across the Flow. If he dived then, Leo found his visibility reduced, but soon jellyfish appeared, comb jellies and moon jellies, neither of which stung humans but both of which fed avidly on the algae. The bloom dissipated. The comb jellies pulsated through the water, refracting light from their miniature swimming hairs or cilia.

Leo took with him a net potato bag from the mess, and searched for periwinkles and scallops. The scallops propelled themselves along the bottom by opening and closing their shells, always moving backwards, so Leo positioned himself behind them, and collected them in the bag, which he afterwards presented to the ship's cook.

The *Benbow* joined the rest of the fleet in regular gunnery exercises and sweeps of the North Sea. Some ships were painted with dazzle camouflage, in the hope of making them more difficult to hit with torpedoes by the German U-boats. They looked like zebra ships. Otherwise the fleet stayed in Scapa Flow.

Beyond organised betting at fleet regattas, gambling on board ship was strictly forbidden in the Royal Navy, yet it flourished. All ships' crews shared certain surreptitious habits, but many also had their own particular vices. HMS *Ajax*, anchored nearby in the Flow in the spring of 1918, was known as a pugilists' ship. Troublemakers were posted to her. Discipline was harsh. Breaches were dealt with by volunteering the wrongdoers in the boxing ring, and large wagers were laid on the outcomes by both officers and men.

On *Benbow*, it was mostly cards and other games. Able Seaman Victor Harris was another diver, whose first words to Leo were, 'Why aren't you sporting a gold ring in your ear, Lofty, like most of you West Country boys?'

Victor Harris gave Leo this nickname and was the only one to use it. Victor told the boy that he had no interest in diving, and like any sensible sailor did not enjoy being in the water, but took the extra pay, for his ambition was to save enough money to buy his own public house back home in Cardiff once his stint in the Navy was over. He'd been robbed blind in this war, he said, for sailors' pay had been fixed, yet prices had gone up and his family was in penury.

'Penury,' Leo repeated. 'Is that a village between Cardiff and Swansea?'

Victor Harris laughed and said that they would get along, and so Leo made his one friend on *Benbow*, a friendship that consisted mostly of ragging each other.

'Our neighbours,' Victor complained, 'who avoided conscription, have jobs in munitions and get massive wages from overtime.'

'What are you moanin about?' Leo asked him. 'You married blokes get your separation allowance, don't you?'

Victor admitted this was true.

'And don't the government give you a load more money just for havin begot children?'

'I get six bob a week for the wife, two bob a week for the first nipper, two bob a week for the second. But the rest?' He scowled. 'I only get a bob each for them, Lofty.'

Victor Harris had various rackets for making money. One was a small unofficial dhobi or laundry firm. He paid boys to wash men's clothes. A stoker hung the laundry in the engine room when he went on watch, and took them down again, all dry, when he came off.

Victor's chief money-making venture was the game of Crown and Anchor, played on a canvas board he could roll up in a moment. On it were painted six squares, in two rows of three. The top middle square had the symbol of a crown, the one below it an anchor. The outer four squares featured an ace of each suit of cards: clubs, diamonds, hearts, spades. Victor ran the board. He had three dice, each with the six symbols upon its six sides. Players put as much money as they wished on any square. If any of the dice landed with the corresponding symbol uppermost, the player would get their money back, and the same again for any or every die.

Leo acted as Victor Harris's scout or lookout. His friend was a genial huckster who jabbered the entire time the game was played. 'Come along now, lads, here we are again, the Old Firm. Put your money where you like, the choice isn't mine, is it? It's yours. The more you put down, the more you'll pick up, think about it. If you don't speculate you can't accumulate, can you?'

It was incredible that Victor wasn't hoarse after a game. The Welshman reminded Leo of Henery the gypsy hawker, when he'd lived with the Orchard tribe, who'd turned the act of selling into a kind of seductive song.

'Come on over, lads. Come yere in a rowboat and go away in a flagship. That's it, smack it down, lad, on the spade there, the stoker's friend. There's a lot resting on the sausage, now, let's roll the dice and see what we get, shall we?'

Victor paid Leo two bob to keep watch, though to be on the safe side he also paid off ship's corporals. Leo asked Victor how he knew he'd make money when it was all a matter of luck which way the dice fell, unless he had some knack or trick in throwing them.

Victor said it was a simple matter of odds, of course. Of probability. He was astonished to find that Leo did not know what he was talking about.

'One roll of a die, Lofty, you've got a one in six chance of any particular side ending face up, haven't you?' he said. 'I roll three dice, each with six sides. You've got six squares on the board. You can calculate the probability. It's mathematics, see, Lofty? If you only roll the dice a few times pretty much anything can happen,

can't it? But the more games you play, the closer the actual result will be to the probability.'

'Do you know what that is?' Leo asked.

'I do.' The Welshman had an intense look in his dark blue eyes.

'Are you going to tell me?'

Victor Harris took a deep breath and puffed up his chest, in the self-important manner of one about to deliver words of wisdom.

'All I'm saying, Lofty, is this. That couple a shillings I give you – don't play the game with it. You may win a little, but you'll more likely lose a lot.'

'And you say you know how much but won't tell me ... and you expect me to believe you?'

Victor frowned. 'Players take away ninety-two point one per cent of what they put down,' he said. 'So what does that leave me?'

Leo lowered his head, shifting his gaze from Victor's, the better to do the sum. Then he raised it. 'Seven point nine per cent,' he said.

Victor nodded. 'You add up all the little stakes the lads put on. I take seven point nine per cent of them. Or thereabouts.'

'I suppose it adds up,' Leo said.

'Well, Lofty, there's a nice pub in Tiger Bay the wife's got her eye on.'

The hands on board the ships in Scapa Flow shared the morose observation that the Orkneys liked to give a man four seasons in a single day. Most days of the year. The morning could begin wet, clear to a blustery noon,

turn warm in an afternoon sun and freeze by nightfall, with hailstones thrown at those on watch. The seemingly ubiquitous wind kept blowing away the prevailing conditions and replacing them with something else. The Gulf Stream, a warm ocean current that travelled from the Gulf of Mexico, brought humid air that kept the winter climate milder than for other regions of the same latitude, yet summers were little warmer.

The Flow was a bleak immensity of water, surrounded by low, barren hills. The spanking wind gave an edge to a long summer's day, and turned into gales in winter. They blew in carrying salt from the sea, and men on deck had to yell to each other to be heard. Though snow was rare, when it did fall the wind blew it into drifts against the gun turrets. The winter days were short and mostly wet. But Leo did not mind the changing weather. With few companions on the ship, he looked outward and felt less imprisoned by their confinement than most. There were frequent, vivid rainbows, and clear nights when the aurora borealis flooded the sky. The first time Leo saw it he thought that the powers of the heavens had been made manifest. That he would see the Son of Man, coming on the clouds of heaven with power and great glory. But other men on watch told him that the Northern Lights were caused by electrically charged particles from the sun reacting with gases in the atmosphere. A natural phenomenon, no more, no less.

The only weather that irked him was the damp sea fog, or haar, that settled on the Flow, erasing the distinction between ships and sea, enveloping all in a

grey cloud. For then he could not watch gannets diving after fish, or shags bobbing on the water.

On one such day, a Sunday afternoon, he sat on the upper deck and Victor Harris sat beside him. Without particularly meaning to, Leo took up smoking while with his friend. He gazed into the fog and wondered if they could be sure they were still in the Flow, since they could not see another ship nor any landmark. Victor said perhaps they had been marooned, and were drifting, and would do so for eternity. He rolled a cigarette and lit it.

'You do not take Communion,' Leo said.

Victor glanced at him and said, 'I do not.'

'You do not believe in God?'

Victor looked at the boy and smiled. 'Does it bother God if I do or I don't? Is He not indifferent? Anyway, He done His work here so long ago, He probably couldn't find His way back to this earth if He tried.'

Victor blew out smoke and looked skyward and cast about the clouds or beyond them.

'He's forgot us, see, Lofty, and when He comes back He'll find what we made of His garden, won't He?'

'You think He'll come back?' Leo asked. 'On the Day of Judgement?'

'A course He'll come back. Why else would He create this world if not for the ghoulish pleasure of seeing what a mess man's made of it? That's His scheme, is the way I see it. He travels through the heavens making worlds, making men, or beings like 'em.'

Leo pondered this idea. 'How will we know when He's come back?'

Victor did not answer for a while. He closed his eyes and smoked. Perhaps he was trying to work out how to make the sublime explicable to this boy. When he opened his eyes, he grinned. 'That's exactly what I was wondering, Lofty,' he said. 'How will we know? In what form might God appear?'

Leo said, 'When Christ was risen, his own disciples did not recognise him. Two a them met him on the road to Emmaus. They told him all about Jesus of Nazareth, a great prophet, who had been condemned to death and crucified. They thought he must be the only visitor to Jerusalem who did not know of all the things that had happened in these days. They presumed he were just some stranger. He spoke to them then of the prophecies concerning himself, he interpreted the scriptures to them, but still they did not know him. Only after they reached Emmaus and invited him to stay with them, when they sat at table, he took the bread and blessed it, and broke it, and gave it to them, only then was their eyes opened and they recognised him.'

Victor nodded. He had not known his young friend to be so talkative before, nor their conversation so solemn.

'They knew this was their Christ, the son of God, and at that very moment of their understanding what did He do? He vanished out of their sight.'

Victor smiled. 'You was listening pretty closely to them Bible readings, Lofty, weren't you now?'

'I always wondered about that story,' Leo told him. 'How could two of his own disciples not recognise the risen Jesus? They'd seen him not three days before.'

'Perhaps,' said Victor, 'even though there he was, right in front a them, because their brains could not believe in a dead man being resurrected, so their eyes could not see it.'

'Yes,' Leo said. 'That is possible. But I do not think so, for Mary Magdalene and the other women had already informed them of the empty tomb. And Jesus himself had foretold, in Galilee, that he would be delivered into the hands of sinful men, and be crucified, and on the third day rise again. No.' Leo shook his head. 'They was prepared for his appearance before them. I believe they did not recognise him because he had changed his form.'

'He was in a different body?'

'Yes.'

'That is possible, I suppose,' Victor said. 'That is possible.'

'But if they could not recognise him, their companion, how can we hope to recognise God Himself, whom we have never seen after he abandoned us for a thousand years?'

'A hundred thousand, more like,' Victor said.

They watched the sea mist drifting before them. Other men strolled across the deck. Victor stubbed out his cigarette.

'Back in nineteen hundred and four,' he said, 'on my first long voyage, we rounded Cape Horn and came up into the Pacific. Lofty, you think the North Sea's big, lad, the Pacific is vast beyond imagining.' He spread his arms out wide to help the boy understand how immense was this vacuity. 'You look and see nothing

in any direction, nothing, for hour after empty hour. Back then I didn't just think, "God has left the world," I thought, "He's never been here in the first place."'

'How then,' Leo asked, 'did the world come into being?'

Victor shrugged. 'They say God was the word and the word was God but who spoke it if not man? I do not know, Leo, but the ocean was vast and empty and I thought the world was too. I mean that there were men and trees and mountains, and trains and chimneys, and chairs and spoons, I could go on, but empty of meaning. You catch my drift? Devoid of intent. Of reason. I was on lookout one day and there I was, gazing out at this empty ocean, dwelling on such matters ... it's what you do, isn't it? Wondering, trying to figure out this world ... when suddenly I saw something.'

Victor fanned his fingers and pressed his hand against his forehead, to shield his eyes from the sun while concentrating on what he had seen.

'It was in the water, beneath the surface but not far down. It come up to the ship and then past, right close.' Victor ceased speaking, engrossed in the memory for a moment beyond the recounting of it. 'A whale,' he said. 'A huge one, the first I'd ever seen. It glided past us like ... I don't know, a fleeting vision, almost beyond our comprehension but available to us if only we kept our eyes open. And just because I was on lookout I saw it, alone out of six hundred men on board.' He chuckled. 'I don't know if the whale saw me. We passed each other and then it was gone but I saw it, and I thought

perhaps there were more. If we are alert, and lucky, we might see them, we might not.'

'You took the whale to be a sign from God?' Leo asked.

Victor frowned. 'That's the problem with you boys weaned on the readings a scripture. You think there's answers, and they will provide clarity.'

'So it was not a sign from God?'

'It was something that happened,' Victor said. 'And it made me consider wider possibilities than I had before. It was a spur to my mind. Perhaps it come from my mind.' He laughed again. 'Who knows what we are capable of, eh, Lofty?'

'Who knows indeed?' Leo agreed. 'We may be an old species nearin the end a days, or we may be a young species with heaven on earth ahead of us.'

Victor nodded. He began to roll himself another cigarette. 'Who can say?'

They sat and gazed out into the Flow. The sky was brightening, the mist lifting. A cormorant flew out of the mist and was just as quickly swallowed up by it again. Victor lit his cigarette.

Twice a week, dances were held on the upper deck of *Benbow*. The band played for an hour, from 6 p.m. The men danced in pairs, one taking the woman's part. They did the valeta, the two-step, lancers. Many men did not dance but stood and watched. On occasion Leo was one such. He listened silently as the other spectators made ribald observations, to cover their confusion.

*

As a rest and a change from the fleet routine, ships were sent in turn to anchor for a few days off the north shore of the Flow. Normal duties were performed in the morning, but at noon a make and mend was granted. Then men could sail or fish or visit the shops in Kirkwall or otherwise do as they pleased.

Boats ferried them to the shore. Leo did not join his fellows but walked off alone. He headed inland along lanes that wound round bleak farms in the open, rolling landscape. There were few trees except for odd specimens around some of the settlements. Coarse-haired little sheep and squat cattle and small, round-bellied ponies inhabited the wind-ridden pastures. There was little cereal grown that he could see.

When he spotted, in a field to his right-hand side, a boy on a white pony coming towards him, it seemed for a moment like some uncanny vision, that Leo was seeing himself as he once was, cantering across the grass out of the past. The sun shone but the breeze was cool, yet the boy wore no shirt. He rode bareback, jouncing off the horse's spine. As he neared the wall between the field and the lane, the boy turned the young horse and rode along in a wide curve around the field, jumping the horse over fences each made from two long rough poles crossed over, like a flattened letter X.

The horse was a white filly. She had long legs, unlike the other, sturdy ponies Leo had noticed on the island. She did not look strong enough to pull a cart. The slight boy was about as much weight as she looked able to carry. Maybe a saddle as well would have been too

much. She was spindly, but fast. The boy hung on as he disappeared over the rising ground.

When they reappeared, Leo had climbed the wall and jumped down into the field and was waiting for them. He waved the boy over. The rider slowed the filly and walked her warily over to the tall young sailor.

'What are ye doin in our field?' he asked.

'That there's a fine animal,' Leo said.

The boy halted the pony a yard or two away. 'Aye,' he said, in a voice as yet unbroken. He had red hair and pale skin. He turned the horse. Should this stranger make an untoward move, he could gallop away.

'You ride her well,' Leo said. He judged the boy to be eleven or twelve years old. He did not speak or otherwise respond to the compliment but sat upon the white filly, waiting to be released.

'The race is on next week,' the boy said, 'and I plan to win.'

Leo asked what race this was. The boy could not believe the seaman had not heard of it and told him it was the highlight of the annual county show. Leo asked if only lads rode. The red-headed boy said men of any age could but the smaller they were, the faster, so riders were mostly young. There was one dwarfish old man who raced every year. He'd won two or three times long ago, but he must be in his thirties now and in the boy's opinion would never win again. 'It's my turn now,' he said.

Leo could not tell how deep the boy's bravado went. Was it sincere or merely superficial?

'Do you wish to ride faster?' he asked.

The boy gazed blankly back at him. Perhaps the question was too difficult. Then he nodded.

Leo stepped forward slowly. He spoke to the horse, and stroked her neck. Then he looked up at the Orcadian boy and said, 'You're holdin her back. You wants to sit higher up, on her withers. She'll fly as swift as a winged beast, if you can bear it. Do you reckon you can?'

The boy had been gazing at Leo with his blank expression. Now he smiled. 'Aye.'

'My name's Leo Sercombe,' he said, raising his hand to shake the boy's, who said that he was called Jamie Watt.

And so Leo had the boy sprint the filly, and each time encouraged him to ride a little forward, as he himself had once done. He showed him how to use his knees, and to loosen the reins. He explained that these were not principles of equitation but skills he himself had discovered by chance.

The Orcadian boy galloped the horse across the field and came back beaming. 'It's brilliant,' Jamie said. 'She's so speedy, I can hardly hold on to her.'

When it came to the jumps, however, Jamie Watt leaned right back, his spine almost touching that of the horse. The boy hung on to the filly's mouth.

'All your weight's over the pony's loins,' Leo told him. 'You're interferin with her liftin and with her spread, and makin it more difficult for her to get her quarters over. And then when she lands she wants to use the muscles of her loins to push off again. You needs to lean forward.'

Once Jamie put this novel instruction into practice, Leo could see that the horse was appreciative and the boy could feel it too. He began to lean forward before he made his mount accelerate for the last strides of their approach to a fence. Leo told him that he should aim to time his own movements in exact conformity to those of the horse, but until this stage of perfection was reached it would be better to be a little in advance of the horse than to be left behind. After a couple of hours the filly began to tire and Leo brought the lesson to an end, despite the boy's protests.

'She won't learn if her's weary,' Leo told him. 'She'll revert to old habits.'

'I thought it was me who was doing things different,' Jamie said.

Leo smiled and said the horse was as much a pupil as the boy was, if a little smarter. Jamie asked the seaman to hold the reins while he pulled on a single upper garment over his bare torso, a thick blue woollen pullover.

Leo said that to understand a horse you had to appreciate how its senses differed from those of man. The boy said surely a horse had five senses just like us.

Leo nodded. 'They do. Your filly sees but she is colour blind.' He turned and with a sweep of his arm indicated the wide vista before them. 'She does not see this landscape as we do. Green fields, blue sky, grey water. All is grey to her, a patchwork, a mosaic of grey. Some parts darker, others lighter. If I stood in the field and my clothes were of the same shade as the grass, she would not see me unless I moved.'

The boy listened intently. 'Can they all see the same, then?' he asked. Were horses not like men, unique?

Leo said that naturally each horse was different. Yet it was useful to know the strong and weak points common to all or most members of a species. Many horses suffered from astigmatism to a greater or lesser extent, for neither the corneas nor the lenses of their eyes were shaped with a true curvature. 'She can hear much better than we can, though. Like a dog, there are many sounds she can hear that we cannot. The officer on my last ship told me that his hunters would sometimes get all excited in their stables for no reason anyone could see. They neighed, broke out in a lather of sweat, and refused to settle until night fell. Why? Because they'd heard the sound of a horn and the calls of the hounds, from miles away.'

The boy nodded, to show he was listening but also to encourage Leo to speak more.

'And, of course, a horse can detect vibrations in the ground in a way we no longer can, if us ever could.' He gestured in the direction of the road down which he had come. 'Another horse walks along that road. Your filly is standing still on her four feet. Her front limb bones, the radius and ulna, the knee bones, canons and pasterns, are locked. So vibrations rise through them, are carried to the skull, and register in the ear.'

'Will you come again?' Jamie Watt asked.

Leo said that he would like to but could not. He had to rejoin his ship and would not get another shore leave for some time. He wished the boy good fortune in the

forthcoming race. Leo turned and walked away towards the road, but the boy called after him, 'Sir.'

Leo turned back and Jamie Watt said, 'What's a horseman doing in the Royal Navy?'

'That's a good question,' Leo said. 'A very good question.' He turned away again and waved goodbye to the boy behind him.

2

The Battle of Jutland was seen as a failure by the civilian population, who had been hoping for another Trafalgar. The Royal Navy lost more ships and many more men than the Germans did. But after the battle, the German High Seas Fleet did not emerge from their base at Wilhelmshaven, to brave engaging again with the British Grand Fleet on open water. As the war drew to a close, Jutland was viewed in a new, more positive light.

Under the terms of the Armistice of 11 November 1918, the German High Seas Fleet was disarmed. At 8 a.m. on 21 November, this convoy of six mighty battlecruisers, ten battleships, eight light cruisers and fifty destroyers, or torpedo boats, seventy-four ships in total, was met at a rendezvous point off the Isle of May. The British Grand Fleet, comprising over two hundred and fifty Royal Navy ships, went out in two lines. When they met the German Fleet, the British ships turned about one hundred and eighty degrees and escorted their surrendered enemy into the Firth of Forth.

On HMS *Benbow*, the crew were allowed up on deck one at a time from their action stations. Leo watched the ships cover the Forth, before and aft, as far as the eye could see, miles of them upon the grey waters. This was the fleet they had met two and a half years earlier, whose guns had killed his friends and comrades. Now they were brought into captivity.

That night the German flags were hauled down. Over the following days the ships were taken north, in units, and passed through the Pentland Skerries and the triple boom defences, into Scapa Flow. There they were moored in pairs to large buoys, the big ships in the west of the Flow, around Cava Island, destroyers south, in Gutter Sound. British boats were moored at strategic points. A battle squadron that included HMS *Benbow* was moored on the east side of the Flow.

The Germans were not permitted to go ashore, nor to visit each other's ships. All their food and other supplies were sent from Germany. These were unloaded to the *Seydlitz*, largest of their battlecruisers. A single rating was taken from each German ship by a British drifter to the *Seydlitz* to draw rations.

The twenty thousand men who had brought the fleet from Wilhelmshaven were gradually reduced to fewer than five thousand, the remainder sent back to Germany on the empty supply ships. The battleships and their skeleton crews remained interned, while the terms of a peace treaty were being negotiated at Versailles.

Fraternisation was forbidden. But when Leo's turn for guard duty came, on one of the armed trawlers, he discovered that there was much contact between the internees and the crews of the Royal Navy drifters that ferried the German doctors, pursers and chaplains to and fro. A black market arose supplying the German sailors with tobacco, soap and meat, in return for medals and items of uniform and small fittings off the ships themselves.

He discovered how monotonous the Germans' diet was. Their home country, from where it was sent, was under blockade. Their food consisted mainly of turnips. So the German sailors fished. Unlike their British counterparts they did so mainly at night, using lamps to lure swarms of small fish which they scooped out in makeshift nets. Many of the men had bad teeth but there was no dentist. The worst sufferers were put on the steam ship home. Scurvy became widespread, as in a navy from an earlier age.

In the mornings, the German sailors maintained and cleaned their ships, with generally poor discipline. Leo learned that engine maintenance was rarely carried out properly. The water for the boilers turned salty. In the afternoons, Sailors' Councils on some ships arranged lessons, in languages, geography and history, mathematics. As the weather improved, they whiled away the hours on deck. They could be heard playing music or singing. Alcohol somehow remained in plentiful supply. Leo sometimes saw men chasing each other round the funnels and masts. It was hard to tell from a distance whether they were involved in violence, or passion, or simply playing a game of tag.

'I don't know who to feel more sorry for,' Victor Harris said. 'Them Huns, or us here keeping an eye on them.'

Leo had been diving from a small pinnace, Victor held his breathing tube and rope line. Leo pulled off his diving suit. 'What are you complaining about?' he demanded. 'You've less than a month left.'

His friend grinned. 'You can picture me, can you, pulling pints behind the bar?'

Leo gestured towards the great ships across the Flow. 'I feel sorry for their commander,' he said.

'They'll be gone within the month too, one way or another.'

'I've heard Sir Sydney don't afford him the courtesy of official visits. His mail is censored. The Admiralty's decent enough to give him a copy of *The Times* only four days out a date.'

Victor shrugged. 'I shouldn't reckon anyone up here gets a newspaper quicker than that.'

Leo ignored the Welshman. 'He must know the peace terms have been delivered,' he said. 'If his government accepts them, we'll take his ships.'

'I don't know, I reckon the Frogs'll bag a few.'

'And if they don't accept, we'll take the ships anyway, and if the unarmed sailors resist, we'll shoot them. Either way, he's going to be handin over his fleet in the next day or two.'

Victor Harris coiled the rope and placed it in a canvas bag. 'That's war, Lofty. We won, they lost.'

Leo shook his head. 'With the sense of honour they Germans have, I wouldn't be surprised if he kills himself before he ever hands over his fleet.'

3

Midsummer's Day, Saturday 21 June 1919. Leo and Victor Harris were on guard duty aboard *Flying Kestrel*, a big tender. The boat had been brought up to the Orkneys from Liverpool under contract to the Admiralty as a water supply and general duties vessel for the internment. The surrendered German Fleet had been anchored in Scapa Flow for seven months. Captain Davies explained to the two seamen that today as on most days his boat's task was to carry water to the Germans from the Pump Well in Stromness. It took him eight days to make a complete circuit of the seventy-four vessels in the German Fleet.

'Unlike Royal Navy vessels, they're not equipped with desalination plants,' he said. 'To distil drinking water from seawater. Do you know why?'

Leo suggested Germans did not drink water but only beer. Victor Harris laughed and declared Leo's answer a good one, but he knew full well that British sailors liked their beer just as much as Germans. Captain Davies said that whereas a Royal Navy ship was built for her men to live in, serving as their home on long voyages around the Empire, German sailors had no Empire and only sailed on short forays. They did not sleep on board and ate only snacks, sleeping and dining in barracks on shore.

Flying Kestrel crossed the channel between Stromness and Hoy and headed down through the boom gates at Houton, and on south across the Flow. The sun was shining and there was only a light breeze. The British Fleet was almost entirely absent today, out on exercise somewhere in the North Sea.

Captain Davies steered the tender at a leisurely pace, to the east of the small Island of Cava. Soon they began to pass between the lines of the great battleships and battlecruisers. One ship was taking on supplies from a British drifter moored alongside. They saw German sailors on the decks of the warships towering above them. Some of the sailors thumbed their noses at the crew of the tender. Victor said he wished Leo had brought his catapult, but Captain Davies said that perhaps they would do the same if they were prisoners-of-war, being gawped at by the enemy.

'We should feel sorry for those poor fellows,' he said, 'who can no more help the misfortune of having been born German than we can claim credit for the privilege of being British.'

The *Flying Kestrel* continued on its course through the German Fleet, towards the destroyers to be supplied that day. Captain Davies told the two seamen that he liked to observe goings-on in the Flow. He knew most of the German ships and called out the names, the tonnage and the gun power of each of them as they passed. 'SMS *Bayern* there, with her sister ship SMS *Baden* – the largest in the German Imperial Navy. Thirty-two thousand tons. Eight fifteen-inch guns in those four turrets.' Victor Harris rolled his eyes, but Leo listened to the skipper. SMS '*Markgraf.* Twenty-five thousand tons. Ten twelve-inch guns in five turrets.'

They carried on south between the Islands of Rysa and Fara, to the destroyers, or torpedo boats, as the captain said they were called by the enemy. Some of the German sailors were fishing from the decks, improvising wooden sticks or staves for rods and string for lines such as children use. The destroyers were low enough in the water for the men to do this. The clothes they wore were filthy, and hardly looked like uniforms any more. Many sported impressive moustaches. One man sat atop a gun turret playing a mouth organ. They passed close enough to hear it, faintly, above the noise of the *Kestrel*'s engines. Captain Davies said he was like a siren, perhaps luring them.

When they reached Lyness, Captain Davies said that the destroyers ahead of them constituted the final flotilla, and he ordered his crew to make ready the water tanks. Victor leaned his Lee Enfield .303 rifle against the wall of the bridge and unwrapped the sandwiches, oatcakes, cheese and dried fish they'd been given.

'Sun shining, decent grub,' he said to Leo. 'The rest of our lot's out there on another exercise. We done all right today, Lofty.'

The *Flying Kestrel* chugged along between the destroyers.

'They've all stopped fishing,' Leo noted. 'Must a got a catch and gone to fry it.'

'They'll have caught nothing with that tackle,' Victor told him.

The captain said he'd often seen them fishing, and they caught all sorts.

They approached the last destroyers, anchored off the tiny Island of Rysa, and Captain Davies steered to the west of Cava, into the channel between that island and Hoy. Victor Harris pointed at the final destroyer. 'Look!' he exclaimed. 'What a bloody cheek. The Germans are flying their ensigns!'

Leo looked up. Ships were hoisting a white flag with a black cross. In its upper-left quarter was the marine jack, Captain Davies said, and he had not seen it before. In the middle of the cross was another shape but as the flag was billowing in the breeze they could not make out what it was.

'That's the eagle,' Victor said. 'The German bloody eagle!'

Victor said they should go up close and find out what the hell was going on, but Captain Davies said that he wasn't going to risk his old boat in any ruckus, with just two armed sailors carrying a single rifle each. He ordered the boat to continue past the destroyer and head out into the Flow.

They came towards a huge ship. 'The *Seydlitz*,' the captain said. 'Look at her armour. Cemented and nickel steel. We hit her twenty-one times at Jutland and she never went down.'

As they watched, a lifeboat was lowered to the water. Men embarked and pushed off. Further along sailors threw a raft down. Some jumped over the side and plummeted into the water, then scrambled to the raft.

'What do the krauts think they are doing?' Victor asked.

Captain Davies was mute. Leo said, 'They look like they're escaping.' As they passed the battlecruiser she seemed to shudder. Then she shuddered again. It was as if this huge ship was feeling the cold and shivering. Then one of *Flying Kestrel*'s crew yelled, 'Jesus Christ! She's turning turtle,' and the men watched open-mouthed as the *Seydlitz* toppled over onto her side. Water came streaming out of the seacocks.

The next ship's stern rose slowly into the air, so that the bows sank first and the rest of the hull slid smoothly into the water, as if the ship were performing an exemplary dive.

Captain Davies ordered *Flying Kestrel* to slacken speed. They passed a battleship whose quarterdeck was awash. They watched her gradually lift her bows out of the water, roll over, and disappear beneath the surface, leaving nothing but a vast patch of bubbling foam.

'What the bloody hell's going on?' Victor Harris asked.

'They're sinking,' Captain Davies said. 'They're scuttling their own damned ships.'

German sailors were abandoning their crafts, dragging kit and throwing it into lifeboats. The sea became littered with boats and hammocks, lifebelts and chests, spars and items of clothing. Debris from the scuttled ships. And in amongst it, hundreds of men. Some floated, others made for the nearest shore. Those who could, hauled themselves onto rafts.

A couple of crew members of *Flying Kestrel* who were not currently needed stood spellbound on the deck. A lifeboat drifted by full of Germans cheerfully singing.

They passed a ship and heard issue from it loud single strokes of her bell. Leo knew this to mean 'Abandon Ship'. What was happening in front of him was awesome. It was impossible to believe that the Germans were doing it themselves, to their own fleet. It made no sense. The ship wobbled, then it upended and plunged down quickly, enveloped in clouds of steam.

The great ships were leviathans. They seemed to have altered their constitution, steel made flesh, to have come alive, like whales, vast grey creatures saying farewell to the upper air and leaving the world of men to sink into the deeps of the ocean.

The bulk of the British Fleet was out on its exercise, but the Flow came alive now with drifters and trawlers, picket boats, pinnaces and ships' tenders. Some began picking German sailors out of the water. Others tried to reach a ship before its sailors had left it and force them to curtail the scuttle. Shots could be heard.

From a ship they passed came sullen rumblings, and the crashing of chains, then its great hull lurched giddily over and slid with a horrible sucking and gurgling sound under the water. Weird and terrible noises the ship made in its death throes. The proud vessel slowly disappeared with a long-drawn-out sigh. On the surface all that remained was a whirlpool dotted with dark objects swirling round and round. These were drawn inwards until they too sank from sight. Captain Davies yelled orders to his crew, afraid perhaps that the *Kestrel* would be caught in the churning turbulence. The whirlpool subsided, then oil rose to the surface, a black stain hugely spreading, as if the lifeblood of some ocean monster were oozing up from the seabed.

Leo watched a British drifter towing a German lifeboat full of sailors. Suddenly one of them stood up in the bow of the boat. He had a knife in his hand. He leaned forward and tried to cut the tow rope. A Royal Marine in the drifter raised his rifle. They saw a puff of smoke and the German drop his knife. Then they heard the crack of the rifle, and watched the sailor fall back into the boat. The other men stood up unsteadily with their arms in the air.

There were shots from on shore as soldiers and Marines repelled boats seeking to land on Hoy, but on the Island of Cava many sailors succeeded in landing. Victor took up a pair of binoculars and reported what he saw. At one cove they could see a boat floating in the shallows, full of German sailors, and people standing guard on the beach. Victor said they were women armed with pitchforks and other menacing implements.

A British trawler came close and an officer raised a megaphone to his mouth and yelled that the German Fleet was sinking.

'You don't say,' Captain Davies shouted back.

The officer called out for the *Flying Kestrel* to make for the *Victorious*, a pre-dreadnought battleship that had suffered much damage and was now the dockyard or repair ship for the Royal Navy in Scapa Flow. Captain Davies seemed to know where the *Victorious* was berthed.

As they came slowly around Cava they could see the bulk of the German Fleet. Vessels listed to port or starboard. Some heeled over and plunged headlong, their sterns lifted high out of the water and pointing skywards. One huge ship sank squarely, rapidly settling down in the ocean, while out of the vents rushed steam and oil and air with a terrible roaring hiss, and vast clouds of white vapour rolled up from the sides. Then it settled, with its masts and funnels still showing, a battlecruiser doing an imitation of a U-boat.

The *Flying Kestrel* went alongside the *Victorious*, sheltering close to its hull. After a while a trawler came up bearing captains and officers of the German ships. Marines in the trawler held their rifles pointed at the officers, who climbed aboard, lugging their own bags.

After some while the *Kestrel* was permitted to return to Stromness. As they left, they saw the first British destroyers, doubtless telegraphed with news of what was happening, speeding back into the Flow, throwing up huge bow-waves as they came.

The last German ship the *Flying Kestrel* passed was the first they'd seen on the way out, SMS *Baden*. For some reason her crew did not seem to have begun the scuttling process. They could see no one on board. Perhaps they had abandoned their ship but forgotten to sink her first. Then when Leo looked back at the *Baden*, he saw a solitary German sailor in a dirty white summer uniform, dancing a hornpipe on a gun turret. He watched him dancing alone, to no tune he could hear. To the east in the distance he could just make out HMS *Benbow* in the midst of the British ships.

Part Four

MOTHER AND CHILD
1919

I

The tall, rangy young man caught the first train out from Taunton. At Wiveliscombe Station, milk churns and baskets of produce were stacked at the section of the platform where the goods van had come to a halt. The young man climbed down from the carriage onto the platform. A few others alighted likewise. Travellers waited to board. He did not wish to be recognised, and tried to pull his seaman's cap down over his eyes, though it had no peak. He put up the collars of his blue woollen coat. One porter unloaded post and parcels and newspapers. The other stacked boxes of provisions on his trolley. A carter in a railwayman's uniform stood beside his horse.

Leo walked under the arch past the ticket office and out from the station, up the hill northward. He strolled along a familiar lane. There was no hurry. Leaves were turning on the trees. The seasons on the ocean bore little relation to those on land. He had all but forgotten the odours of autumn that entered his nostrils. Wet rotting plants decomposing into rich dark soil, distant bonfires, fungi erupting, sweet fruit decaying. They mixed into a scent that he inhaled deeply. He took a path across a field. Mist rose like smoke from the wet grass.

The war was over but Leo had signed up shortly before hostilities commenced. He was now merely on leave. Other hands with nowhere in particular to go spent their leave in riotous debauch, much of it insensible. The less they could remember, the more acclaim they received upon their return to ship. It was the British way, almost a patriotic duty. Leo might have joined them if a friend had invited or persuaded him, but since Victor Harris had left the Navy and returned to Cardiff he had none. He had become a loner on board, a ghost among men.

There were those among the survivors of the ships lost at Jutland who believed they must have died there and were ensconced now in some parodic afterlife, for who could have survived that conflagration? There was humour in this world, after all. Might not God have allowed Himself some share of it? Such a thing would surely amuse Him, to have the dead believe they yet lived, a miraculous elect.

A light rain was falling. The few people Leo saw had lowered their gaze, were unlikely to see the tall lean figure ambling northward. He entered a wood and remembered how he had once got lost here when sent on an errand, had ridden round in circles and feared that he was spellbound and would never get out. The drizzle ceased. Leo disturbed a cock pheasant out of undergrowth beside the track. He watched it rise, panicking, and fly noisily away. He could have brought it down with a catapult. A breeze came up through the wood. The sun shone. Wind shook the rain from the trees.

Leo did not wish to enter the estate by the customary route. Instead he skirted the village in a wide arc to the east then cut back and walked into the scrubland of the old quarries. By the time he reached his destination it was almost noon. The great pool, where he had learned and loved to swim as a boy, was as he remembered it. He sat upon the grey slab of rock where he and Lottie Prideaux had once picnicked, and looked upon the black water and across the pool to the granite cliff on the far side. The sun warmed the autumn morning. Leo unbuttoned his coat and laid it out to dry. He lay back some feet away and closed his eyes and soon slept.

When the young man woke he shielded his eyes from the sun and sat up. He looked out and saw, on a ledge of the cliff across the pool, a few feet above the water, a heron. It stood on spindly legs, wings folded. Leo pondered the bird. He could not tell whether it was gazing back at him, or at the water, or merely lost in contemplation of something other. Had it been watching over him while he slept? Perhaps herons completed a holy trinity of sentinels, along with horses and trees, put on the earth for this purpose. The bird bent its wiry knees and took off from the rock ledge, and with a stately flapping of its wings flew off towards the sun.

The young man rose from the slab. He picked up his coat and tossed it over his left shoulder and walked around the edge of the pool to the track leading away. It became a winding metalled lane through the old quarries. Then he entered the wood known to all as the Bluebell Wood. Of course they only flowered in spring. Now the leaves from oak and ash, hazel, beech, were falling, the compost of the wood, beneath which the bulbs lay dormant. In six months' time they would release that blue rhapsody of colour and the faint subtle sweet fragrance.

Leo walked past cows grazing on tired pasture and down into the valley. He followed the stream lined with willows that had been pollarded since he last walked here and now resembled the heads of huge medieval weapons – cudgels, bludgeons – whose handles giants had thrust into the soft earth.

He walked up onto the gallops. This was the spot he feared being spotted, on the open terrain where Herb Shattock's lads exercised the master's hunters. To his relief there was no one riding there now. Leo walked on, past the hillocks called the Burial Mounds, and through empty pasture, then along a track between the burnt stubble of wheat fields on Home Farm. Soon plough-men would turn the earth over, furrow by endless patient furrow.

Leo entered the small spinney Lottie had called 'the jungle'. This was where he had waited for her, with the skeleton of a hawk his brother Sid had given him. He walked stealthily between the trees. Ahead lay the terraced lawns. Beyond them the big house, which came into partial view as he approached.

What he needed was a plan but he had none. Instead he stood well hidden and looked up across the empty lawns at the quiet house. The garden seemed altered to him. There was a pond he could not remember being there before. Over on one side near the walled kitchen garden stood an elegant wooden bench beneath a bower across which some climbing plant had been trained. On the far side of this was a gap in the hornbeam hedge that he could not explain. Perhaps these things had always been there and he had not noticed. Why would he? He was interested in other things.

Why was he standing here? He had come because he wished Lottie to know that he had not forgotten her, or his pledge to return. But how? Perhaps he should go to Head Keeper Aaron Budgell's cottage, to see if Sid still lodged there or at least to find out where he now lived, and to give his brother a message for her. Or else to the stables, to converse with Herb Shattock. Leo understood that none of these people might be working here now or even still living. Yet he preferred to imagine nothing had changed.

His attention was drawn to movement up at the house. A glazed door opened and a young woman emerged. She walked across the terrace in his exact direction. Leo stopped breathing. He eased back behind the nearest tree. It was her. She was taller, a little fuller in the figure, but unmistakably Lottie. She wore a black skirt and white shirt; her brown hair was longer and tumbled about her shoulders.

Had she seen him, perhaps, from a window up in the attic? While he was peering in from the wood, was Lottie peering out from the house? She had seen him and was striding towards him. He could feel his heartbeat hammering in his chest.

Then she turned, gestured and perhaps said something to someone still inside. Out of the door came a small child. A boy. He toddled towards Lottie. She did not wait for him but stepped backwards off the terrace and retreated further across the lawn. The boy kept coming towards her. Even from this distance Leo could tell that the child was laughing. He gazed, rapt, unable to believe what he was seeing.

Halfway across the upper lawn, Lottie stopped and bent and waited for the child to reach her. She opened her arms and scooped him up and, holding him close to her, spun round and round. The boy hung on tight, his arms around her neck, spinning. Eventually she stopped, and somewhat clumsily set him back upon the grass. Lottie staggered a little. The boy reeled drunkenly and sat down, perplexed. Immediately he struggled to his feet again and tried to walk, but tottered and collapsed once more.

Lottie had surely regained her balance but now she too lost her bearings. With theatrical exaggeration the young woman lurched one way, froze, tripped awkwardly back the other. Leo could just hear the child's high-pitched laughter. He could not help smiling himself, so fine was the performance. Lottie completed it with a flourish, falling gracefully a few feet from the boy. For a moment she lay prostrate, still, as if dead. The boy watched her. He stopped smiling. He seemed to be speaking to her. When she did not respond, he crawled over to her. Just as he reached her Lottie burst awake and grabbed him, and rolled over with him. When they stopped rolling it was hard to tell whether Lottie was tickling the child or wrestling with him, but he was certainly giggling again.

Leo watched her with the boy, as he had once watched her ride, suppling the doomed blue roan, Embarr. He had understood then, observing her, how fine a rider Lottie was, what understanding of horses she possessed. He understood now or believed he did something of what kind of mother she was. He had adored his own mother Ruth but she had never played with him in this manner. She'd had no time.

Mother and child rose from the grass. Holding his hand, Lottie led the boy to the pond on the lower lawn. Now as they came closer Leo could hear her talking to her son. He could not quite make out the words but he listened to the recognisable cadence of her voice. Imperious, familiar, undissembling. He thought she spoke to the boy as she would to anyone, or to a horse. Or to himself.

There was a low brick wall around the pond. The boy stepped up onto it. Lottie grasped his hand as he walked along the wall. She traversed a wider radius, around the outside, like a horse turning a wheel. Perhaps parenthood demanded such sacrifice. A parent had elected to become, to some extent at least, a beast of burden.

Leo could not understand. He'd believed his destiny lay with her but how could that be? Must he simply become her stable lad? Her groom? He watched the boy stepping carelessly along the wall, secure in the knowledge that if he slipped he would not fall but be saved by his mother. He seemed to Leo for a moment to be not a child but a goblin, mocking him. What had he thought? That he would be more to Lottie than a servant? It was absurd. Yet he was too proud to settle for less.

Leo stepped slowly backwards, deeper into the shadows of the wood. Lottie and the boy circled the pond. Then she looked up and Leo stood stock still. How pretty she was. A lovely woman. Another man was luckier than he. Leo was overtaken by an urge to cry out. His heart was breaking. Then the boy lost his footing momentarily. Lottie steadied him, and they resumed walking. Following the wall, they turned away from Leo. He too turned and ran through the wood, away from the house. He ran across the estate the way he had come, away from it forever.

Part Five

SALVAGE
1919–1927

I

In the summer of 1919, Ordinary Seaman Leopold Sercombe was transferred to HMS *Ajax*. The ship's role, along with the rest of the Mediterranean Fleet, was to fly the flag on cruises around that sea. Men were issued with white tropical uniforms. Canvas awnings were raised on poles and spread across the aft decks as protection from the sun.

Operational readiness was maintained by exercises, manoeuvres and inspections. There were flotilla regattas and fleet competitions, on board or ashore.

They anchored off cities: Nicosia, Piraeus, Port Said. Civilians were invited aboard for dances, and for general visits. From Barcelona came a party of children, for whom games were set up. For one game, lots were drawn in Leo's mess and he lost. His face was blackened with shoe polish and red paint applied to his lips. Thus adorned he had to hide behind two canvas screens, set up on deck some yards apart. As Leo dashed across the gap between them, children threw tennis balls at him. 'Aim for his face,' his shipmates urged the children.

Leo lived in a broadside mess with fifteen other men. A long wooden table was hinged to the side and hung from the deck above by a swinging bracket. The long benches could be secured in rough weather with deck bolts. At the head of the table was a locker containing cutlery, plates, basins. There were nests of galvanised steel lockers, one for each man, in which Leo kept his uniform clothes. His daily working rig was a white duck suit worn with a silk lanyard. He wore overalls for dirty jobs out of sight, and his cap at all times. There was also storage for small ditty boxes, containing each man's private possessions. Photographs, letters from home. Leo had none of these. In his ditty box he placed skeletons of small birds and tiny mammals that he found on his rare forays ashore in the Mediterranean.

There was no privacy in a broadside mess. Leo began to read. There was a small library on board, odd readers scattered amongst the ship's company who identified each other reading in their hammocks, and passed books back and forth.

The commander's priority was the appearance of his ship, especially when in harbour, on show. The side party was charged with ensuring the ship's side was always immaculate, without a single blemish. The quarterdeck was made of oak, rather than teak. A twice-weekly holystone scrub with sand gave it a whiteness teak could not match. The turrets and guns and superstructure shone with fresh enamel paint. Wooden hatches and bollard covers were scrubbed smooth. Brass tompions in the turret guns glistened. Leo's division worked the upper deck, painting and keeping the forecastle clean. On Sunday mornings, when the skipper inspected the deck, Leo was placed up in the bridge wings with a rifle and a pocket full of blanks, to scare away from the paintwork any insolent seagulls.

The men washed their clothes at set times and dried them on wire clotheslines riven through blocks under the foretop and shackled to eye bolts. The clothes were pegged and the lines triced up taut and the laundry dried in the wind. Only these authorised lines could be used. No clothing could be hung up in the superstructure or on the guard rails that might be visible from outboard the ship. Many foreign ships displayed their crews' clothes drying. Leo's fellow hands poured scorn on such indiscipline.

Their day began at five in the morning and ended at nine in the evening, when the commander moved around the ship, preceded by the bugler, the corporal of the gangway and the master-at-arms. At each messdeck the men stood to attention. When the rounds had passed, hammocks could be unstowed and slung overhead.

When HMS *Ajax* was in transit, seagulls fell away, and other birds appeared. The Mediterranean Sea acted like a huge barrier between Europe and Africa. Each autumn some large birds went east and made their way to Africa through Turkey and the Levant. Others went west and gathered at the tip of Spain. Thousands of storks and kites waited for thermals to lift them high enough for the wind to help them over to the African continent.

Small birds like chiffchaffs and nightingales flew straight across the Mediterranean. When they grew exhausted, some took the opportunity of a rest on a passing battleship. One early morning on the upper deck, in the middle of the sea, Leo was woken in his hammock by a familiar sound. For a moment he could not make sense of it, and thought that it must have been remembered from his dreams. It seemed to be calling to him from out of his childhood. Then he heard it again, and looked up and saw, sitting on an arm at the top of the mast, a cuckoo.

Across the Royal Navy, the men's rates of pay were reduced. Those with families had less to send home. Morale fell on the ageing ships. Officers worried they would lose their jobs. At least married officers could bring their wives out to Malta, at their own expense, but crewmen could not. Ratings often ran out of money by the middle of a month and could not afford to go ashore to visit a canteen or cinema. Some scarcely ever left the ship. Leo was one of these. He was resolved to quit the Navy with savings. He bought soap and tobacco cheaply from the paymaster, the cost stopped from his pay. He did not intend to open a pub, like his friend Victor Harris who had sent him a postcard from Cardiff, but he turned other ideas over in his mind. He stayed on board, reading or playing shove-ha'penny in the mess, or else on deck gazing at the land that was always in sight. In Valletta harbour, a fragrance of spice, perfume and oranges wafted out from shore. Occasionally he scented cigar smoke. The buildings on shore were a light sandstone, the cloudless sky pale blue, the Mediterranean Sea a deeper shade. After tea the rig of the day was no longer compulsory. Leo changed into night cloth-ing, an old serge suit worn without collar or lanyard, and watched the lights of the waterfront bars and the bobbing lights of the *dghajsas*. He listened to the bells of horse-drawn *karozzins*. His life was temporarily becalmed and there was nothing he could do but wait for the time it would resume.

Leo kept up his diving. On a stormy night in Malta, when HMS *Ajax* lay to buoys in the Grand Harbour, a steamer came adrift and collided with the bow of the ship. Leo inspected the damage and over the following weeks carried out underwater repairs.

In the summer Leo went swimming. Sometimes others went with him. They took a *dghajsa* over to the harbour breakwater. At its inner end was an area of flat sandstone, which he made his base for a picnic and a doze in the sun. Periodically he rose and dived into the sea and swam to a buoy moored a hundred yards out. There he heaved his dripping body from the shimmer-ing water, and sat on the bobbing float.

The ship's plumber bent copper pipe for him with which Leo fashioned a snorkel. He acquired a pair of submarine escape goggles. With these Leo floated in the deep blue water, entering another domain, and watched multicoloured fish dart before him. He saw octopi and eels. His skin turned the colour of hazel.

In the summer of 1923, optional swimming periods were introduced. Between 7 and 7.30 in the morning and 5 and 5.30 in the afternoon, men could rise from the clammy atmosphere below decks and dive into the sea.

Leo rarely missed an opportunity. He swam well away from the ship.

HMS *Ajax* was involved in occasional operations to keep the peace in trouble spots around the Med. From Gibraltar they oversaw the Tangier Patrol, ensuring the security of Tangier against incursion by Berber separatists. There was briefly action against Turkish Nationalists in the Sea of Marmara. In 1922 the Sultan of Turkey was deposed, and the *Ajax* conveyed him to exile in Mecca.

In April 1924 *Ajax* returned to Devonport, assigned to the Reserve Fleet. The clear waters and bright sun of southern Europe were replaced by grey seas and grey skies around the grey metal ship. June was dull and unsettled. July was wet and thundery, and cool. August the same, with frequent rain.

Leo asked to see the chaplain. He knew Reverend Martin from the library, and now visited him in his cabin. The chaplain sat at his desk and invited Leo to sit in an armchair beside it. He asked the young seaman if he knew of the damage that insects could do on board. Leo said that of course every sailor gets used to crushing a cockroach beneath his heel. And the cooks complained constantly about weevils in their flour.

'Silverfish,' the chaplain said. 'They're the most damnable little philistines. I've discovered they're eating our books.'

'That's awful, sir,' Leo said.

The chaplain admitted that in truth the small insects were consuming paper very slowly. The library was not in imminent danger. He asked what it was Sercombe needed.

Leo said that he wanted to ask a question.

'You may ask anything you like,' Reverend Martin said. He gestured to the closed door behind Leo and told him that whatever was said in this cosy cabin was confidential.

Leo nodded. He frowned, and bit his lip.

The chaplain waited. Then he said that he had heard so many men express one anxiety or another, he did not believe anything could surprise him. 'Do you smoke, Sercombe?' he asked, and offered Leo a cigarette from a silver box.

The tobacco, or perhaps the action of lighting the cigarette and inhaling and exhaling, seemed to make it easier to speak, and Leo said, 'Do you think it be possible, sir, for a man to find himself in a life that is not his own?'

The chaplain smiled and said he was sure that it was. In fact, it was closer to the natural condition of man than any other.

'Out a place?' Leo asked. 'Out a time?'

'We are all wanderers,' the Reverend said. 'We are exiles upon the earth.' He reached up to a shelf above the desk and brought down a Bible, leafing through its thin pages. Then he found what he was looking for and, with a finger upon the page, read out, '"Here we have no lasting city, but we seek the city which is to come."'

Leo stubbed his cigarette out in the ashtray on the chaplain's desk.

'Of course, if you have lost God,' the chaplain said, 'I suppose this is scant consolation.'

'I ain't sure, sir, that God did not lose me.'

The chaplain shook his head. 'No, Sercombe. No. If there's one thing I am sure of it is that God loses no one. He will always be there when we truly need Him.'

Leo nodded slowly. 'I hope so,' he said.

'As you doubtless know, it's the padre's job on board ship in time of war to censor letters. To explain to the men what could and could not be said. I must say that I'm very happy to be divested of that obligation, but it did teach me something.' He passed the box to Leo, and took another cigarette for himself and lit it. He blew out the smoke and said, 'What I learned is that language is a puzzle. Words can be replaced and taken out and moved around to try to say the same thing in a different way, only for one to find they say something new, or the same thing in an improved fashion.'

Leo said he believed the Reverend was surely right about that, and thanked him, and left the cabin.

In June 1926, a few days after his twenty-seventh birthday, Leo Sercombe completed his twelve years' service in the Royal Navy, with the rank of Able Seaman, and resigned.

2

'A field.'
'A field?'

'Enough for a vegetable garden, some fruit trees. A paddock for a horse.'

Victor Harris had asked Leo what he wanted. They sat in the small saloon bar of the public house Victor had bought in Cardiff while his wife tended the bar. There were only two customers visible at noon, both old men, sitting alone on different benches along the walls.

'I'd build a cabin in the field.'

'From the way you've spoke about horses they'll need one, but what about you, Lofty, where are you going to live?'

Leo smiled. 'You're right, Vic. First I'll build a shelter for the horse. Then I'll build myself a cabin.'

Victor Harris nodded. 'I can see that, I can,' he said. 'It's a picture. But I can't see where the money's coming from. You've spent money on the land. What are you going to live on?'

'I'll hire myself out,' Leo said. 'Me, my muscles, my horses. And I'll buy and sell them. Break them in, train them.'

Victor shook his head. 'You never struck me as a man mean enough to break horses. And where do you reckon on buying this field a yours?'

'I guess I'll head back home,' Leo said. 'To the West Country.'

'How much more d'you reckon you need?'

Leo took a deep breath through lips pressed close together. 'About two hundred and fifty.'

The men supped their beer.

'At least,' Leo said.

'Your trouble is, you only saved,' Victor Harris said. 'You never speculated.' He asked Leo whether he had heard about the salvage operation up in the Flow.

'A rumour,' Leo said. 'But I couldn't rightly believe it. We saw what happened. Most a them ships are deep under the water.'

'Aye, the Admiralty said they'll rust where they rest. But then the price a metal started rising on the markets, see, and some Brummie scrap dealer's got the contract to lift 'em.'

'So it's true, is it? I heard about this scrap merchant.'

'He's a madman, is what I been told, like. The rest of us saw rustin metal hulks, see, Lofty, sinkin in the silt. This bloke went up there and had a poke around and saw money underwater. He sent divers down, and they're seeking ways to raise the ships.'

'What's he pay?'

'I heard he's payin labourers ten shillins a shift, and divers twice that. He works them hard. A bloke from here it was who told me. Went up, come back inside a month, said this feller, Cox is his name, works his men like beasts. The only one he works harder is his self. It's dirty work and it's dangerous. He said the money wasn't worth being flogged to death for.' Victor shrugged. 'You might see it different.'

Leo remembered Cyrus Pepperell, a farmer who drove himself insanely hard. He was not sure he wanted to work for such a tyrant again.

'Taff said this lunatic has raised the destroyers but he ain't satisfied. Got his eye on the battleships, see? Goldmines. He'll be needing more divers, Lofty.'

Victor's children wandered in and out of the bar from the family's quarters out the back. Leo could not see how Victor Harris could have fathered so many children. Victor said it was simple. Each child represented a different visit home on leave.

'I've not checked the dates too closely, mind you. Whether the day they was born come a little sooner or later than nine months after my leave. If they did, I don't need to know, do I?'

The men sat in the gloomy corner, watching Victor's wife Myfanwy at the bar, serving a third man, who had just come in, with a pint of draught ale. She had a grim unsmiling countenance, but in response to what she said, which Leo could not hear, the man was laughing.

'I couldn't ask for a better wife, boy,' Victor Harris said. 'If you find one half as good, keep a hold of her. Though she might not be over impressed, like, by life in a little cabin.'

Leo smiled. 'If I find such a woman, I'll build an extra room for her.'

Victor nodded. 'Now you're thinking straight,' he said.

3

On the train to Scotland, passengers in Leo's compartment spoke of the General Strike. One man claimed that strikers in Northumberland had derailed the Flying Scotsman. A large woman said that Baldwin was right, we were threatened with a revolution, and she didn't care how many Communists were arrested, they could have arrested twice as many as far as she was concerned. A second man said that the strike was a sin, as the Catholic Church had pronounced it to be.

Another asked if they did not feel some sympathy for the miners, who struggled on alone, but none did. He asked Leo for his opinion, but Leo said that he regarded himself as too ignorant of the facts to make a sensible contribution, and so kept his own counsel.

The steam train chuntered through the North of England. Past dirty factories, surrounded by piles of rusty iron and stagnant pools of oily water. Through cuttings, the rock on each side blackened by the coal smoke of the trains. Between rows of houses squashed together, with tiny gardens squeezed between their back doors and the metal fences of the railway. The train chugged across open country for a mile or two then back into the industrial grime of foundries and factories and railway yards.

When Leo travelled this way before, was he asleep in the darkness while they came through the North? Or perhaps the Jellicoes had taken a different line, further east. Smoke rose from factory chimneys. They passed collieries, with grey and black slagheaps. Narrow streets wound away up steel hillsides. He stared at a refuse heap on which small figures scavenged.

Beyond York the countryside opened up once more. It was haymaking season. Leo did not know if summer breezes carried scents into the railway carriages stuttering past or memories defrauded his senses, but he knew the raw smell of fresh grass in the morning, the honey scent of clover. The damp earthy odour of the underside of hay as they turned it to expose it to the sun, the sweet dry fragrance of it being loaded in the evening. But there were fewer people in the fields than he remembered as a boy. And there were fewer horses. For on some farms tractors now pulled the mowers, and rakes that turned the hay. Men who had once worked with horses now rode the machines belching smoke over the fields. Perhaps his father was now driving such a vehicle. No. He could not see Albert Sercombe on a tractor. That would never happen. It was not possible. His father was surely a horseman for life.

4

The man seated on the other side of the desk read the piece of paper Leo had given him. Once or twice he looked up, perhaps to correlate the tall, young ex-seaman standing before him with what was written in the reference letter. To equate the person with the words used to describe him.

'To whom it may concern,' he said at length. 'Yes, it does concern me. Who is this Chief Petty Officer fellow, singing your praises? He could be your uncle for all I know.' He picked up the letter. 'This could be a forgery.'

Leo shook his head. 'It isn't, sir.'

The man narrowed his eyes. 'It says here you can dive to ten fathoms. Which if it's true means you're plumb fit, sonny. You'll need to be.'

'It's true, sir.'

'Just out of the Navy and you want to jump back in the water, eh?'

'I heard you pay well, Mister Cox.'

'I pay good men good money. You'll have to earn it. If you're no good, you'll be on your way.'

'I don't mind hard work.'

The man stood up. He was of average height and looked across his desk and up at Leo. 'You want to know who you're dealing with, sonny. I'm not some upper-crust, blue-blooded gentleman. I left school at thirteen. No one taught me anything apart from the writers of the books I read. Manuals. Textbooks. I'm an engineer, and I'm a merchant in metal. The people who know about these things said these ships couldn't be raised. The experts. Well, I raised 'em. I've proved 'em wrong with the destroyers, and I'll prove 'em wrong with the battleships.'

Leo listened to the blowhard. Another of them. Maybe there was something in his own withdrawn nature that brought forth their boastful soliloquies. He hoped that there might be more substance to Ernest Cox's bragging than the empty bluster of Henery Orchard selling dud horses or Victor Harris on HMS *Benbow* fleecing his gambling customers.

'Put a piece of metal in front of me, sonny, any metal. You can blindfold me … all I need is a spanner to tap it with and I'll tell you what metal it is, just by the sound of it. What do you think of that, eh? How many men do you reckon could do it?'

Leo did not know the answer, but he guessed the one Cox wanted to hear. 'No other, I reckon.'

'Yes, that's right, sonny,' Cox said, nodding. 'No other bugger could do it. You've done your twelve-year stint, you've spent years on board big ships, and I'll wager you've no idea what metals there are on these Hun boats. Well, I'll tell you. Cast steel was used for the stern, the stern frame, the rudder frame and suchlike. Wrought iron was used for cables, davits and so forth.' He did not count these items off on his fingers but with each one slapped the back of his right hand into the palm of his left. 'There's armoured cable, sonny, steel rope, anchors, turbine blades.'

He might have been describing the fruit of the Tree of Life, the paradise of God become a scrap metal yard.

'And when we go inside what are we going to find? Non-ferrous metals. Brass, copper, lead. Phosphor bronze, gunmetal, manganese. You see, Leo Sercombe, I don't give a tinker's cuss what objects were once used for. Their function means nothing to me. Irrelevant. All I see is the metal and how we can get it. Come along, I'll show you round our little kingdom.'

Ernest Cox wore a clean white shirt beneath a tweed waistcoat, jacket and plus-fours. His brogues shone. At the door of the office he lifted a trilby from a hook and put it on his head. 'Mac!' he yelled, marching along a corridor and into another office. Leo followed.

'I may have got you your sixth diver, Mac, just in time,' Cox said to the man studying ship's plans at a table. Cox made it sound as if he had recruited Leo himself. 'He's a Navy man, stationed here in the Flow back in the days of the internment. His name's Leopold Sercombe. Leo, meet Sinclair McKenzie, chief salvage officer. He's a diver too, so there's no pulling the wool over his eyes.'

Another man came into the doorway. Cox and MacKenzie were middle-aged. This one was younger, not much older than Leo.

'Ah, Ern. We've got a fellow ex-Navy man to keep you company. Not on submarines, I'm afraid, this one, but a good diver, he claims. Ernie McKeown's my chief engineer, Leo. Come along. It's almost time for lunch.'

The base of Ernest Cox's operations at Scapa Flow was in the old naval quarters and depot in Lyness on the Island of Hoy. Cox rammed his trilby further down onto his head against the stiff wind and walked out into the sunshine.

'We've cleared Gutter Sound of its destroyers,' he said. He took Leo to the old barracks, whose huts now accommodated his workers in a series of dormitories. 'You'll be in here with the other divers,' he explained, opening the door of a hut. There were half a dozen beds. Clothes and equipment lay scattered around, though there were a number of cupboards and lockers. Leo noticed a wireless set on top of a dresser.

There were other huts for mechanics, carpenters, electricians. Perhaps there was a hierarchy as onboard ship that would become clear soon enough. Cox showed Leo all the accommodation – for labourers, linesmen – to impress upon him the scale of operations. They walked back, past a hut that had been converted into a cinema. Another with billiard tables and a bar.

They approached a larger building from which voices could be heard, and the sounds of plates and cutlery clanking. Cox pushed open the door and strode in.

'All right, Father?' a man addressed him. Cox did not reply, but picked up a fork from a table, and a glass. He rapped the fork against the glass. Men ceased talking in a widening circle from him.

'Listen up, lads,' Ernest Cox announced once there was silence and full attention directed towards him. 'We've got a new diver here, name of Leo Sercombe. He's a Sassenach like myself so you Jocks better not give him any grief on that account.' He pointed to a table. 'There's some divers,' he told Leo. 'They'll settle you in.'

5

William Peterson was the dive leader, a fair-haired, stocky man in his forties. That afternoon he took Leo out in a launch. They sailed up Gutter Sound and into the channel between Hoy and the small Island of Cava. It was all as Leo remembered. A battlecruiser was lying on her port side, with thirty feet of her starboard side above the high-water line. Two cranes were situated on a floating platform beside her, their grabs gutting the ship. The crane-drivers were extracting black matter from her innards and transferring it to a barge.

'With the strikes, the price a coal's gone up four-fold,' Peterson said. 'That's if ye can get it at all. We need two hundred tons a week fer the tugs and all the machinery. Father Cox had the idea to open her up. Found her bunkers full. We've got enough free German coal here to see us through tae Christmas. The wee big man's a genius. Ye'll see.'

The ship was the *Seydlitz*. Peterson said that there were four further battlecruisers below the water in a line running north. One was so big that her bridge, funnels and two masts were still above the water. Leo remembered her well. The others were fully submerged. Each one weighed more, Peterson said, than the weight of all the twenty-six destroyers they'd already raised.

'He's a genius but he's a madman,' William Peterson declared of Cox. He showed Leo where coloured floats or marker buoys floated above the first battleship to have been surveyed and selected for salvage. SMS *Moltke*.

The Admiralty had decided to transfer all operations south. It was strange to look across the Flow and see no Royal Navy ships, just as it was strange to see the naval base at Lyness taken over by the salvage company of Cox & Danks. The sight was uncanny to Leo, used to seeing the British Fleet in occupation.

'She's upside down,' Bill Peterson said. 'As if there's not enough to be worrying about.' He explained how they'd used the spring or flood tides to help raise the destroyers. How they got wires under the hulls at low tide, drilling through the silt the ships were sinking into, and lifting them at the highest tides, pulling them clear from the suction of the ocean floor.

6

On the day following, the divers got to work on the wreck of SMS *Moltke*. She weighed over twenty-six and a half thousand tons, unloaded. She was six hundred and twelve feet long, and ninety-eight feet abeam at her widest point. Her draught was a little over thirty feet. The great ship lay upside down in eighty feet of water.

The German destroyers or torpedo boats had been raised with wires attached to two floating platforms, tightened by twenty hand-operated ten-ton winches. It was a revolutionary method that had worked amazingly well but it would not be sufficient for these far larger battleships.

The divers went down in pairs, each with an assistant on the boat plus a reserve diver, ready to descend to their aid in an emergency. As well as Bill Peterson, three of the other four divers had been with Ernest Cox from the beginning. Their names were Sinclair MacKenzie, Nobby Hall and William Hunt. The fourth, named Harry Grosset, had been there almost as long.

Leo was kitted out. The men wore deep-sea diving suits of rubberised twill. The sleeves had vulcanised rubber cuffs for a watertight joint at the wrists. They wore heavy round helmets made of copper, with a glass aperture or window at the front, and a smaller one to each side. These helmets were screwed to the breast-plate or corselet by a slight turn.

The divers worked two three-hour shifts per day. Leo went down in the afternoon with Bill Peterson. Harry Grosset was the reserve diver up in the boat. Leo was connected to his linesman, Magnus Scott, by a breathing hose and a lifeline. The air supply was fed to him from a hand-winched compressor. A pressure gauge on this pump indicated the depth Leo had reached and regu-lated the air pressure accordingly. The hose was made of tough rubber and fed into the helmet. As he breathed, Leo found the window steamed up with condensation. To clear this, he had to open a small tap or spitcock and gulp in a mouthful of seawater to spit on the glass.

The lifeline was a rope used to pass signals up or down by means of tugs according to the simple code he had used in the Navy and that fortunately was universal. The lifeline was passed around Leo's waist, between his legs and up under his right arm. Bill Peterson assured him that it had a breaking strain of over a thousand pounds and that if he was in trouble Magnus Scott would pull him to the surface. All the assistants understood how to prevent the divers suffering from the bends, and knew to pull them up gradually, in stages. There was also a telephone line attached to the lifeline, but Bill warned Leo that this quite often shorted, especially when you'd been obliged to use the spitcock.

The diving suits were filled with air, which was pumped into the suit through a line from above. The diver himself could regulate this, and thus adjust his buoyancy, by means of an outlet valve. If he opened this valve, air would escape and so he descended. When it was time to return to the boat, he closed the valve and the suit would fill with air and so help his ascent.

Leo wore lead boots weighing fifteen pounds each that anchored him and helped him keep upright while walking on the seabed or the wreck. He bore forty-pound weights, one strapped to his chest, another to his back, that aided his balance beneath the water.

Leo Sercombe and Bill Peterson descended slowly into the waters of the Flow. Even now, in midsummer, beneath the surface the water was cold. Under his suit Leo wore first an all-in-one suit of cotton underwear, then another of wool. Over this he wore a full set of clothes. Shirt, pullover, trousers. He wore two pairs of thick socks and a woollen hat.

They descended into a strange world. When they reached the capsized, upturned SMS *Moltke*, Leo did not realise it was the ship they had come to, he thought it a huge rock or reef no one had told him about for it was covered by an aquatic forest of seaweed, taller than a man. The hull was blistered with barnacles, soft corals, anemones. The two divers took the small knives from the scabbards at their waists and hacked at the trunks of the seaweed, but these were thick and tough, and they made little progress. When they rose to the surface and reported on what they'd found, the next pair, in the afternoon, went down with axes.

The seaweed had to be cleared so that the external vents, torpedo tubes and side valves could be found, and any other holes opened when the ship was scuttled, for in order to be raised it had to be made watertight again. The first weeks were spent clearing these limbs and saplings from the hull. Small openings were filled with wooden plugs, which were taken underwater and hammered in tightly. The wood then expanded as it absorbed seawater. Larger holes were measured and the divers made templates out of thin plywood. These were sent to the workshops on Lyness Pier, where stronger versions in metal were produced. The divers then used bolt-punching guns to attach these plates onto the hull, and rendered them waterproof with so-called pudding joints made of canvas strips or gaskets packed with loose fibres of old rope oakum. These joints were compressed when the bolts were tightened.

Leo Sercombe and Sinc Mackenzie were performing the final part of this operation one afternoon, smearing the joints all over with tallow. They'd been underwater for a couple of hours, applying the tallow with a large paintbrush, when the water above them went black. Before he could begin to make sense of what might be causing this, Leo was yanked upwards by his rope and breathing tube, and dragged through the water. He collided with Sinc Mackenzie, who was hurtling by likewise. In the turmoil, Leo fell still, lying face up, and caught a glimpse above him of massive creatures gliding over his head. Then he was yanked askew again. It occurred to him that this was a strange experience, spinning around in the sea, he must remember what it felt like. Then as suddenly as the whirlpool had engulfed them the water stilled. Leo came to rest. He saw that Sinc was all right. When he looked up, the creatures had moved on. There were pulls on the lifeline that told the divers to ascend. When they reached the surface and clambered back into the boat the two men there told them with great excitement that a school of forty-foot whales, larger than either of them had ever seen, had just passed over the wreck site. One of the whales must have tickled the divers' lines with its huge tail.

Once the outside of the upturned hull was secured, the divers ventured further down. They found, still attached, a large boat made of two-ply oak in fine condition. They detached this boat from her fixtures, floated her, and towed her ashore. She was still in such good shape that from then on Ernest Cox used her as his own launch in the Flow.

The divers worked their shifts six days a week, through the autumn and into the winter. The occasional Orcadian gale stopped all work, but otherwise the divers agreed with each other that beneath the bleak grey northern sky and the bitingly cold winds, underwater was the best place to be. At least every other day each man did a shift as the reserve diver, which should have been a rest, but none of them enjoyed being stuck in a boat that bobbed and bucked in the surface swell. The reserve diver and the diving assistants were customarily soaked by water washing over the deck. It was better by far to sink beneath the surface from the furious wind and waves above.

The divers worked with their bare hands in the cold water and their fingers became numb and swollen, but the deeper they went, the calmer the silent world into which they descended. As they could only move sluggishly so it seemed to Leo that time itself slowed down. He did not know if this was some mysterious quality of the ocean, combined with their transit closer to the centre of the earth.

The divers were cordial enough with the other members of the workforce yet remained separate from them. All the men went to the flicks, and to the bar and canteen, but most of the time the divers sat at their own table, or retreated to their dormitory to play cards or listen to the wireless. They lived within a larger community of men but at one remove from them. At first Leo thought it was because they were the highest-paid workers and so saw themselves as superior, or others saw them so, but it was not that. It was something else. Perhaps the danger of their job. Perhaps others could feel that danger and smell it and kept away for fear it might somehow threaten them.

Ernest Cox brought his wife and daughter up North on occasions, and the engineer Ernie McKeown lived in a small hut with his wife, but otherwise it was just like the Navy, a world without women. Apart from Leo and Cox himself, Nobby Hall was the only other Englishman, another ex-Navy diver.

Leo read books Missis Cox obtained from a library on the mainland. When the divers played vingt-et-un it was for matches, not money, for none wished to waste wages that were hard-earned.

At Christmas some of the men went home, but others stayed in Lyness. Either they were from parts of Scotland far from Orkney, or they had no home to go to.

On New Year's Eve they gathered in the canteen to see the New Year in. The cook made them haggis with mashed swede and cabbage and mashed potato. They ate by candlelight, the candles stuck with their own dripped wax to the wooden planks of which the tables were made. When they had finished eating the men all sat and drank steadily. Leo sat with Nobby Hall at their table. None of the other divers had stayed and there were empty seats at the other two tables, occupied by no more than a dozen men in all. The cook joined the men on the furthest table.

One of the labourers called across, 'You's drinking beer even tonight?'

'That firewater don't agree with me, mate,' Nobby told him. 'It burns me up.'

The labourer did not respond. He only stared at his own glass and continued to do so. Leo had a bottle of malt whisky before him, Nobby a dozen bottles of ale. These were sealed by ceramic stoppers with rubber gaskets, held in place by wire bails. With each bottle it took Nobby a little longer to lever the wire loose. By the sixth or seventh he'd acquired the need to examine this contraption closely, blinking, before attempting to open it. It became a steadily increasing challenge as the night wore on.

'How the fuck do ye drink that piss water anyways?' the labourer called out. Nobby grinned stupidly. Leo poured himself another glass of malt. He drank the whisky neat, but with a glass of water beside it, which he swallowed in between sips of the liquor.

'On this night of all nights,' the labourer said, his voice loud and slurred. 'Suttin over by their selves like a pair a fuckin Toby jugs.' He did not look over but continued to gaze into his own glass of dark brown liquid.

Every now and then a man would rise clumsily from his chair and stagger out of the canteen. Either to stumble to his dormitory or more often to throw up then return for more drinking. The labourer and the other men at his table sat in sullen silence, but the furthest table seemed to accommodate comedians, for there was badinage and laughter. Leo considered joining them but he was not sure his legs would carry him there. He told himself that he could not hold his liquor, he was an idiot, he should abstain from alcohol. Then he wondered if he had said this aloud and looked around, but so far as he could tell, no one responded. Well, it was hardly interesting. Then he realised he'd forgotten what was not interesting. He tried to remember but could not. His brain did not work. Neither did his vision. The canteen building was not built on firm foundations, it tilted and swayed. Someone should tell Mister Cox.

'Ye'd rather sup that gnat's piss than good Scottish whisky,' someone said. Who said it? It was that man over there again, with the black beard and the red skin, gazing into his glass.

A man at the far table was singing, another had produced a small squeeze box, and a third was dancing. Leo watched him. All the other men on that table were laughing, but Leo considered the man's dancing to be elegant, even graceful. From out of his stupor he enjoyed watching this candlelit performance. Yes, it was mightily impressive. He wished only for that hectoring man to say nothing more.

'On New Year's Eve ye've nae wish tae drink with us,' the labourer called out. 'Are ye stuck up because ye're a divin fuckin swankpot or because ye're a pair of English cunts?'

Leo was stupefied. Then all of a sudden he was not. He was sober. His vision was clear. His mind was lucid, though he had no thoughts as such. He simply acted. Leo stood and walked over to the closer table. The labourer glanced up and saw his approach and rose awkwardly, his chair clattering on the floor behind him. He stood on his own feet for no more than a second. The diver Leo Sercombe hit him with two punches, each to the man's jaw. The first with his left fist spun the labourer's head, the right shortly following caught the man's jaw while it was still turning. Everyone heard the crack. The man was unconscious as he fell, collapsing like a boneless doll.

The singer ceased singing, the musician stopped playing his squeezebox. The men around them stopped laughing. The dancer still cavorted, for he was as drunk as anyone in the room and lost in his flailing. After a while he began to become aware of the fact that things had changed, though even as he looked up and around him he stamped on his boot toes to and fro. Then he came to a halt, swaying.

Leo looked at the prone figure of the man he'd laid out. Then he walked out into the bleak Orcadian night. He strode away from the barracks, down to the jetty, shocked by what he'd done. He'd thought he lacked the capacity for violence. He felt sick, not from the alcohol but of himself. Where did it come from? Did a man's seed condemn his progeny to defects similar to his own? The same flaws? A son becoming his father. Was there no escape? That pure wash of anger that drove him into action, it was instinctive, and had felt as natural as anything he'd ever done.

The waters of the Flow were filled with stars, but the surface of the sea was choppy and the stars bucked and swam in his vision as if the heavens themselves were not fixed but all in flux. Perhaps they were, and their stasis in the firmament above was an illusion created by the great distance between them and the earth. All was impermanent – the rocks, the seas, the planets – to imagine otherwise was obtuse. All he had here was a brief span. Was he compelled to be someone he did not wish to be? Better surely to fill his pockets with stones and jump from the jetty.

'Don't let 'em get to you, mate.'

Leo felt a hand press his shoulder.

'Jocks love to get aggressive when they drink,' Nobby Hall told him. 'It don't mean nothin. Bobby back there'll be his friendly old self come Monday. At least he will if his jaw ain't wired up. If I weren't drunk myself I'd a give him back the banter. That's all he wanted.'

'How'd you stop yourself?' Leo asked. 'Gettin angry?'

'Just let it sail over me, mate,' Nobby said.

'A wise man,' Leo told him.

Nobby laughed. 'I s'pose it helps that I weren't never much cop at fightin. Come on, mate, let's get to the dorm. It's freezin out here and I'm about done in.'

7

As they took the launch out to the wreck each morning and afternoon, it was tossed on the waves. The wind blew loud and wild. Rain fell, soft or hard, from vertical to wind-driven horizontal, in large sharp drops that stung the face or else so fine Leo did not know it was falling until he realised his face and hair were damp, his clothes covered in tiny droplets barely visible to the naked eye. Thunder rolled and rumbled over the Flow. Lightning crackled. The black sky loomed over them.

Yet there were other days when the sea was eerily calm and the sky clear and blue, the air warm, a summer's day in the middle of winter. On one such, Leo went down with Bill Hunt, the second lead diver, to survey what had been the upper decks of the ship, but were now underneath. They found her funnels and masts and the upper bridge all buckled under the weight and skewered into the ocean floor. The *Moltke* was stuck fast, but her bow was higher than her stern, and she was on a list, so that there was room to attach explosives. Tom McKenzie performed the demolition, placing charges of gelignite made from guncotton, nitroglycerine and potassium nitrate, with which they blasted the funnels and other impediments off the superstructure of the battleship.

The divers entered the interior of the vessel, to seal holes they could not access from outside. They carried submersible electric lamps, which gave out a dull, foggy glow. They found that lobsters had made their homes in compartments, and defended their territory with large claws. One afternoon Leo went down with Harry Grosset. He was cutting a ply template for a hole when he looked to the side and saw, in the dim yellow light of the lamp, that he was being watched. He could not see the man's body, only his head. He was sure that Harry was behind him somewhere, this was someone else. A bald man with dark, sad eyes and fine whiskers. The man beheld him. Leo returned his gaze. After some seconds had passed it occurred to Leo that the man was not wearing a helmet. This was not possible. It seemed to him that the man's face was unusually small, and somehow unnatural, but in what way he was not sure. He could not make it out. He wondered if he was looking at a ghost. The shade of a German sailor. Or a creature, one of those of whom the Scottish divers had warned him, who came up to the Orkney shallows from their home in the deeps of the oceans to grab a human mate.

Then the odd little man turned and swam off. Leo watched him swim away, and realised it was a seal that had been observing him.

Conger eels were everywhere. As Leo pushed an air-pipe through a porthole one bit him on the hand. It did not seem too bad, as he could not feel it and the cut did not bleed much underwater. But when he came up to the surface the blood began to gush out and he had to have the wound hurriedly dressed.

The divers worked their way through the ship blocking holes. For those too large to be plugged yet too awkward to be covered with a plate they poured *ciment fondu*, a cement that dried chemically rather than by evaporation. It was pumped into an opening through a long pipe like a fireman's hose.

One morning in late January Leo went down with Bill Peterson. They followed guide ropes that had been left by the last pair working in the ship the day before, and passed down through the decks until they reached the upper deck now at the bottom of the ship. Every door and porthole had to be sealed so that the entire hull was rendered watertight.

When the scuttled ship had turned turtle, everything loose had been tumbled about and settled on the ceilings that were now floors and covered in a slimy carpet of oil, coal dust and decaying matter. Fuel oil and liquid from the bilges had spilled everywhere. When they disturbed the sludge, no light from their lamps could penetrate it; they had either to wait for it to settle or to work in darkness. The light was dingy anyhow and with every step the two of them raised the oily silt, which spread through the filthy water darkening it further so that Leo felt he was walking through ink, unable to see more than the faintest glow from his lamp. He lowered himself through a hatchway into a mess room. Bill

Peterson remained outside to make sure his partner's air and lifeline did not get snagged.

Leo felt around until he found a wooden ladder. He climbed down it towards the ceiling of the room, where he expected to find an open door that they hoped to be able to close tight shut. Suddenly the ladder came loose from the wall. It squirmed free from his oily grip and shot up through the water, propelled by its own liberated buoyancy.

For a moment Leo waited. He believed that he could sense the wooden ladder beside him rising like a vertically propelled torpedo through the black water. Then he felt his lifeline and his airline pulling themselves taut, lifting him up with them. He rose a yard or two and stopped. The ladder was stuck. He tugged the lifeline. It was caught fast, pinned by or entwined around the ladder. If the ladder had also ruptured his airline he was a dead man. He might be anyhow.

Leo hung blindly in the inky darkness, his heavy boots and the lead weights around his torso pulling him down but his trapped lines ensnaring him. He shut the air valve in his diving suit. After some moments he realised to his relief that the suit was filling with compressed air through the airline, and soon he began to rise. He held his arms above his head. When he found the ladder he grasped hold of a rung and tried to pull it down but it was stuck fast.

Leo took one hand off the lowest rung of the ladder and opened the valve to let air out of the suit. He thought that the lead weights added to the weight of his body might help to pull the ladder down. He held onto the rung as his suit lost buoyancy, but the ladder did not budge. All that happened was that he became aware of heat in his arms that he realised was pain from taking the strain of his own weight and the lead. He changed tactics and closed the valve again and after a minute or two felt the tension in his arms relax, and soon he began to rise once more. He rose beside the ladder now, keeping hold of it rung by rung.

Suddenly the ladder bucked out of Leo's grasp. He thought that the whole ship had shifted, listing on the seabed. He floated in the blackness. He wondered if death would come now violently or if he might curl up and hang blindly in the strange fluids of that womb-like tomb. There seemed to be no further movement or reverberation. He felt around for the ladder and found it again, then had it sprung from his grip once more. It banged against his helmet. This time he did not try to find it but pulled the lines and discovered that one of them, the lifeline, was now free. He rose, following the remaining, pinned, airline. He was aware of turbulence in the water nearby, presumably the ladder being shifted downwards then bobbing back up, but as it did it yanked him after it on the airline. Someone was doing this. Some insane bastard was messing about with the ladder and with his lines.

Leo rose. His hands came into contact with something that moved. It was oily as everything else and so difficult to decipher. He tried to keep hold of it but it was slippery and was moving, then he grasped something that seemed also to grasp him in an oily handshake and he understood that this was Bill Peterson. They came together and though they were unable to see each other they could tap on each other's helmets. Painstakingly, by taking Bill's hand and putting it to the ladder, and to his lifeline, Leo hoped that he might make his colleague understand what had happened and the plight that they were in. They wrestled with the ladder and with Leo's airline, slithering around in the murk, trying to help each other and work together though it was impossible to know if they actually were, blindly groping for what felt like hours and hours. Until suddenly the airline came free.

Leo rose and felt the floor of the room above him and followed the lifeline to a hatch and half-swam, half-clambered through it. Bill ascended beside him. As they rose together Leo understood that their lines were entangled and they had no choice. He wanted to hug Bill Peterson with relief but, as two men in diving suits in deep water, this was impossible. He signalled by tugging on his lifeline to those in the boat above that they were coming up, and they made their way back. They rose side by side. When they had been pulled into the boat and their helmets removed, Magnus Scott said, 'Have ye two fellows been doing the tango doon there or what?'

Bill Peterson related what had happened in the boat there and then, as he would do many times in the hours and the days following. To the boss, in the dormitory to their fellow divers, in the canteen to the other men. He liked to tell the story with Leo there beside him, for every time he told it he finished by assuring those present that, 'This laddie's got one calm head on his shoulders. He has that, I can tell you. He's one cool customer.'

Then it was Leo's turn to speak. 'Bill saved my life,' he said.

Someone else had once saved his life underwater. Lottie Prideaux. He did not tell Bill, or anyone else, about it, but he began to think of her again, he could not help it. Of his promise, despite her son and any other encumbrances. Of what it meant.

8

When the holes were finally sealed in February, six twelve-inch centrifugal pumps were set up on the floating dock. A further dozen six-inch submersible pumps were placed beneath the surface. Water began to be sucked out of the great warship, and continued, hour after hour. Over the days following thousands of tons of water were pumped out. It was not possible to say exactly when the ship might be salvaged, but after a week Ernest Cox and his team knew there should be some indication. Some movement. There was none. They stood on the floating dock.

'Turn them off,' Cox ordered.

Divers were sent back down. Sinc Mackenzie and Nobby Hall descended in the morning. At first they could not find a problem. No holes that had been missed or some other unforeseen problem peculiar to the battleship. Then they saw that water was seeping back into the hull, through tiny leaks in the pudding joints.

Leo Sercombe and Harry Grosset were the next pair to go down, on the afternoon shift. They were told to collect a plate and bring it back for inspection. They chose the one closest to the surface where the light was best, though the sea was choppy and it was not easy to begin unscrewing the first bolt. Leo was attempting to apply the spanner when he felt a tap on his shoulder. He looked up and saw Harry pointing. Leo obeyed the direction and saw small fish nibbling at the outside of the pudding joints. They did not unscrew the plate but went up to the boat and returned with a fishing net.

The fish were identified as saithe, a species of cod, and they had been feeding off the tallow that had been spread on the outside of the joints. Tom McKenzie had a tank set up in one of the sheds, filled with seawater and populated by saithe. Then he experimented with new sealants. After a few days he found that if he mixed a little Portland cement with the tallow the fish did not eat it. With this new mixture the divers painstakingly re-covered all the pudding joints.

Once the new compound was set, Ernest Cox ordered pumping resumed. The stern of SMS *Moltke* was embedded in the gravel and silt of the ocean floor, her bow up off the ground. On the third day of sucking water from the ship the bow began to rise. This was no good. If there was a quantity of water trapped amidships the ship's back could break under the strain and she would be lost, her scrap worthless. Leo watched as Ernest Cox, Tom McKenzie and Ernie McKeown tried one thing after another.

To lighten the ship's weight at the stern, the giant propeller was loosened, worked off the shaft and hoisted out. This did not seem to help. Water was let back in and the bow lowered, and a destroyer scuppered to add its weight to that end. They pumped the

water out again until the ship began to rise but it did so in a volatile manner, rolling and see-sawing, and they let her down again.

All this took weeks. Leo was amazed at the time it took. Victor Harris had said that what Cox did was to speculate to accumulate, but this was speculation on a grand scale. Every action Ernest Cox took was a new experiment, for who had ever salvaged battleships this size? An entire sunken navy? Every problem was a new one, and there was no guarantee it had a solution.

Perhaps the stern needed a little help to free it from the suction of the gravel and sand. Cox ordered the divers to attach a series of nine-inch cables to the gun turret and to other strong points aboard the stern section. These were connected to the winches they'd used to raise the destroyers, attached to one of the floating platforms. Again water was pumped out of *Moltke*. The cables were made taut. This time, when, on the third day, the bow began to rise, labourers turned the winches. There were twelve winches, with four men on each holding one of the handles. Leo stood smoking with Harry Grosset at the back of the platform. Harry told him how when they'd raised the destroyers there would be another platform on the opposite side, with the same number of winches, so that they'd lifted those boats in a wire cradle.

The bow inched out of the water but there was still no movement in the stern. Ernest Cox barked out orders through his megaphone. It was imperative that the labourers all pulled in unison. Cox yelled for each twist and with a great effort, heaving and grunting and

sweating, the men slowly turned the handles. The taut wires began to sing or hum with the strain. Suddenly there was a loud crack. Leo flinched for he thought that someone had fired a gun. He looked up and saw a length of severed cable rear up into the air and come down towards the floating dock, writhing and whiplashing like some steel-wire snake. He threw himself to the floor. He heard another gunshot, then another, as one cable after another snapped, and he heard men yelling, and the sound of the cables as they swished through the air, thrashing, and struck the dock and the winches on the dock and other such machinery.

Leo did not raise himself up until the noises had abated and there was only one sound other than the wind, which was that of a man groaning. When he rose he saw that others had done so before him and were tending to the groaning man, one of the labourers. Another lay still on the deck. Two men knelt beside him. Then they rose and turned away. Other men stood watching. One of these took off his jacket and stepped forward and laid it over the head and shoulders and upper chest of his former colleague.

All work stopped. The injured man was recovering in hospital. The funeral of the other took place two days after the incident. The men accompanied the coffin by boat to the harbour on the mainland and thence by foot to the church in Kirkwall.

9

On the morning following, they were told to gather in the canteen. There Ernest Cox addressed them. The divers sat at their usual table.

'I don't know what's gone wrong, boys,' he said. 'Either we can't lift the stern or when we can her weight seems to shift around. Maybe turning turtle's loosened everything up inside her. There's air trapped in some places and water sloshing about in others. The only way to find out what's happening when we try to raise her would be to have men inside, and that's too dangerous even for these thrill-seekers.' He gestured to the divers' table. 'I wouldn't ask you to do that,' he said, shaking his head. 'I would not. What happened to those two lads was a terrible accident. We all know the risks in this work, and I know you're all brave as lions, especially you Jock lads, but I won't go beyond a reasonable limit, no, I won't, not for any one of you.'

Cox looked around. He was dressed as smartly as he always was, whether he was office-bound or about to spend the day aboard the boat or dock in terrible conditions. His brogues shone with brown polish, his white shirt was freshly starched. There was a woman on Hoy who did his laundry, and new clothes arrived

in packages that his wife Jenny Jack had regularly sent to the Flow.

'But I'll tell you this, boys,' he said. 'Don't let anyone tell you Ernest Cox knows when he's beaten. He doesn't. I'm going to explain to you now what it is we're going to do.'

Cox nodded to someone at the door. A young lad carried in a large chalkboard and rested it across three chairs, leaning it against their backs. Cox took a stub of chalk from his pocket and drew a side-on outline of the hull of a ship. Then he drew three pairs of vertical straight lines from the top to the bottom of the ship. With crude cross-hatching he filled in the narrow space between each pair of lines, so that the ship was graphically divided into three parts.

Ernest Cox turned back to the company. 'The hull of a warship,' he said, 'is built with many different watertight compartments, partitioned by metal walls or bulkheads. Now, boys, we've been making her watertight and pumping out the water. It hasn't worked. So do you know what we're going to do next? We're going to do something different. In fact, we're going to do the opposite.'

Leo glanced across at Tom McKenzie and Ernie McKeown. It was apparent from their bemused expressions that whatever was coming was going to be as big a surprise to them as it was for everybody else.

'That's right,' said Ernest Cox. 'Instead of pumping out water, we're going to pump in air. Compressed air. We're going to make these three bulkheads airtight, so that we've three separate sections of the ship and can

control the air pressure in each section separately. Then we might be able to lift her in a controlled manner, do you see? Make the bow less buoyant or the midships more buoyant, as the case may be. We are going to do something, boys, that has never been done before, and in the work you do in these next weeks and months you will write yourselves into the history books.'

IO

Now that Ernest Cox had decided what he wanted done, he brought in experts to advise him. The head diver Bill Peterson took part in these consultations and relayed their conclusions to Leo Sercombe and their other colleagues.

The three bulkheads ran through the many decks and countless compartments in the ship. It would have taken the divers years to seal them underwater. Enough air had to be pumped into the hull to enable men to work freely within it. In order to maintain this state, and allow men to pass from the open air and enter the ship whose air was in a pressurised state, airlocks had to be made.

Ernie McKeown found disused boilers six feet in diameter and twelve feet in length. Their tops and bottoms were cut away to render them tubes. Eight of these were welded and bolted together in the workshop in Lyness. Steel ladders were fitted the length of these new pipes, inside and out. This long airlock was carried out to the *Moltke* on a calm day on one of the tugs and taken to the fore end of the upturned hull at low table, when it was not far below the waterline. The spindly airlock was lowered into place by the tug's outriggers and chains, and bolted onto the ship. It was then secured with dozens of wire stays riveted to the hull like the guy ropes of a tent.

Tom McKenzie climbed into the airlock and down the ladder and cut through the bottom plating of the hull. An upper hatch was fitted at the top of the airlock and another, inner, hatch, twenty feet further down.

Two further airlocks were made and attached to the hull likewise, one for each of the three new sections to be formed.

Leo went out on the tender to the floating dock moored by the *Moltke*, from which compressed air was being pumped into the upturned battleship. He followed Tom McKenzie on a swaying rope gangway across from the dock to the airlock then climbed the metal ladder up the outside. They opened the upper iron door and climbed down the ladder into the lock. Tom McKenzie swung the door upwards into place, and turned the air valve. Compressed air flew shrieking through the valve with a sound like a hundred whistles.

McKenzie put his mouth to Leo's ear and yelled, 'It's a wee bit strange the first time.' He leaned back and gestured to his throat so that Leo could see him making a swallowing action. Leo did the same, repeatedly, responding to the sensation in his ears under the increasing pressure. He thought that something in his head would burst, but did not know what. His eardrums or blood vessels or brains. Soon he had no saliva left, his mouth and throat were dry. Again he copied Tom McKenzie who gripped his nostrils between the thumb and forefinger of his left hand and blew, easing the pressure in his ears. Leo watched the needle on the dial

of the air pressure move slowly round until the whistling and shrieking faded away. He did not think that
anything could be worth repeating this experience for
every time he came out to the ship from now on.

'Aye,' Tom said, 'you'll get used to it soon enough.'

Now they opened the inner door and climbed down
the ladder and into the ship. The water-filled world they
had moved through in their diving suits, and viewed
from inside their copper helmets, or felt through darkness like blind men, they now traversed in breathable air.
Everything was covered in a thick slime of oil and coal
dust. A dark and stinking world. They wore oilskins
and rubber macintoshes which became smothered with
this filth. Lights were strung along passageways.

The three bulkheads ran up through the levels or
decks of the ship, in various compartments. Throughout
the spring of 1927 the divers were joined by others,
labouring to seal them. They were like miners, but
working under the sea instead of underground. Pipes
were cut with oxyacetylene burners. These consumed
much of the fresh air in order to maintain their heat at
three thousand degrees, so the atmosphere was often
foul. Pipes were blocked with wooden plugs set in
red-lead putty. Buckled doors were replaced by cement
patches and fills. With the ship upside down, doors
were often now twenty feet above the ceiling that had
become the floor, so new ladders had to be attached to
armour plate.

In the German crew's accommodation, they found
photographs, clothing and personal effects in lockers and
lying scattered amid the debris. Leo found bottles of fine

wine, but it could not be enjoyed, for the pressure of the compressed air had blown the corks in. Harry Grosset found chocolate bars in a cupboard in the canteen, which he brought up and passed around. They still tasted good. Of course there was no evidence of the German sailors, who had scuttled their ships and escaped. Somewhere out on the bed of the North Sea lay the wreck of HMS *Queen Mary*, and the bones of Leo's friends interred within her.

In bad weather the men emerged from the top of the hundred-foot airlocks into wild blowing sky and had to hold tight and climb down the ladders on the outside with the locks pitching in the savage wind.

In May of that year all was ready. The bulkheads were airtight, and each was separately fed with compressed air. All the men left the ship and on a calm day late in the month gathered around her at a high spring tide, on the tugs and tenders and floating platforms. The last stage of the job was not rushed but instead slowed down, as the ship filled with air under ever-greater pressure, towards the point where negative buoyancy would give way to positive buoyancy. Leo stood on the tug *Sidonian* with the other divers. All of them had worked on some at least of the destroyers and they told Leo that if this worked as Father Cox hoped it would then he was about to see something he would never forget.

Ernest Cox strode the deck of the largest platform, equipped with his megaphone. He checked the gauges that showed the pressure, on fourteen-inch dials, to the nearest quarter of a pound, and told the men on the various machines to give more air, or slow down, or shut off.

The compressors throbbed and generators chugged. Labourers stood smoking on the floating docks, waiting if needed for they knew not what. As well as the airlocks protruding from beneath the surface of the Flow, with their multitude of guy wires keeping them stable, rubber pipes now squirmed in the rough water like sea snakes, and electric cables ran down to feed the lights and other equipment inside the submerged ship.

'Look around,' Nobby Hall told Leo. 'We're all here waitin, like for a miracle. Father Cox there's like one of them old prophets, ain't he?'

Leo smiled and said it had not occurred to him but perhaps this was right. Nobby said he hadn't been one much for worship, but they'd had readings in school, and he seemed to recall vaguely a story in the Bible about making iron swim.

'You're right,' Leo said. 'Elisha led the Israelites to the River Jordan, and as they were cutting trees to build dwellings, one man dropped his axe in the water. Elisha made it float back to the surface, so the man could retrieve it.'

Nobby Hall grinned. 'There you go then, mate. Father Cox is like the Prophet Elisha. There you go.'

The day was unusually calm. Men chatted and smoked on the boats, then gradually they stopped speaking and turned their attention to the site of the wreck. Leo could not see anything happening. Yet they all sensed it. Workers on the floating platforms stopped what they were doing. Everyone looked towards the water.

'She's rising,' said Bill Peterson quietly.

Leo watched the three pillars of the airlocks creep upward. There came a long low groan from under the

209

water. Harry Grosset said he had once heard a whale make such a sound. Bubbles of air appeared on the surface and popped. The sea began to ripple and roil and pitch like something cooking or fermenting. It frothed and foamed. It seethed and simmered.

The tugs pitched and swayed in turbulence; men lost their footing. Compressed air escaped from underneath the ship in twenty-foot bubbles. Suddenly there was a rush of water and the great broad hull reared up out of the sea, groaning, long tendrils of seaweed flailing from her sides in the sun.

Once positive buoyancy had been reached, and the suction of the mud in the seabed had given way, there was no way of controlling the ship's ascent. They could only watch as a million and a half cubic feet of surplus air was expended in seconds. The driving force shot the *Moltke* to the surface, sending waterspouts soaring upwards around her, as if heralding this monstrous arrival from the deep. Holding his breath, Leo watched the huge ship, all her twenty-four thousand tons of metal, rise above the surface and tower above them, seeming to breathe there in that ferment or get her breath back from the enormous effort of her resurrection, while sprays of water containing the filthy slime inside the ship turned the surrounding sea a dirty brown, oil and air and bubbling seawater all gurgling together.

Sinc Mackenzie yelled, 'She's up!' and Leo realised that all the men around him were cheering. He joined them. What they had just seen was a sight given to few men. Gradually the great upturned battleship settled, afloat. Ernest Cox ordered the tugs brought alongside her and secured.

11

On the days following, the battleship was towed alongside Lyness Pier. The pier railway was extended with a long curve, and re-laid on *Moltke*'s upturned hull. A light engine towed a three-ton crane along the tracks. Openings, six feet square, were cut into the hull. Men went down with oxyacetylene burners and cut loose whatever they could. Everything metal, large or small, that could be lifted out of the ship was raised by the cranes through the hatches in her hull cut for this purpose. Gun steel, with its high content of nickel and chromium. Boiler plates, with their low content of phosphorus and silver. Cox knew what everything was worth. Three thousand tons of metal were removed.

The open holes were plated over, and the ship was once more airtight. It floated, still upside down. Two corrugated-iron huts were riveted on the hull, each painted white. One was a machine room to house the three compressors required to maintain a constant air pressure for the journey. The other a kitchen, bunkhouse and mess room for a fourteen-man runner crew. Leo volunteered to join it. Ernest Cox planned to tow the ship, lighter than it had been but still weighing over

twenty thousand tons, to the Admiralty dry dock at Rosyth in the Firth of Forth.

Two towing bollards were fixed a hundred feet from the bow of the upturned hull, and lines from these were taken up by a large tug. A hundred feet further back a bollard was bolted on the port side, another on the starboard, and a small tug secured to each.

Lifeboats and rafts were attached to the *Moltke*, and the tugs towed the huge overturned German battleship out of the Flow, through the Pentland Firth and out onto the North Sea. The tugs hauled the ship south, her great weight pulling them back, so that their progress was slow but steady in the swelling sea.

On the morning of the fourth day the *Moltke* approached the Firth of Forth. Ernest Cox stood surveying the channel before them. Somehow he managed to look as smart as ever in his Harris tweeds and brogues and the trilby pushed down tight on his head.

'You'll tell your grandchildren about this,' he said, turning to Leo. 'I know you've got no children yet, lad, but you're young, you surely will.' He stamped on the metal plate they stood on. 'Aye, Leo, you can say that you were one of Ernest Cox's men. No one's lifted such a ship as this. No one's towed a ship so far upside down either. How about that, eh, sonny?'

Leo did not think he had ever seen a man so satisfied. With good reason. ''Tis been quite a year,' he said. He could not do as others did and address Ernest Cox as 'Father'.

'The first of many,' Cox said. 'It'll be like the destroyers. We learned from all our mistakes on the first one. The rest came up quicker every time.' He put

his hands on his hips and squared his shoulders. 'You're a good diver, Leo Sercombe. Mac thinks highly of you, you know. Bill Peterson too. I intend to raise your pay. You'll be earning good money with me.'

Leo nodded slowly. 'I appreciate what you're sayin, Mister Cox. But this is it for me.'

Ernest Cox looked at Leo with a mystified frown upon his face. He did not seem able to understand what he'd heard.

'I've been long enough in the North,' Leo said.

Cox scowled. His face reddened and it seemed he was about to curse. But he was in too good a mood to be angry. He shrugged. 'I'll be damn' sorry to lose you, sonny,' he said. 'Have you had bad news?'

Leo shook his head. 'No.' He drew on his cigarette. 'I've been a wanderer, at other men's beck and call, long enough. I should make something of my own.'

'What kind of thing?' Cox asked.

'A field. A horse.' Leo smiled. 'A home. It don't sound like much.'

'If you've got none of those things, sounds like a lot,' Ernest Cox said. 'To make it work might not be easy.'

'I doubt it will.'

Cox rested one hand on the young man's shoulder. 'Few things worth doing are, sonny.'

Leo looked around. He had to admit that the man spoke from a position of authority. Cox looked up at Leo and said, 'But we're not done here yet. We've still to bring this piece of scrap to the dock.'

*

Ernest Cox radioed ahead for an Admiralty pilot, and arranged for him to come out and meet them at Inchkeith, at an agreed time, to guide them through the Firth of Forth, under the great bridge, and on to the dock at Rosyth. The galley cook announced that breakfast was served. They ate their morning meal of porridge followed by bacon and the last of the eggs they'd brought, with fried bread, and mugs of tea. The radio operator came in and reported contact with the leading tug.

'The pilot's on board, Father.'

Ernest Cox swallowed a mouthful of tea and said, 'He can't be yet.' He strode out of the corrugated-iron hut onto the hull and marched along towards the fore end. Other men followed him. 'Binoculars,' he said without turning round.

Tom McKenzie had a pair slung around his neck. Stooping forward, he removed them and walked faster to catch up with his boss. Cox took the glasses and stopped and raised them to his eyes.

Leo came up level with the two men and followed Ernest Cox's gaze. He did not need binoculars to see that a boat was now tied to the leading tug, a hundred feet ahead of the *Moltke*. Beyond, a second boat was approaching out of the Firth, with the Royal Navy ensign flying.

Without lowering the glasses, Ernest Cox said, 'Get me a boat.'

Leo looked at Tom McKenzie, who gestured towards the aft of the upturned hull. 'The rowboat'll be quickest,' he said. Leo accompanied him to the small lifeboat.

Tom McKenzie waved others over too. They untied the boat and lowered it to the water then unrolled the rope ladder, with its wooden spars. Leo climbed down first and fixed the rowlocks in position while Tom McKenzie and two others followed. They found their oars and raised them as Ernest Cox climbed down the ladder and stepped into the boat.

The men on that side pushed off from the *Moltke* with their oars and they rowed out and on, around the side tug tied to the ship, towards the leading tug. The sea that had appeared calm from on top of the hull was choppy in the small boat.

'Faster, men, faster!' Ernest Cox yelled. Leo rowed hard, his unaccustomed muscles on fire.

When they reached the leading tug, Ernest Cox directed them to steer the boat between the two larger ones already tied to her. As soon as one of the crew on the tug had grasped the rope thrown to him and pulled their boat flush with the side, Ernest Cox rose and clambered out. The others could hear him yelling, 'What the bloody hell is going on here?'

'It's gettin crowded on that tug and no mistake,' one of the rowers said.

Tom McKenzie caught Leo's eye again and said, 'We'd better go after him.'

They heaved themselves aboard the tug and walked across its deck. Mac climbed the short ladder to the bridge. Leo stayed at the bottom and watched from there. On the bridge of the tug the skipper introduced a man he said was a Firth of Forth pilot. He explained that the man had hailed him, and come on board.

'We're towing this hulk to the Admiralty dock at Rosyth,' Cox said. He pointed to a man in naval uniform. 'And this Admiralty pilot is going to guide me.'

The Firth pilot shook his head. 'I can't allow that.'

'You'll do what the bloody hell I tell you,' Cox said.

'The tug skipper here accepted me,' the Forth pilot said. 'Once I'm appointed I can't be removed until the vessel's docked.'

Ernest Cox turned to the Admiralty pilot. 'You're a naval officer,' he said. 'Pull bloody rank or something.'

'I've been contracted to do the job,' he explained to the Firth pilot.

'That's no concern of mine.'

'I can't be removed either,' the naval pilot said. 'I refuse to leave this bridge.'

Tom McKenzie stepped forward. 'Can you two not work together?' he suggested.

The pilots looked at Mac, and at each other, with similar expressions that seemed to combine distaste with incredulity.

'Pilots working in pairs?' one asked.

Leo turned and walked back across the deck of the tug. He leaned over the side. The two men in their life-boat looked up and Leo shrugged. He stood and walked to the back of the tug and rolled a cigarette and lit it. As he exhaled the smoke of the first drag he heard faint cries in the distance and looked behind him. The men of the runner crew on the upturned hull of the *Moltke* were waving and yelling. One of the other tugs sounded its horn. Leo turned and looked forward. He saw that though the tugs had stopped towing some while earlier, all the vessels were drifting on the ebb tide. He reckoned the tide had about a five-knot run. He looked ahead and saw to his horror the massive Forth Bridge looming.

Now the men above him on the tug saw what was happening. They were heading for the central pillar of the bridge! One of the pilots took command, or they worked in unison, Leo did not know, but the order was given to the tugs to cast off their tow lines. They did so, and all watched the twenty-thousand-ton hulk of out-of-control metal float towards the pillar.

If that pillar was struck by the tremendous weight and motile force of the *Moltke* it would be a disaster. If a train was crossing at the time many people would surely be killed. Cox would be ruined anyhow. All the men's jobs would be lost. Leo would never receive the rest of his pay. He watched in horror, unable to breathe. The miracle of the raising followed so soon by catastrophe. *The haughtiness of man shall be humbled, and the pride of men shall be brought low.* Leo stood on the leading tug and watched the hulk turn broadside and glide through the left-hand bay, missing the pillar by no more than a few feet. He gasped a huge gulp of the Forth air.

The tugs caught up with the *Moltke* on the far side of the bridge and once more took her in tow, one lashed to either side, the leading tug pulling her forward. They brought her to the dry dock and inched her in, Ernest Cox yelling orders from the hull with his megaphone. Spectators came and went along the side of the dock to view the extraordinary sight. Leo and the rest of the running crew stood upon the hull like hunters who had captured this wild and huge beast of the deep, this iron leviathan, and brought its corpse to land.

When the docking was complete Ernest Cox threw his megaphone into the air, and one by one embraced his men. The dock was closed and drained. The *Moltke* rested on pillars in the dry dock. Her upper decks, now beneath her, were covered with barnacles and sponges, blue mussel shells, and anemones in the full range – red, orange, blue-yellow – of subaquatic colour.

On the days following the men gathered the gear off the hull of the *Moltke* and took it on the tugs back to Scapa Flow. Leo said goodbye to them. Ernest Cox arranged for his pay to be delivered, and Leo carried his bag and got a lift to Waverley Station in Edinburgh, to find a train and begin the journey down to the South West of England.

Part Six

THE GREY
THOROUGHBRED
1923–1926

I

In 1923, female students were admitted to the Royal Veterinary College in Camden, London, for the first time. Two women, Lottie Prideaux and Muriel Furst, took six-month courses. Both had previously worked as assistants to veterinary surgeons, Muriel to her father in Birmingham. Since assisting Patrick Jago during the war, Lottie had worked on her own, attending to animals on the estate. Digs were found for them to share close to the college.

'Well, my dear, you're off to live in the great metropolis,' Arthur Prideaux said to his daughter at breakfast on the morning she left. 'A day I never thought would come. Perhaps you might even find time to enjoy some of the delights of our capital.'

'I shall not,' Lottie told him. 'As you well know, Papa, I intend to work hard, learn all I can, and return as soon as possible.'

Her stepmother's teacup was returned to its saucer with a loud chink. 'I cannot believe you,' she said. Alice could not hide her envy. She wished to bring her children up in London. She allowed that bucolic isolation might be acceptable for their infancy, but maintained that the stimulation of city life was an absolute necessity once they acquired the use of reason, which she believed to be at the age of seven. Arthur pointed out that from that age the boys would be away at school most of the year, and whatever other arrangements prevailed, they'd surely spend summer in the country. Their eldest child, James, was not yet quite seven, and Alice's parents had made their town house available for as many visits as she might wish.

'I don't care how hard you study, Lottie,' her stepmother said. 'I'm going to come and sweep you off to Liberty's. They've new premises and I can't wait to visit.'

Lottie raised a sceptical eyebrow. 'Thank you, Alice,' she said. 'You are far too generous. But I warn you, you'd have to drag me into town.'

The main doors set in the façade of the college were opened at 8 a.m. Most mornings the two female students stood there waiting. The doors gave access to a vaulted archway that led to the main quadrangle, laid to lawns and flowerbeds. The only evidence of its veterinary function were the gravel setts or walkways, and the quadrangle resounding to the clatter of shoes and cracking of whips as horses were trotted, being studied for lameness. The buildings surrounding the quadrangle housed a bone room, botanical classroom, dissecting room, pathological laboratory, and the offices of the professors.

On the ground floor of one side of the quadrangle were stables, generally occupied by horses awaiting assessment for soundness, and a loose box for use while examining horses' eyes.

'I don't think I ever really believed such a place as this existed,' Lottie told Muriel during their first week. 'Devoted to the study of such animals. I might have dreamed it.'

The middle quadrangle had a massive glass roof supported on iron columns. At the northern end was a table at which small animals were attended to in the Poor People's outpatient clinic, which took place each morning between 9 a.m. and noon. Owners came with their moggies and mutts, and sat waiting their turn on a bench along the wall. Muriel spent every morning here, for virtually all her work in Birmingham had been with domestic pets. Students had to work in pairs. She and Lottie interviewed owners, examined the patients, made a diagnosis and proposed treatment. If an operation such as castration or spaying was required, they led the patient to the small-animal operating theatre off the archway between the quads. Under a professor's guidance the women performed the operations, taking it in turns to act as surgeon or anaesthetist.

The veterinary work that occupied Lottie at home was chiefly with large animals on the estate, and it was to these she turned her principal attention while at the college. She attended lectures on hygiene, surgery and the pathology of farm animals. There were always cattle, sheep and pigs awaiting examination in a yard behind the lecture theatre. An area of the middle quadrangle was covered in straw and in this bed horses were cast and operated on in the afternoons. This was the domain of final, fourth-year students, but Lottie observed whenever she could. Not that she reckoned she'd be able to manage the arduous and awkward work while dressed in a long skirt. Back home on the estate Lottie wore what she liked.

At first, Muriel beseeched her friend to stay with her so that they could work on the small animals as a pair, but as male students queued up to offer themselves as colleagues she let Lottie go. Muriel was a plain, stoutly built young woman, a couple of years younger than Lottie, yet there was something that drew men to her. Lottie could not quite see what it was. A teasing lilt in the way she spoke with them, perhaps. A sense of self-awareness when she moved, how she moved, that attracted them.

In the room they shared back at their digs Lottie asked Muriel if she knew what she was doing.

'I do now,' Muriel said, 'though I didn't used to. I don't ask them to push themselves forward. It makes no sense, does it? You're twice as pretty as I am.'

'I didn't mean that,' Lottie said. She did not tell Muriel that she herself did not intend ever to trust a man again. She was simply curious.

'Ten times prettier. And they're mostly sons of vets, just like I'm the daughter of one. They know you're from nobility.'

Most of the students were younger than Lottie. She was approached, but she told one prospective suitor that she was engaged to be married to a peer of the realm, another that she was a divorcee, and the invitations ceased.

*

The Professor of Surgery was a pioneer of equine abdominal surgery, and Lottie attended all his lectures. She spent as much time as she could in the dissecting room, and volunteered to assist at post-mortem examinations. She was permitted to attend the London, Scottish and Midland Railway stable to the east of the college on Saturdays, when lame horses were examined. Most Sundays she came back into the college to help the laboratory assistants. When Alice sent a telegram saying she would pick her up from her digs the following Saturday morning, Lottie replied with the words: REGRET TOO BUSY. SEE YOU BACK HOME. She made no trips to the West End, or Oxford Street. The six months were gone before she knew it, and she returned with renewed confidence to the West Country.

2

Lottie Prideaux beheld the vicar's pair of cocker spaniels. The younger one scurried around her, rose on its hind legs, demanding food or attention or simply out of uncontainable excitement. The other lay on a rug in the drawing room, glancing up at her with a defeated expression.

'She's been poisoned,' Reverend Doddridge said.

'Who on earth would do such a thing?' Lottie asked him.

'A thief.'

'You've been robbed?'

'No,' the vicar said. 'He got poor Mabel but Edna chased him off. I dreamed I heard her barking in the night, but did not wake.'

Lottie did not believe the excitable young spaniel at her feet would chase away any intruder, but rather welcome them.

'Or possibly some other blackguard,' the vicar said.

'Do you have enemies?' Lottie asked. She knelt and examined the stricken bitch.

'The call to righteousness has many enemies,' the vicar replied. 'Myself, personally, none that I know of. Unless some member of the Chapel believes cruelty to animals a legitimate expression of schismatic dissent.'

Lottie wondered if this was the vicar's attempt at humour. She suspected not. His devotion to his dogs was well known, and he took their well-being more seriously than that of members of his flock. He had been the incumbent for over forty years, and always kept two female spaniels. As one neared her end he bought a puppy, always unrelated. He did not breed but had the puppies spayed as soon as they had had their first season, during which he protected them from male canine attention under lock and key. Mabel was a little over six years old. Lottie herself had lethalled the previous ailing spaniel, Reverend Doddridge hovering over them like some grim guardian angel as she applied first chloroform, then when the dog was unconscious a concentrated vapour. Reverend Doddridge had the gardener dig a grave in a spinney in the vicarage garden, where the old girl could rest with her predecessors.

'Or perhaps it is distemper,' he said. 'I'm sure Mrs Dagworthy has some castor oil. And syrup of buckthorn. Is that what she needs?'

'I don't think so,' Lottie told him.

'Can't you see the poor girl is fading before our eyes? She's paralysed ... that's what distemper leads to, is it not? Or clots in the blood vessels, they're deadly too, aren't they?'

Lottie massaged the quiet spaniel. The younger one tried to lick her fingers as she did so. She asked the vicar if he wouldn't mind removing Edna to another room, as the youngster's antics were distracting. He said he could not leave Mabel in her distress and instead lifted a small bell that was on a reading table and rang it vigorously. They heard footsteps approaching along the stone-flagged passage from the kitchen, and the housekeeper Mrs Dagworthy appeared in the doorway.

'Please take away this unquiet dog,' the vicar said. He gently picked Edna up and, cradling her in his two large hands, passed her to his housekeeper, who turned and carried away the yapping puppy.

'You may have been right the first time,' Lottie said.

'Mabel's been poisoned?'

'It looks to me like dropsy. It feels like there is an obstruction of the portal circulation.'

Reverend Doddridge said nothing, and when Lottie glanced up at him she saw the puzzlement on his face.

'The liver,' Lottie said. 'She might perhaps have consumed something with lead in it. We all know how greedy spaniels can be. They'll wolf down all sorts of muck, indiscriminately.'

The vicar looked pained, as if he could hardly bear for one of his dogs to exhibit a human vice. Lottie reassured him that Mabel was young enough to recover, if given calomel, and also a decoction of broom, which could be got from the chemist in Wiveliscombe.

'But most important,' she said, 'is to rub her right side, from the last rib to the hip, with embrocation.'

'Every day?' Reverend Doddridge asked.

'Certainly,' Lottie told him. 'The influence you produce on the nerves of her skin will be carried to her liver, it'll be just what she needs.'

'I shall do it, without fail,' the vicar said.

'And if Edna exhibits signs of jealousy,' Lottie added, 'you may give her a massage too.'

Reverend Doddridge smiled. This produced a somewhat sinister effect upon his face. 'That is a fine idea, Miss Charlotte,' he said.

'Don't worry,' Lottie said. 'Mabel's greed is not life-threatening. Unlike some incidences. A fortnight ago, cows got through a fence into Mrs Tucker's garden, over at Manor Farm.'

'I suppose they gorged themselves on her vegetables?' the vicar asked. He rose to his feet. Mabel already looked perkier. 'Or her flowers, perhaps?'

'A reasonable assumption,' Lottie said. 'But false, I'm afraid. They went for her washing on the line. Most of the beasts were little affected. They passed the various socks and vests through their four stomachs. But one greedy Ruby Red tried to eat an entire bedsheet, and choked on it. She was dead when I arrived.'

Lottie rode her motorcycle back to the estate. Villagers and farmworkers watched her pass. A plume of snuff-coloured dust rose from her wheels. Her home was a cottage once inhabited by the Wombwell family. Mr Wombwell had died young, neither of his sons had returned from the Great European War, and when crippled Florence Wombwell died a fortnight after Lottie came back from the veterinary college in London, in 1924, she'd asked her father if she could live there. Arthur assured her there was no need to move out of the big house, there was plenty of room for everyone. Alice said she should have a larger house, they could build a new one in the grounds for her, it was unbecoming for Lord and Lady Prideaux's daughter or stepdaughter to inhabit a labourer's tied cottage. But Lottie insisted it would suit her perfectly. She had it emptied and stripped. Floorboards were freshly oiled, rotting window frames replaced. Plumbing was installed. An extension was added onto the back of the cottage with one room for her surgery, another for storage and preparation of medicines.

On Saturdays Lottie saw domestic animals in her surgery. The queue of patients and their owners often stretched into the afternoon, attending from an ever-wider radius around the estate. On weekdays she visited the farms.

3

Each day dawned hotter than the one before in the summer of 1926. Without rain, many crops struggled. In his study Arthur Prideaux watched the needle on the slowly turning drum of his barograph, hoping for a sign of change in the atmospheric pressure, but the line on the graph only scrawled upwards. By the middle of July the mercury in the thermometer on the wall in the hall rarely dropped below eighty degrees even after nightfall.

On Sunday 11 July Arthur and Alice and the three boys were joined for lunch by Lottie and also Alice's mother, Maud, Lady Grenvil. They began with a chicken broth. Alice asked Lottie how she managed in this heatwave, riding her noisome motorcycle in those heavy clothes, and manhandling large animals.

'I must confess, I wouldn't mind a little rain,' Lottie said. 'A light breeze.'

'It's ghastly,' Maud Grenvil said. 'I was brought up in India, where one went up into the hills when the heat in the plains grew unbearable. Here, what can one do? Climb Dunkery Hill? One would simply expire in the attempt and that would be that.'

Garnished ham and galantine of veal were brought from the kitchen, served with a hard-boiled egg salad, another of beetroot and potato, a third of tomato and watercress, which Alice's mother proclaimed was efficacious not only for women in their confinement or recovery from childbirth, but also for those heavily outnumbered by male members of their household.

Alice laughed and said, 'Thank goodness you are here, Mama. But don't worry. The odds will be shortened at the end of the holidays, when Edward joins James at Tyttenhanger Lodge.'

George heard this and demanded to be allowed to join his older brothers at preparatory school. 'There won't be anyone left for me to play with,' he protested.

Arthur Prideaux turned to his eldest son, James. 'Could you ask your younger brother,' he said, 'not to be in quite such a hurry to dash off and leave me at the mercy of these women?'

James smiled, but George frowned and said, 'Couldn't you call in reinforcements, Papa?'

Alice repeated 'reinforcements', and said it was an impressive word coming from a five year old. Edward explained that it had occurred in the book Aunt Lottie was reading to them. George denied this. He knew the word anyway, he hadn't got it from anyone.

'Do you know, I read an article the other day,' his father said. 'It claimed that, far from coining new words all the time, increasing our potential to express all we experience, in fact the English language is losing more words than it gains. More slip out of use, are forgotten, become archaic, than are invented. The language is impoverished, and so are we.' He looked around the table at his sons. 'Rather sad, don't you think? You chaps, it's up to your generation to reverse this sorry trend.'

The boys had milk jelly for pudding while the adults took coffee and chocolates in the drawing room. Afterwards, a wicket was set up on the lawn, stumps hammered into the hard earth, ruining one bat, and bails laid on top. Arthur and Lottie joined in the game. James said it was a belter of a wicket, and his father warned him not to bowl any bumpers. Lottie bowled underarm. She said it was as cumbersome to play cricket in a skirt as it was to do most other things. She regretted that she didn't wear breeches on a Sunday as on weekdays.

George swung wildly and missed. Edward possessed a pair of pads but would not let anyone else use them, and wore them himself even when fielding in the slips. They used a tennis ball, though James could easily send it for a six into the jungle. The Labradors nosed round after it while a replacement was tossed down from the terrace, where Alice and her mother watched from beneath parasols.

Play was interrupted by the housekeeper Gladys Whittle, who informed her ladyship that his lordship had a message from the stables. *It has arrived.* Alice passed this on. Arthur called out, 'Draw stumps. Play over,' and marched off towards the side of the house leading to the stables. Edward said it was unfair, it was his turn to bat next, Gladys should be twelfth man and bring some drinks out to the pitch and they could resume after. But the others were already following their father.

4

The horse was unlike any that had ever been seen on the estate. He stood some seventeen hands high. His glossy hide was grey. He had deep shoulders and a strong chest, a short back and powerful hindquarters. His withers were well defined, the neck long and his head refined, handsome. Altogether he was an incredible combination of muscularity and elegance. Lottie looked at his eyes. They were bright and shining, commanding. She had witnessed such creatures before, in the enclosure at Epsom, and they were striking then, led round by their dwarfish riders. But to see a pure thoroughbred here in the stable yard of their home in a hidden corner of the West Country was quite different. He stood there like some magical creature, a visitor from a higher realm.

Even her father and Herb Shattock, inspecting the stallion, seemed diminished beside him.

'I thought you should wish to have a look, master,' the groom said. 'Before he goes over to the stud farm.'

'I should indeed,' Lord Prideaux said. 'Let the poor chap have a day or two to recover from the journey.'

As they spoke, the two men ran their hands over the animal's skin. Perhaps they were aware of doing so but

Lottie thought not. They could not help themselves in their appreciation of his conformation, his beauty. He had a certain nervousness, rising off his hooves on the cobblestones of the stable yard. Yet he gave no indication of a desire to escape. He possessed a regal bearing, a poise, that suggested his awareness of the impression he made on these human beings and enjoyment of their attention. His restlessness was the expression of the energy latent within him, ready to explode into action when required.

Lottie wished to caress the stallion too, but held back, letting her father enjoy the moment. Watching the two men, master and closest servant, so alike in physical stature, it occurred to her that with a slight calibration or adjustment of class relations they could be best friends. Or perhaps without, in fact, realising it, they actually were. She did not know. Perhaps the differences between them, of wealth, of power, of freedom and opportunity, were insignificant compared to what united them. Horses, the land, their love and care for herself, and her mother before her.

The boys were in the yard. Alice implored them to keep away from the stallion. 'Come back here,' she cried as each boy took a step closer than his brothers. Lottie turned and looked behind her. At the end of the stable block a crowd had gathered. Word had spread through the house, the gardens, across the estate amongst those perambulating on their afternoon off. A maid, a gardener, farmers and their wives, children, ploughmen who worked every day with heavy horses, all stood and beheld the remarkable beast.

*

On the day following, Lottie returned to the stables after breakfast. There was no one around but she heard noises and followed them to the paddock. Herb Shattock's eldest lad led the grey horse on a long rope, circling him. Arthur Prideaux and his head groom leaned against the upper pole of the fence, watching. Lottie joined them, and stood beside her father. She asked how long they had the stallion for. How many mares did her father intend him to cover?

Her father turned to her with a grin upon his whiskered face. 'I've not hired him, my dear,' he said. 'I've bought him. He's ours. We'll breed from him, but we'll also hire him out. I'm convinced there's nothing to compare with him in the entire West Country. Unless they're deeply camouflaged.'

'I had no idea, Papa,' Lottie said. She shook her head. 'I thought my father was a man of caution.'

Arthur Prideaux removed his hat with his left hand and with his right wiped the sweat from his forehead. He nodded in the general direction of the big house. 'Not a word to Alice. I've not told her yet. She still hopes to persuade me to make our main home in London, when George goes off to school. But once I've explained it to her, she'll realise that with this new commitment to the stud farm, I couldn't leave it in someone else's hands. I mean, behold this fellow. This beautiful hot-blooded horse. I intend to come and regard him every day.'

Lottie's father was rarely so exuberant. He told her that the stallion had raced thirty times over five seasons. He'd won only four races. 'But he was placed a further eighteen. If he'd won one or two more races I'd have had to pay a lot more for him, do you see? But he was often unlucky.'

The lad led the horse towards the spectators, then turned and led him away, his hooves kicking up the dry dust. The lad was in his shirtsleeves and there was sweat at his armpits and on his back.

'You can see,' Arthur Prideaux said, 'what outstanding straight paces he has.'

'Abundance a bone, there, sir,' Herb Shattock agreed. 'Excellent feet an all.'

'He'll add size and bone to our lighter mares, and quality to the heavier ones.'

'That he will,' the groom agreed. 'And he seems to have a good temperament from what I seen so far.'

'Indeed,' Lord Prideaux said. 'I wish to ride him.'

When Lottie turned to look at her father, she saw that Herb Shattock had done likewise. She herself wore, no doubt, a similar expression of consternation or dismay. Her father still gazed at the stallion with a benign grin. Herb Shattock narrowed his eyes. Lottie caught his gaze and glimpsed an infinitesimal shake of his head.

'Is that a good idea, Papa?' she said.

'After lunch, Shattock,' he said. 'I shall ride him on the gallops.'

'With all due respect, your lordship, do you not think he might be a bit high-strung for you, sir?'

'I've ridden some of the meanest hunters in the Quantocks. With far worse tempers than this fine chap.'

'But with nothin like his power, master. Look at him quiverin. Unless you hold him back. If you're even able to. I mean, I don't know as anyone could, the speed of him. You bain't as young as you was, sir.'

Arthur Prideaux chuckled. 'You're saying I'm too old, my dear Shattock?'

The groom looked at a loss for words. 'Maybe if Miss Charlotte wished to ride him for you, sir. Or there's one a my lads I reckon I'd trust.'

Lord Prideaux laughed as if his groom had cracked the best joke imaginable. 'My daughter ride him,' he said, 'but not me?' He turned and began to walk away, still chuckling. Half-turning, he said over his shoulder, 'I shall come back after lunch. See if you can sort out a half-decent saddle.'

5

'Is it merely indigestion?' James Sparke asked. "Tis merely indigestion, yes? I think so.'

The boar lay upon the straw of his sty.

'I let 'em give 'im too many raw spuds, Miss Charlotte, that's what it is, no?'

Lottie stepped into the sty and examined the pig. He did not object.

'I mean, 'tis not swine fever, that's for sure. He ain't so languid as all that and his skin ain't cold, see?'

Lottie had been halfway through her lunch when Gideon Sparke knocked upon the door of her cottage and stood there, sweating and breathless in the heat of the day. He apologised for coming on a Sunday. Perhaps he had run there, but he was an overweight man, of much the same age as Lottie, so it was possible he had only walked.

'Please, miss,' he said, 'Father asks if you'll come and look at our prize pig.'

James Sparke held the tenancy of Wood Farm, the smallest on the estate. Though like all the others it mixed animal and arable, with varieties of each, he had a monopoly on breeding pigs. He sold a piglet or two for fattening to almost every farmer and labourer, and when the time for slaughter came he travelled around and did the job himself. The pigs were his main concern. He believed he had a gift for both understanding their character and tending to their welfare. He worried constantly that should he fail to reach his usual high standards the master might relieve him of his unique responsibility.

As a rule James Sparke kept two boars and half a dozen breeding sows at any one time, as well as one or two of his own fattening pigs.

'How long has he been so inactive?' Lottie asked.

'No more an a day,' James Sparke said. 'Two at most.'

'Has he taken any food?'

The farmer shook his head. His son Gideon watched from outside the sty. One or two other members of the family hovered there too. Whenever Lottie made a visit to a farm, she often found her diagnostic examination being witnessed by a small crowd.

'If it was merely indigestion he would eat a little and would move about the field like the others.'

'But those red blotches, miss.'

'Symptoms, I believe, of measles.'

James Sparke groaned. 'No.'

Measles was a parasitic disease caused by small bladder-worms in the substance of a pig's muscles. On consumption by human beings in pork these developed into tapeworms. Measly pork was one of James Sparke's worst fears.

'Just because he has measles,' Lottie said, 'doesn't mean the others have, but we'll keep an eye on them. And separate him for the time being.'

The farmer asked her what the treatment was, and she said that oddly enough it was much the same as for indigestion. 'Add ten drops of croton oil to a small teaspoonful of sugar, and put this on his tongue. Give him some warm-water enemas if he needs them, which I imagine he probably does, and put some bicarbonate of soda in his drinking water. You might add some milk to it to tempt him. What's the matter, Mister Sparke? Do you not have these substances to hand?'

James Sparke was frowning. 'I do, miss,' he said. 'It ain't that. It's just that I don't believe he'll let me put nothin in his mouth never mind his rear end. I do adore him but he's a cussed beast and he don't like me.'

Lottie smiled. 'Then he is a most ungrateful creature, Mister Sparke. Will he take it from Gideon here?'

'He might, Miss Charlotte. The trouble is, I wouldn't let Giddy nor no one else near him.'

Lottie shook her head. 'Get an old clog,' she said. 'Drill a hole in the end. Mix the oil and sugar in a solution of warm water. Press the clog into the pig's mouth and pour the medicine in.' Lottie knew how impatient she sounded but could not help herself. She doubted whether she would ever develop the soothing manner required of veterinary surgeons. She knew that she should be more indulgent of her patient's owner's foibles, and reassure him that he cared for his animal with unrivalled solicitude. But at least the more she asked James Sparke to do for his pig, the happier he would be. 'Use a clog and he will swallow the medicine, and do so without choking.' She turned to go. 'Oh, and as soon as he begins to resume eating, mix one or two teaspoonfuls of both bicarb of soda and flowers of sulphur in his meal.'

James Sparke nodded. 'Mornin and evenin, Miss Charlotte?'

'Yes. Both.'

Lottie walked home from Wood Farm along a footpath that ran across a wheat field, her veterinary instruments in a rucksack on her back, her shirt damp beneath it. She wore a wide-brimmed hat that shaded her eyes from the full force of the sun. She reached out and tugged loose an ear of corn, and worked a grain from it with her thumb and forefinger. She put the grain in her mouth, and chewed it as she walked along, enjoying the nutty taste on her tongue.

Lottie had planned to watch her father ride the grey stallion. James Sparke and his prize pig had taken two hours of her time. Perhaps, she thought, her father had come to his senses and let the stable lad ride instead. Or would let Lottie herself. Despite Herb Shattock's declaration of her competence, the prospect frightened her.

The ground on the path through the wheat field was hard as stone, and fissured with cracks. It was amazing how the crop thrived in the arid soil.

There was no doubt that the farmers called on Lottie now more often than they ever had on a vet, for whose services they'd had to pay. Hers were free, though being proud men or perhaps married to proud women they paid her in kind. Items of food were delivered to her cottage. Joints of meat, fruit, vegetables, butter, cheese, eggs. Often she could not eat it all herself and took her bounty in turn to the big house and handed it over to the cook.

It was equally not in doubt that under her ministrations there were already fewer animal fatalities, illnesses, contagious diseases. Lottie's father had given his daughter an allowance to live on. Now they called it her salary and both of them were happy. Arthur reckoned this arrangement was enormously beneficial to the success of the estate. Word spread. An article about them had recently appeared in *Country Life*. Lord Prideaux was held up as a model landowner.

Lottie walked past the empty paddock and through the spinney and up past the stable block. There was an almost buried sound of buzzing in the air, a hum in the background in the afternoon heat of the day. A crow rose from some shrubbery, croaking and squawking like one affronted by a rude remark and leaving in high dudgeon. Lottie gazed towards the gallops and saw a shimmering figure approaching out of the middle distance. She stood and watched. Through the haze, Herb Shattock led his own horse, a brown hunter of medium height, towards her. Then he altered direction, away from the stables, towards the manor house, and as he turned so Lottie saw something slung across the saddle. A dark object. It was the body of a man. His legs hung to the side Lottie could see, boots swaying slightly with the movement of the horse.

She ran towards them. As she came closer Lottie called out, but Herb Shattock did not seem to hear her. Neither, it seemed, could he see her through his tears.

They laid her father's body on his bed. A boy was sent to fetch the doctor, another the vicar. While they waited, the valet Adam Score asked to undress his master and wash him and dress him in clean clothes, but Alice said they must wait for the undertaker. She did not seem shocked or saddened but rather enraged by what had happened, her jaw clenched, bunched fists white at the knuckles. Maids kept the boys away. The house was silent.

Alice knelt beside the bed and took Arthur's hand in hers and squeezed it and yelled once, furiously, then leaned against his body and wept. Lottie looked out of the window. She saw Herb Shattock walk towards the gallops accompanied by two of his stable lads. He carried something with him. At first Lottie thought it was a stick. Then she realised it was a rifle.

She had once, in very different circumstances, dissuaded him from destroying a horse. She would not do so this time, and did not move from the window. She recalled that blue roan with a twisted gut, the vigil she had held in its loose box as it died in agony, how selfish she had been. She should have let Herb Shattock destroy the horse and held her vigil for it after death.

Lottie recalled too the boy who had joined her and would not leave until after the roan had expired. When would Leo Sercombe return? He had said that he would, and she reckoned him to be a person of his word. Perhaps he had perished in the war, like so many. She did not think of him as often as she used to.

No, Lottie thought, even if she could get there in time, she would not stay Herb Shattock from his plan of action. Instead she turned and walked to the bed and knelt next to Alice and put an arm around her shoulders and allowed herself to weep beside her.

6

The vicar told the congregation packed into the village church for the funeral of Arthur, Lord Prideaux, that in the midst of life we are in death. Man that is born of woman hath but a short time to live, and is full of misery. He cometh up, and is cut down, like a flower. He fleeth as it were a shadow. And if the Lord God saw fit to take the master from us at the age of fifty-seven there must be some purpose to it, though he, a mortal priest, could not see it. He said that he wished to provide consolation to Lord Prideaux's young widow, his three boys, his daughter, his friends, and all those who lived and worked upon the estate, not to mention their kin in the village. But he could not do so. Only the Lord God could. They must seek consolation from God, there was nowhere else. Put your trust in Him.

'And now, Lord, what is my hope? Truly, my hope is even in Thee. Deliver me from all mine offences, and make me not a rebuke unto the foolish.'

Arthur Prideaux's coffin rested on trestles in the chancel. Despite the season, and the congregation packed inside, the church was musty and damp. Lottie could smell the candles too. She was not the only unwed woman in the church. Even all these years after it had ended, the absence of men lost in the Great War was evident.

The atmosphere amongst the mourners was strange. Lottie glanced around. She understood that beneath the grief and sadness lay a thick sediment of fear. So many livelihoods relied upon the master. A hundred people on the estate, in the house, in the timber yard, on the farms. Others in the village, like the blacksmith and the wheelwright. Including Reverend Doddridge himself, for Lord Prideaux was patron of the living. All feared for their futures.

Soon they would lower his coffin into the grave in the corner of the churchyard reserved for the Prideaux family, beside the plot holding Arthur's first wife, Lottie's mother. She imagined she would join them there one day. She looked at her three half-brothers. And presumably they would follow. One child after the other, time leading them like beasts in procession through the abattoir. It was impossible to imagine life in any other configuration than finite, mortal, doomed from birth to ultimate destruction. A more miserable scheme could not be imagined. Lottie looked up through the high windows. The sky was grey as the grey stone of the church. But the windows were oddly in flux, liquescent, as if the glass were reverting to the molten form from which it was once fashioned. Then all at once Lottie understood that, after these blue cloudless weeks, it was raining outside, water sliding down the long windowpanes.

*

Rain fell on the thirsty earth, but the surface was hard and impervious and so at first water filled the streams, which overflowed and overwhelmed the field drains, or coursed across slopes or pooled in puddles. When the rain ceased, water still dripped from trees and buildings. The earth softened. It rained again and soil turned to warm mud.

Some days later Lottie went to the stables for the first time since her father had died. Herb Shattock was not there. A lad was in the bothy but she did not bother him. She walked to the field and haltered her horse, Pegasus, a big grey gelding, and led him back to the stables. The day was hot, the sun shining then disappearing into white clouds, then coming out again. Lottie saddled up the horse and mounted him and rode out to the gallops. Although her grey gelding was nothing like the stallion, she could feel what power lay latent in his form as if for the first time. She asked the horse how fast he could go and urged and kicked him to make him find his limit. The grass was slippery and the turf sodden. She rode the horse hard. When they came back to the stables, woman and horse were both sweating, Lottie's clothes splattered with mud and the grey gelding muddy too. She slipped her boots from the stirrups and dismounted, sliding to the ground and staggering backwards, exhausted.

The stable lad appeared and came forward to help her if she fell but Lottie regained her equilibrium. When he asked if he should take care of the horse, she thanked him and said he could. Then she asked him where Herb Shattock was. He would not say.

'Do you not know?' Lottie persisted. 'Or you know and refuse to tell me? Is he not well?'

'He is well, miss,' said the lad.

'Where is he?'

'You'd best ask her ladyship.'

Lottie strode up from the stables. She felt the urge to run but restrained herself and so marched, breathing hard, to the house. She walked straight to the back yard and through the kitchen. She was aware of one or two people that she passed but only at the edge of her vision, outside her concern. She glimpsed them pause and watch, without addressing her.

Lottie found Alice in her father's office, seated at his desk. She asked if her stepmother had a moment. Alice looked up, through her spectacles, and blinked.

'Lottie, my dear,' she said, 'I have these letters to write. Why don't you go and change out of those filthy clothes? Come back and join us for lunch, then you and I can talk afterwards.' She returned to the letter she was writing.

'Just tell me one thing,' Lottie said. She tried to keep her voice even. She was not sure how successful she was. 'Where is my father's groom?'

Alice did not look up, or take off her spectacles. 'I do not know', she said, 'where he's gone.'

'What do you mean?' Lottie asked. She began again. 'Do you know then *why* he has gone?'

Alice shook her head slightly, perhaps to express her irritation at being disturbed. She removed her glasses and looked up at Lottie and said, 'I have dismissed him.'

It occurred to Lottie that she should sit down, for her legs felt unsteady, but instead she leaned forward and placed her hands on the desk and remained standing. 'On what grounds?' she asked. She could hear her voice wavering.

'On what grounds?' Alice said. 'He let Arthur ride that monster.'

'So did I,' Lottie said. 'I mean, we both tried to dissuade him, but we could not. Papa insisted.'

'Then I shall blame you too, if you wish.' Alice shrugged. 'He then shot the beast, without my permission. Have you any idea what that horse cost? Yet the groom took it upon himself to ...' She raised her hand and swept some invisible object off the surface of the desk. 'Dispense with him.' Alice shook her head. 'What else could I possibly do? Shattock left me no choice.'

Now Lottie stepped back and sat down, in the chair against the wall. Her head spun, the room turned, the world was upside down. Or the world was turning, coming round to where it had been before. Didn't her father believe he had no choice, when he dismissed Leo's father all those years ago and threw the family out of their estate cottage? Perhaps the world was locked into a groove and though people thought they had free will, in truth they were condemned to repeat the actions of others and all men were little different one from another.

'In the countryside people may act without reason,' Alice said. 'I'm afraid they cannot presume to do so with impunity. I had no alternative. None.'

'Who do you intend to take over the stables?' Lottie asked. She heard the words issue from her mouth, and understood them to be meaningless.

'I don't care.' Alice shook her head again. 'Dear Lottie, I have lost Arthur. I am twenty-nine years old, with three young sons to look after. I do not care about the stables, or about this ugly great house.' Lottie looked up and saw that Alice's cheeks were flushed. 'I do not care about the garden, or the farms. I do not care about any of this, do you understand?'

'What are you planning to do?'

'We shall move to London now, of course.'

Lottie nodded. 'Of course.' The world was collapsing. 'You will sell the estate?'

Alice laughed. 'Oh, no,' she said. She had an expression on her face that suggested she had bitten into an orange only to discover it was a lemon. 'Your father inserted certain stipulations in his will. In the event of his death, the eldest son should inherit the estate when he comes of age. In the meantime, the estate will be held in trusteeship.'

Lottie nodded. 'What does that mean, for now?'

'I'll mothball the house. We might visit in the summer holidays, but I doubt whether any of the boys will want to be country bumpkins, do you? As for the estate as a whole, you are welcome to stay and manage it if you like. Since it is your brother's birth right, no doubt you'll be motivated to look after it better than some land agent.'

Lottie leaned her head back against the wall. There was a rose or dome around the chandelier in the middle of the ceiling, with some kind of patterned inlay decoration. She wondered how many times a month or year it was dusted, by one of the maids standing on a stepladder, to keep it so clean. She lowered her gaze and looked at Alice. Her stepmother was only a few years older than she was. She had been so pretty, it was hardly a surprise that Arthur Prideaux had fallen for his best friend's daughter. Yet she looked older now, her child-bearing figure no longer that of a slender maiden, the once sweet youthful face hardened.

'What about the staff?' Lottie asked.

'Some may join us in London,' Alice said. She fiddled with the papers on her desk. 'Others will need to find new employment.' She glanced across at Lottie. 'Don't look so disapproving. I shall provide them with good references.'

Lottie nodded slowly. She rose to leave. 'All right,' she said. She understood that she had no say in any of it, none at all. Even staying in the little cottage would be at Alice's discretion. She walked to the door but turned and said, 'If you thought Papa was a country bumpkin and you don't like living here, tell me this. Why did you marry him?'

Alice lowered her gaze, summoning up memories. She looked up. 'I returned home from Switzerland, agreed to come to a ridiculous pheasant shoot here with my father, and fell in love with yours.' She smiled sadly. 'I thought I could change him, Lottie,' she said. 'But he was more obstinate than I'd realised, and I could not. Perhaps Arthur was too old. Or I was too young.'

Lottie wiped her face with her hand. She shook her head. 'But why?' she asked. 'Why change a man you love? Why would you want to?'

'That is what we women do, dear Lottie,' Alice said. 'You'll find out soon enough, if you haven't already. They are simple creatures. We mould them. That is why they need us. We make them into the men they can become.'

Lottie sighed. She turned and opened the door and walked out. She went through the house and out of the front door and along the drive. Then she cut across the lawn in her customary short cut to the cottage. A light drizzle had begun, warm rain falling softly. Lottie walked on alone.

Part Seven

THE RETURN
1927–1929

I

Leo Sercombe surveyed the rolling land north of Maundown. Growing up, he'd seen the wooded cleeves in the distance, looming beyond the village, and now was drawn in that direction and walked here and there. Exmoor rose to the west, the Quantocks to the east. Leo had neither map nor plan, but he knew what he was looking for. A field. And so he strolled to and fro, round about, at random.

Leo stowed his old Navy kitbag in undergrowth and walked out for the day and came back to it in the late afternoon. The days were warm but the late-August nights were cooling. Leo lit a fire and slept close to it. If he woke in the night, he leaned over and set fresh wood upon the embers and left it to catch of its own accord. If such it did then in the morning he had only to blow into the coals to rejuvenate the fire and heat up his billycan for tea.

He entered the village of Clatworthy to buy food in the stores there but did not linger. He passed road workers who had made a fire. One fried bacon on his shovel while the other made tea. He passed a pair of tramps, each travelling one side of the road, eyes down, on the lookout for fag-ends.

One hot day Leo picked his way through bracken and gorse, in a valley of rough-split, broken shale. He saw sloughed-off skin. A place of snakes. As soon as he saw one alive, he saw another, then another, and trod slowly. The adders came in a range of colours. Reddish, yellowish, charcoal grey. One was almost black.

The summer was ebbing but haphazardly. Flowering grasses were going haywire. On hot nights gorse pods popped with a cracking sound like a horse whip, provoked to seed by the day's sun.

When it rained Leo plodded on in his oilskin, his boots clobby with mud, rain dripping off the sodden rim of his felt hat, or took shelter beneath a tree, leaning against the trunk. He rolled a cigarette and smoked it while looking out at the rain falling in the wood, listening to the sound of it, a background roar over which were laid the taps and tocks of raindrops on the ground. A cigarette was sometimes ruined by a single splodgy drop.

One afternoon the rainclouds rolled north and the sun shone from the south and a bright rainbow with a full spectrum of colours such as Leo had never seen arced across the grey sky over Exmoor like a dazzling gateway to another world. Then the sun dimmed, and Leo turned and watched a cloud move across in front of the sun, and when he turned back the rainbow was gone and all was as before. There was this world only, no other.

The wandering man doubled back on himself, criss-crossing his own designless tread. He dogged his own footsteps. He imagined he might crest a slope or

enter a gully and see before him the back of his own figure walking. Or hear boots on the ground behind him and turn and behold himself in unremitting pursuit. Was such a thing possible?

Leo explored the coombes and woods, the sloping fields and steep pastures of the crooked landscape. Like some deluded cartographer he mapped that territory but haphazardly, and kept no record writ on paper or even scrawled in his mind. The perambulations of a crackpot.

He remembered his brother Sid once telling him of mornings after snowfall, tracing fresh nocturnal tracks of the animals with whom he shared this earth. Their unseen presence revealed. He told Leo that you could trail the habitual paths of badgers or study the logic in how foxes traversed the ambit of their domain. But sometimes you came across an animal's prints that had no pattern. Bereft of logic.

Sid had paused then. Leo waited for him to continue.

'Well?' Sid said.

'Well what?' he replied.

'Bain't you goin to tell me the reason?'

Leo frowned. 'How should I know the cause of such behaviour?'

'Well, bain't you goin to hazard a guess?' Sid had sat back, watching his younger brother, and grinned.

'Has such an animal been wounded?'

Sid shook his head. With the forefinger of his left hand he pointed to his temple. 'Them prints tell me,' he said, 'that creature's gone doolally.'

'How?' Leo asked. 'Like rabies?'

Sid shrugged. 'Could be rabies. Or some such. All manner a malfunctions of the brain, which is but an organ and one that animals possess just like humans, so stands to reason some a them's mazed as a brush. Don't tell me none of your horses is.'

Leo gasped at this recollection of his brother. He heard the sound come out of his throat. How he missed Sid. He'd shut the thought from his mind all these years. Along with memories of his mother Ruth, his other brother Fred, his sister Kizzie. This familiar landscape brought them back. He missed them all. Then he took a deep breath and swallowed the memory again, pushing it back down into his guts where it was hid.

On he wandered. Then one evening he came across a hidden coombe, a depression between the hills of buckled rock thrown up from below in the heat of the earth's eruption. Here the ruins of a hovel were surrounded by fruit trees, some gnarled, ancient, others self-seeded recently, randomly, from the pips that had passed through the bodies of hungry birds or simply from fallen fruit. A small untended field lay below the rubble. It curved steeply down then up again, little more than an acre scooped out of the south-facing hillside.

On one side of the ruin extended a shelf of land that might once have been a vegetable garden. The whole was bounded by wild hedges. It was like a child's idea of where a smallholding might be created. It was perfect.

Leo found a spring a short distance from the ruins and placed his jerrycan there and watched it fill with cool water that tasted of clean stone to him. He ate the

last of his bread and cheese and some ripe plums off one of the trees. There was plenty of wood lying about. Leo built a fire and heated water and made tea, and he sat gazing into the ungrazed pasture in the hollow below him, drinking tea, smoking, watching bats that came out as dusk fell and flew in veering circuits to catch insects in the twilight.

In the morning his blanket was covered in dew and his face wet with dew but he was not woken by it. What woke him came into his sleep as water flowing over stones. Downhill, but also uphill, which in the dream was strange but acceptable. Leo opened his eyes and saw that a blackbird occupied the branch of a tree above him and sang notes of a liquid song, over and over, urging him to action. If only to get up, and leave its domain.

Leo rose and drank the clean water from the spring and packed his rucksack. He crossed two fields and walked along a lane towards a farmhouse. Grass grew along the centre of the lane. There was no movement and little sound but as he approached the yard two dogs came around a corner running. They bared their teeth and snarled at him. Leo stopped.

'What's up with you?' he asked them. He stood. The dogs crouched low to the ground and slunk about, unsure what to do following their initial hostile welcome. One still eyed him sideways, growling, her hackles raised, but the other ceased. Her hair lay along her back and she came towards him bent low and submissive. Leo did not know dogs. This one's meekness might provoke the other to further aggression. Or its servility give way to a resentful snap. He waited.

Then he heard a voice calling. A figure appeared around the corner of the house, a stout moon-faced girl who did not stop moving when she saw him but came forward.

'Sorry,' the girl called. When she reached the angry dog she grabbed it by the scruff and with one meaty arm lifted it clear of the ground, turning it to look into its eyes. 'Don't be a gurt noodle,' she said, then lowered her arm, directing the dog towards the yard. When it was a foot from the ground she let it go but at the same time propelled it in that direction. 'Git on,' she said. The dog landed and padded away. The other followed meekly.

The girl turned to Leo and enquired as to how she might help him, trespassing as he was on their land. He asked if this was her farm. She frowned.

'Me?'

'Are you the farmer?' he asked.

She laughed at him. 'Do you want to speak with the farmer?'

'I do.'

The girl turned and walked back towards the house. Leo followed. Two other girls appeared around the corner and stood watching. They stared at him unblinking, unabashed. The pair looked much alike and though not identical were both similar to the first girl. He stole glances at them. They each had blonde hair so fair it was almost white, and round faces. They were solid, sturdy. He guessed their ages to be around eighteen or twenty, but could not discern which was the elder, which the younger. Perhaps they were triplets.

The farmer was their father. He received the visitor in the kitchen. The family, such as it was, was evidently partway through breakfast. The farmer invited Leo to join them. One of the girls laid a fifth place, another fried bacon, the third brewed more tea. The farmer asked where he was from and Leo told him he was from around here originally, but he had come down from Scotland only recently.

The farmer rose and walked to the far wall. He indicated with his left hand the large framed painting he stood before. Woolly-haired cattle with extravagant horns grazed in rough pasture beneath misty mountains. 'Glencoe,' he said. 'My father painted it. Your grandfather,' he told the girls, as if they could not work out such a connection for themselves. The farmer was built on sturdy legs like his daughters. His round stomach pushed out against a white shirt and red waistcoat. His face was circular like theirs but in addition he had lost most of his hair so that his round face and the dome of his bald pate made his whole head look like a globe. He came back over to the table and sat down. Then he spoke of Glencoe and other parts of Scotland that he himself had seen as a young man. 'A wild country,' he said approvingly. 'A wild people.'

Leo listened and ate bacon and eggs and drank strong, sweet tea. The farmer spoke about the painting. He said that his father was a good painter as their guest could see for himself, but not good enough. Farming was his second choice and that was why they were here now. Then he said, 'And you, young man. How can we help you? I'm told you've been mooching about our land.'

Leo looked at the three daughters. Each gazed back at him unperturbed. He explained that he was looking to purchase a small plot of land on which to rest and grow a few vegetables and graze an animal or two. He described the scooped-out field beneath the ruin. The farmer stared at him. He turned to his daughters and shrugged, then turned back to Leo. 'Show me,' he said.

They walked in the warm but overcast morning. The dogs joined them. The sun was there behind grey clouds but struggled to break through. Leo led the way over the farmer's own land. The daughters followed three abreast behind and the two dogs ran ahead of them, pretending to know where they were going but checking every few seconds that they were right. It felt like some extempore Sunday excursion from the farmhouse.

They stood on the shelf of flat land and looked at the rubble of whatever hovel had once stood there and at the fruit trees and saplings and at the little dip of a field. Spiders had strung cobwebs over the tall grass and the flowers in the grass, and the dew was still caught on the webbing and revealed them all across the field. The dogs went sniffing amongst the grass, chasing animal scents only they could smell, and they came out with their coats soaking wet from the dew and with spider-webs all over their faces and their eyes so that they were blind, and lay beside the ruin trying to clear the mess from their faces with their forepaws.

The farmer looked upon this pocket of his farm as if it was a surprise to him. His daughters gazed in silence.

Then he turned to Leo and said, 'If me and my three girls here are to have you as a neighbour, we'd best see how we get on afore I sell you the land.'

Leo nodded.

'Dost thou know aught of animals? Of farm work?'

'I know best of horses,' Leo said. 'But the rest I know a little, and am quick to learn.'

'Horses,' the farmer said, turning to one of the girls. 'Could be useful, Myrtle.' He turned back to Leo. 'I ask,' he continued, 'because I shall gladly rent you this portion of our estate. You can pay me five pound a year and also give me one day a week of your labour. And if we all get on as I hope we will, I'll sell you the land in one year's time. How does that sound to you?'

Leo looked once more around the field. 'That sounds fair,' he said. 'It sounds good.'

2

The farmer's name was Wally Luscombe. He gave Leo timber for a hut and the three girls helped him build it with their tools. Each of them was muscular and competent with hammer and plane and saw. They gave him two of their laying hens. One or other girl came over every day with a scythe or a loaf of freshly baked bread or a jacket their father had grown too fat ever to wear again. Leo cut the grass. The year was too far gone for haymaking yet in those calm, dry autumn days the grass quailed in the pale sun and he turned it with a rake. It dried right through and he raised it in stooks.

Then one evening rain came, and it fell for much of the night. In the grey damp morning the soil and plants and flowers gave off rich odours, like beings that had been woken and breathed out the breath of a long sleep. Leo inhaled the smell. He tried to hold it in his nostrils. He'd known it each autumn, each year of his childhood.

That day the earth looked just as brown and parched as it had these last weeks, as if there had been no rain. But on the day following Leo woke and saw the colour of the landscape had altered, all was green and alive once more.

*

At first he was able to tell the girls apart only when they spoke. Agnes, the eldest, who told him she was twenty-one and had first addressed him, had a confident, commanding voice. Ethel, the middle daughter, aged eighteen, spoke softly and slowly. Myrtle, the youngest, who said she was sixteen and a half, spoke quickly, her words tumbling over themselves and sometimes catching in a stammer, over which she gabbled swiftly in the attempt to outrun it. Soon Leo could distinguish them by sight, too, even at a distance, by their slight differences of gait.

He dug the level plot. When he asked for advice, Wally Luscombe said, 'I never touch the garden, oh, no, that's all Agnes's work. I'm a farmer, Leo. A farmer don't make a good gardener, and a gardener don't make a good farmer.'

Agnes gave him some of her autumn onion, winter lettuce and spring cabbage to plant. Asparagus and rhubarb crowns too. As well as gardening, she was the housekeeper. She also did her family's laundry. She lit the furnace and boiled a big tub of water and boiled up the clothes. When she'd washed them, she wrung them through a mangle and hung them out to dry. On wet days she kept the furnace going but got rid of the water from the tub, bucket by bucket, to rid the room of moisture, then hung the clothes on lines run from hooks on the ceiling.

Ethel tended the stock. She bred calves and milked eight cows. She scalded the milk and made cream. She sold skimmed milk and cream at market in Bampton, and she carted vegetables there to sell too. One market day Leo saw her come home with a cow and a calf she'd bought, the calf in the cart and the tethered cow walking along behind.

Myrtle assisted her father with the horses. All helped each other as necessary. Leo worked one day a week as agreed for whoever needed him.

On Sundays the Luscombes did not attend church or chapel but worked as on other days. They insisted their tenant join them for lunch.

Wally regaled Leo with tales of his youth. The girls served the food and listened, or pretended to. Roast beef was tender and tasty, served with roasted vegetables and greens and thick gravy. Pork skin was crunchy and crackly. Leo told Agnes she was the best cook he'd known but for a certain gypsy woman by the name of Rhoda Orchard. The girls wanted to know more of this gypsy but their father overbore them, saying Agnes's true talent lay in wine-making.

'This young woman can make wine from anything,' he said. 'Parsnip, rhubarb. Her peapod wine was a rare vintage. And her runner bean … You would not believe it, Leo.'

None of the girls drank. Perhaps their father would not allow it. He wanted all the wine for himself. Or they chose abstinence. After lunch they insisted Leo make up a four at cards while their father nodded off in his armchair and slept off the great quantity of food and wine he'd ingested.

'Which games have you played?' Agnes asked.

Leo said he reckoned that from his days in the Navy he likely knew the rules of every game men had devised using a pack of royal cards. But the girls seemed to have invented rules of their own. In rummy, sevens were wild. In whist, the jack of hearts beat the king. Random aberrations. House rules, they called them, and obliged their guest to learn.

Leo snared rabbits, and pigeons. He caught small trout in the nearest narrow river. He walked the fields. He scouted horse mushrooms and made ketchup. He picked the last blackberries of the season. In his haphazard orchard were apples, pears, plums, damsons, green-gages, of which particular variety – recorded or not – he had no idea.

One evening he heard yelling and stepped outside his hut to find Ethel running along the fence around his vegetable plot. ''Tis Shadow the big gelding,' she gasped. 'In an awful terrible state. Come look.' She took his arm as she spoke and pulled him along. Ethel was out of breath from rushing to Leo's smallholding and slowed down. 'Go,' she uttered, and he let her fall behind.

The other Luscombes were all in the stable. The four horses stood in their line, three of them pulling lucerne through the ash bars of the high hay racks above the wooden manger. Shadow the big black gelding did not eat but stood still. Wally and Myrtle stood beside him, studying him.

'He broke a fence into our orchard,' Agnes told Leo. 'He's a greedy sod, that one. Filled his guts with apples.'

Shadow subsided on the cobbled floor, kicking and groaning in pain. His chain pulled taut his leather neck band.

'He'll choke, Father,' Myrtle said.

Wally Luscombe bent and unbuckled the chain and Shadow clambered to his feet. With his mouth open and teeth bared he came at the man and girl.

'Whoa,' Wally said. 'Whoa, boy!' And the gelding stopped advancing and settled back in line.

Leo came forward. He saw that the horse's skin was hugely distended beneath him and tight as a drum. When Wally Luscombe turned to him, the expression on his face was one of despair. 'I can't recall,' he said. 'I just can't mind what you should do with gripes.'

By now Ethel had arrived in the stable. Leo asked her if she had linseed oil and turps in her cowshed. She nodded and he asked her to mix some half and half in a long-necked receptacle.

'I'll fetch a wine bottle,' said Agnes, and she followed her sister out of the stable.

'There's a loose box next door, ain't there?' Leo asked. 'Put him in there away from these others now.' Wally attached a head collar to the gelding and led him out. Leo followed, Myrtle coming after. It was still light outside, and it made them realise that their eyes had been adjusting in the stable to the dimness at the edge of night.

In the loose box, Leo looked around and saw rope hanging from a nail. He took it and cut a length. He twisted this and knotted it and brought it over. Leo stepped between father and daughter and up to the horse, speaking to it in his calm, gravelly voice. 'We're here to help you out, old fellow,' he said. 'You be blown with gas, we needs to release it.' He put his quick-spun rope twitch on Shadow's nose and looped it in his mouth while Wally held the head collar.

Leo climbed up on the manger and fastened the twitch to a beam above, obliging the horse to stand open-mouthed, with his head up. Leo jumped down. Agnes came in with a wine bottle which she gave to him. Ethel held up a hurricane lantern. Leo raised the bottle and poured the drench of linseed and turpentine down Shadow's throat. Restrained by the head collar and by the twitch, the horse was helpless to object.

Myrtle clambered onto the manger and stood there unsteadily, reaching up to loosen the rope twitch from the beam. Leo advised her to hang on a moment in case Shadow tried to spew the drench back up. He waited until he saw the horse swallow, the muscles of his brisket bulging. Myrtle loosened the twitch and climbed down. Leo undid the rope from the horse and asked Myrtle to put her ear up against Shadow's ribs and listen to see whether his belly was working.

'How do you mean?' she asked.

'Rumblin,' Leo said.

Myrtle bent and listened to the carthorse. She glanced up at Leo, keeping her ear to the horse's stomach, then looked back down towards the floor. She stood up. 'Nothing,' she said. She turned to Wally. 'I can't hear nothing, Father.'

'Full a gas, right enough,' Wally said.

The gelding knelt on the floor again and rolled onto his side, groaning with the griping pain. Wally let go of the head collar. When the horse came up again, his mouth open, he bit the wooden lip of the manger.

Leo grasped the head collar and spoke to the horse, telling him they needed to keep moving, and pulled him away and led him out of the box. Myrtle ran after him with a length of rope which she clipped to the head collar so that Leo could lead Shadow from a foot or two away. They walked up the yard and back. Ethel came out with her lamp and walked along off to one side, lighting their way. Wally and Agnes stood by the stable door, watching.

'If we keep him movin, the gripes won't be so bad,' Leo told Myrtle. 'He'll be more comfortable. And it'll give the drench time to work its way through.'

'To loose a passage for the gas?' Myrtle asked. 'The wind?'

'Aye, though he'll need to empty his bladder first, I should think. Let's have another listen.'

Leo halted the horse and Myrtle put her ear once more to the gelding's stomach. She straightened, shaking her head. They resumed walking the horse. They led him up the yard and when they came back Agnes had retired to the house. A while later Ethel hung the lantern on a metal bar sticking out from the wall of the stables, and followed her elder sister indoors.

They walked to and fro. The movement seemed to ease the horse's pain or perhaps he understood that this strange constitutional was for his benefit, so he submitted to it. Leo stopped him periodically and Myrtle listened to his insides, then they resumed leading him around the yard. He did not groan but once or twice he stopped and spread his hind legs apart and tried to piss but could not. Leo spoke to him at these moments, but it did not help.

'My father had some horses he could whistle for to help them stale,' he told Myrtle. 'The turps might aid him, but there's other things I should carry with me if I were a horseman.'

The girl asked him what such other things might be.

'Sweet nitre would be one. To be honest, I do not know why a blown horse should be unable to piss. Perhaps the blown gut presses on the bladder. Or perhaps the apple juice here has had some ill effect upon it. I do not rightly know.' He shook his head. 'Oil a juniper was another my father kept close to him.'

Myrtle stopped. 'Wait,' she said. 'We've got some of that. I swear I've seen a little bottle in the stable cupboard with "Juniper" writ upon the label.'

The girl ran across the yard. Her father was no longer standing in the doorway. Leo walked the gelding up the yard and back and Myrtle came out with the bottle and a syringe. She gave them to Leo and took the rope from him. He drew a little of the oil into the syringe and injected it into the horse's mouth. They led him on.

Beyond the feeble light of the lantern the night was dark. Leo told the girl how horses used to suffer widely from asthma, or broken wind. More often in the old days than today. The worst form they suffered was an emphysema of the lungs. He told her how in the past, unprincipled dealers practised all sorts of tricks when selling an animal thus affected. One was to pour a pound or two of lead shot, mixed into a pound of melted butter, down the horse's throat.

Myrtle asked how on earth that had any beneficial effect. It sounded mad. 'Are you teasing me?' she
wondered.

Leo assured her that he was not. 'The shot weighs
the stomach down,' he said. 'It takes the pressure off the
diaphragm, so the lungs have more play, and the horse
can breathe almost natural. A course it don't last long.
And if the new owner has the wit to study the animal's
dung over the next day or two, he'll see in what way
and how badly he's been had.'

So Leo spoke of horses. He told the girl stories that
he remembered from his childhood, and his voice was
for the black gelding too, calming him in his discom-
fort. The gelding stopped once more. He straddled
again in the middle of the yard, close to where the
lantern hung. He stood with his hind legs apart and
his penis hanging down and the apple-sour urine at
first dribbled, then flowed. It ran onto the cobbles and
along the gutter.

'He'll be fittle now, I reckon,' Leo said. 'He'll make it.'

They walked the horse on. Myrtle said the swellings
on either side in front of his hips remained. Leo said it
would be about the right time to take the horse back
into the box. No sooner had they entered than Shadow
raised his tail and farted for an inordinate length of time,
the whole stable echoing with the sound and the air filling with a stink of cider, until his huge extended belly
had returned to its normal size. Leo advised Myrtle to
give him a drink of water and to bed him down in the
loose box for the night. 'He'll be right as rain in the
mornin,' he told her. 'Let him off work, I should. Give

him a bran mash and he'll empty his bowels and be back to normal.'

The girl thanked Leo and he turned to go but stopped and turned back and said, 'And I'll fix that broken fence for you. By tomorrow that horse will have forgotten what bad the apples done him, but he'll remember how much he liked the taste of 'em.'

3

Leo walked across the fields. A sound like singing came on the wind, eerie voices. As he walked on he realised it was ewes and lambs, mothers and their lost children, calling plaintively to one another. In another field two horses stood, one with its bent leg raised as if cocked ready for movement, still as statues.

He stepped on pine needles through a gloomy conifer plantation, trees packed close together. The wood's silence was unsettling. No sound of birds.

He crossed a meadow where cattle lay. Then a chestnut horse came from a distance towards him, neighing and prancing, and the heifers rose and moved off out of its way. The mare was unafraid and came to him and stood. He stroked the horse. Her skin quivered under his hand.

Leo walked through the village, past the church, the shop, the school. Everything was smaller than it should be, the buildings had shrunk or perhaps he had grown to gigantic size and wandered through an eerie land. Two old men stood in the lane beside the lychgate. They greeted him. He did not recognise them, but touched his cap in reply. He passed the wheelwright, then the smithy. He stopped for a moment and watched Jacob

Crocker's swarthy son, alone, hammering some metal on the anvil. How often as a boy Leo had stood watching the Crockers shoeing horses, putting iron tyres on waggon wheels. He looked around but there was no sign of Jacob, nor the tall crooked son.

Leo walked on out of the village and on to the estate. Men and women worked. Some saw the tall young man with the rangy tread but none looked twice at him. He did not believe even his cousin Herbert would recognise him.

His memory had flattened the land. He'd thought of it all these years as little more than undulating plain, but it was carved up and crooked, bumpy, with woods on hillocks and coombes in shade.

Leo went first to the home of Aaron Budgell and his wife. Perhaps he would be given word here of his brother Sid, who would be over thirty years old now, and surely no longer still lodging with them. Perhaps long gone from the estate. All was quiet. He knocked on the door. No one answered.

Leo walked on to the stables. Even as he approached, he knew much had changed. There was no sound of horses or of human activity. He stood in the yard. There was a faint smell of horse but also of petrol. He looked around. One of the boxes held not an animal but a motorcycle. The others were empty, and but for a single one with straw bedding were all swept clean.

He walked up from the stables to the manor house. He walked past the kitchen yard. The back door was closed and there was no activity there or the sound of such from within. He walked on along the path around the side of the house. There was something ghostly inside but he could not tell what, for the glare of the sun on the windowpane prevented it.

The lawns and the flowerbeds were tended. The windows at the front of the house were shuttered on the inside. There were no vehicles of any sort on the gravelled drive. Leo knocked on the front door and stood waiting. No one came. He tried the handle of the door but it was locked. Leo stood insensible as if some understanding might come to him but it did not.

Rufus Devereaux had once tried to persuade him that ownership was nothing. That he who looked upon a landscape owned it as much as the man with a piece of paper in a safe. More so, in fact. Leo told him that was easy to say for one who passed across the land like a shadow. For those who resided in one place it was different. Without the paper they were merely cottagers, powerless.

'Then they should take to the road like us,' Rufus had said, and the two of them had laughed together at the prospect. 'We are all tenants,' Rufus added, 'if only of our mortal form.'

Leo walked back around the side of the house and across the lawn. After a brief hesitation he stepped cautiously through the flowerbed and leaned forward and pressed his nose to a windowpane. With his hands he formed a shield and peered into a room whose every item of furniture was covered with white sheets. He began to lean back away from the pane but then he saw a man, a ghostly figure, moving about amongst the furniture. Then this man stood still. He raised a gun.

'Come away from there,' said a voice. It issued from behind Leo. He stepped back and turned around.

The man stood upon the lawn. He held a shotgun raised towards the intruder. He had a thick beard and wore rough working clothes. 'I seen you traipsin about,' he said. 'Get your thievin carcase off this property. Now.'

Leo put his hands up in the air and trod carefully back across the flowerbed to the lawn.

'I was just ...' he began.

The man cut him off. 'I done told you to quit. So shut your mouth and go. And don't try nothin or I'll blow your bowels out.'

Leo nodded and turned and walked away.

4

Lottie Prideaux hitched Pegasus to the buggy and drove out of the estate. The horse was too large, barely fitting between the shafts. He trotted with his neck upright and his head high and his trot was more of a prance. This job was beneath him and he wished to make that clear.

At Wiveliscombe Station Lottie put the brake on the buggy and told the horse not to be foolish. She walked towards the station then stopped and looked back. The horse was not watching her but gazing in quite another direction, eyes fixed apparently on a distant horizon.

Lottie stood on the platform. Her guests had stayed the night in Exeter and were expected on this early train. Others on the platform waited to be taken to Barnstaple, or stations in between. Lottie spoke with a woman whose pig she had once treated for gastritis. She asked the porter to be ready to help with her guests' luggage.

The train came in to the station. It had two carriages. The guard stepped down from the first and called to the porter. The people on the platform began to board the train. A woman emerged from the second carriage. She looked about her then turned and helped a man down the step and then to the platform. The guard passed luggage down and the porter stacked it on his trolley.

Lottie walked along the platform. The man stood, turning his head slightly from side to side. The woman held his right arm. In his left hand he held a cane. The woman said, 'You must be Miss Prideaux.'

The man said, 'Lottie,' and pulled his right arm free and held it out in front of him. Lottie grasped his hand and shook it.

'William,' she said.

The man withdrew his hand and gestured to his right and said, 'May I introduce my sister, Helena Carew. Helena, this is Lottie Prideaux.'

The women shook hands. Lottie turned and walked slowly along the platform, and the Carews walked with her. She enquired after their journey while the porter wheeled their luggage to the buggy and loaded it. Helena helped her brother up onto the seat. Lottie gave the porter a threepenny bit and he thanked her and pushed the empty trolley back into the station, then Lottie drove back to the estate.

The Carews stayed in Lottie's cottage. They ate a cold lunch and in the afternoon Lottie left them while she answered an emergency call to Wood Farm. In the evening she served them cottage pie with peas and carrots, apologising for the quality of her cooking, followed by trifle made for her by one of the farmers' wives.

'Do you remember how you used to cut up those dead animals?' William asked her. He tilted his head towards his sister. 'While other girls her age filled their heads with length of skirt and style of hair, Lottie was finding out for herself how animals are put together.' He turned back towards Lottie, as if to look at her though his eyes were sightless. Perhaps it was habit, from when he could see. But he never quite faced her directly. It was as if he was gazing past her, miscalculating a touch. Or perhaps he imagined there was someone else standing there, and it was this ghostly figure he addressed.

Helena said that Lottie was pretty enough to be able not to bother herself about styles. As William shifted his head a little, Lottie understood all at once that it was not his eyes but his ear he was directing. His head was tilted the better to hear what she or Helena said.

Helena told Lottie that she worked as a nurse in a children's ward in the South London Hospital. The hospital was for females only, except for boys under the age of seven, and all the staff were women. Helena expected to become a Matron eventually. She said that she did not envy the younger women studying medicine and training to be doctors. They were forced to make brutal decisions and the women now qualifying had to ignore the prompting of their natural compassion and develop callous masculine traits.

'Perhaps you have a more benign view of women than I do,' Lottie said. 'I fear we're no different from men. Just as capable of cruelty.'

'How can you say that, less than ten years after the worst bloodbath the world has known?' Helena demanded. She made a vague gesture towards her brother. William listened closely to the conversation.

'If women had power,' Lottie said, 'or wielded the weapons, would it all have been different?'

'Of course,' Helena said. She wore her hair cut short, almost shorn like a nun's, as if like them to renounce any claim to femininity. She wore no lipstick. Her clothes were those of an older woman, or else a young woman of the previous epoch. Her eyebrows were paler than her light brown hair.

'Then might it make sense to let us have the power, in the hope that you are right?'

Helena made a sound with her mouth as if spitting something out from between her lips. 'You're trying to trip me up with sophistry,' she said.

William turned towards Lottie. His eyelids were closed, not upon curved eyeballs but sunken sockets, and Lottie suspected that the skin of one lid was not the original but had been taken from elsewhere on his body and grafted there. 'My sister', he said, 'has a pessimistic view of the world. If not a tragic one. She prefers the fallen world as it is to an unknowable future.'

After supper Helena insisted that her brother go to bed. She helped Lottie with the washing-up, the two women working around each other in the cottage's small kitchen. With a tea cloth Helena dried the utensils they had used. Lottie reached around her, putting cutlery or crockery away, on shelf or in cupboard. She asked how William was coping. Helena said the worst thing was having nothing to do. He lived in her flat, where he listened to music. The wireless was a further distraction. He could go for walks alone, in a gradually increasing radius, but she sensed that it gave him little pleasure to grope along the pavements of Clapham. And on the one or two occasions he'd broken free onto the Common he'd become disorientated and distressed, and was brought home cowering.

'This is the first time he's spent a single night away from my flat. To be honest with you, I don't think it's a good idea. But I foolishly read out your invitation for us to visit, and once William heard it he was set on accepting.' Helena gave Lottie the wet tea towel. 'I constantly worry about him while I'm at work,' she said. 'That he'll be robbed, or beaten, or step into the road and be run down.'

'How ironic, considering his adventures,' Lottie said. 'When he travelled all over the world.'

'Oh, yes,' Helena agreed. 'Ironies abound. Do you know, William was the best shot in his regiment? He should have been a sniper, but such work was considered beneath officers.'

'And now you support him,' Lottie said.

'Oh, he has his pension,' Helena said. 'I have to work.'

'And *your* life?' Lottie asked.

'Apart from my job, William is my life,' Helena said. The Carews' mother had died and their sister taught in a school in Yorkshire. 'Look at me,' she said.

Lottie frowned. 'What should I see?'

'A plain Jane,' Helena said. 'Oh, no, don't make a face. It's true and I know it. Someone like you wouldn't know what that's like and why should you? Nature fashions us according to her whim. No doubt you have many suitors at your hunt balls and country parties.'

She waved her hand towards Lottie to indicate, or perhaps to dismiss, Lottie's looks.

Lottie reckoned that if she wished to, Helena could make herself far more appealing. She chose to hide rather than accentuate her looks. Perhaps she had embraced her sisterly martyrdom as a calling, a vocation, twinned with her nursing.

'I'm an old maid now. There are many of us in the hospital. It's not so bad.'

Lottie said that surely Helena was still young.

'Men have had their pick. For women like me, our would-be suitors lie in the fields of Flanders.' She shook her head. 'Listen to me. I can't bear people who feel sorry for themselves.'

On the morning following, they walked to the big house, all boarded up, and wandered through the garden. Lottie told William that he would hardly recognise it now. Alice sent the gardener Alf Satterley instructions throughout the winter. Plans, drawings, the names of fashionable plants. And when she brought the boys down for their holiday she oversaw new developments, standing over the gardener or his boy as they worked.

Lottie laughed. 'I thought he must hate it and would leave as soon as he could find another job, every alteration a desecration of the garden he'd created with my mother. But then I realised that I was wrong. Old Mr Satterley began to enjoy it. A new collaboration. He's getting younger by the month.'

From the other side of the kitchen garden wall an engine suddenly roared into life, sputtering, then backfiring, and Lottie saw William flinch, bending low and covering his head with the arm that was not holding the cane.

'It's a lawnmower,' Lottie said.

Helena took her brother by the shoulders and reassured him that it was only the mower and all was well. All was calm. William stood up once more and smiled, though he was trembling, and said what a chump he was. Helena caught Lottie's eye and opened her own wide and raised her eyebrows as if to say, you see? You see?

They walked further. Lottie admitted she now managed the estate, the job William had held, briefly. They walked up the hill to Hangman's Wood and looked out. Lottie named the farms they could see. Helena said that when William had described the estate she didn't somehow imagine it to be as large as this.

In the evening, after their meal, William gave Lottie some new records and she played one on her gramophone. She confessed to never having heard of Jean Sibelius. The work was the *Karelia Suite*. William said that although Sibelius was inspired by his native Finland, and indeed the work had been adopted by the patriots of that country, it summoned for William this place, Lottie's own West Country. They sat and listened, and the scratchy recording of the boundless music filled the room as if it came from far away, from Finland itself perhaps. Yet Lottie understood what William meant. It could have been inspired by this land.

Helena nodded off. When she jolted awake she apologised and said she was exhausted from the journey and no doubt the fresh air. William suggested she go to bed, he would be fine with Lottie here, and to her surprise Helena acceded and went upstairs to her room.

Lottie poured William a brandy and they drank. He suggested another piece of music but Lottie said no, she would like him to meet her horse properly. William smiled and said that he would be delighted.

The moon sat like a boat in the sky and stars blazed across the firmament as brightly as they did on only a few nights as clear as this in a year. It was fortunate timing. Then Lottie was reminded that for William the darkness was total, all year round, in or out of doors, wherever he might be. But the silver light was helpful to her, and it meant that Pegasus was not spooked when they reached the gate and she called him up out of the field. Lottie opened the gate and walked through, and when the horse came to her she fed him a carrot she'd brought with her and put the halter on him.

'Come in,' Lottie told William. He followed the bars of the gate and found the metal loop over the post and lifted it. He opened the gate a little and squeezed in and closed it behind him.

'Over here,' said Lottie, and he stepped towards her. She took his hand and placed it on her horse's neck. 'He's called Pegasus,' she said.

'He's tall,' William said.

'Almost seventeen hands. He's strong, but gentle. And with a lovely soft mouth.'

William caressed the horse and put his head to the horse's neck and smelled him. Pegasus turned his head and snuffled against the strange man's skin.

'What does he look like?' William asked.

Lottie described her handsome grey gelding.

'Do you know,' William said, 'I miss riding.'

Lottie said that she had a notion. She reopened the gate and led her horse to the stable yard. William followed the sound of their steps. In the yard Lottie tied the rope to a ring in the wall and fetched the bridle from the tack room, which jangled as she carried it. She removed the halter and replaced it with the bridle, throwing the reins over the gelding's head, then reaching the bridle over his ears and under his jaw and feeding the bit into his mouth. Over the bridle she attached a head collar.

Lottie fetched the saddle, and swung it over Pegasus. She bent and reached down and pulled the girth strap under his belly and secured it. Then she stood and waited. William had come up and stood a few yards away.

'He's a terror for blowing himself up,' Lottie said. 'Then holding his breath. I have to wait for him every single time I saddle him. It does him no good but he never learns.'

William listened. Eventually Pegasus breathed out and Lottie cinched the girth strap another two notches tighter. The horse did not neigh or strut or make any noise that would give the impression he thought it strange to be harnessed in the dark. William remarked upon this. 'As you told me, Lottie, he has equanimity. Or perhaps one should say equine-nimity.'

Lottie smiled. She invited William to step forward to the horse. 'You're on his left side.' She took the reins in her left hand, and lifted William's right hand and gave them to him. Then she stepped to her horse's head, and held the head collar, and told William to mount whenever he was ready.

William reached his right hand up and felt for the cantle at the back of the saddle. He stood for a moment, not moving, and it occurred to Lottie what an overwhelming prospect this must be for him, how unfair a challenge she had presented him with.

Then she saw him lean forward and to the side until his face was up against the horse's neck. William was smelling the animal. He leaned back, and took his right hand off the saddle and felt for the stirrup, and when he had found it he lifted his left foot and inserted it. Then he put his right hand back on the saddle. Her horse was so tall. And William had not mounted a horse in ten years.

Only now did Lottie remember the mounting block, on the far side of the yard. How stupid she was. She was about to suggest they go over there, when William flexed his muscles and pushed off with his right leg from the ground and pulled with his left leg in the stirrup and rose up and swung his right leg over the saddle. Pegasus's back dipped to take the rider's weight. William sat in the saddle and gave a gasp of satisfaction or relief.

'All right?' Lottie asked.

William smiled. 'A piece of cake,' he said.

Lottie fetched a longer rope and a whip from the bothy and came back and clipped the rope to the horse. She held the rope in her right hand close to Pegasus and carried the rest of it coiled in her left. She led the horse away from the yard on the path down through the spinney towards the paddock. Wood pigeons cooed in their sleep on the branches. Two or three flew up. William held the reins loosely in his hands. Lottie walked into the middle of the paddock feeding out the long lunge, then she made a clicking sound with her teeth and told her horse to walk on and circled him anti-clockwise around her. She reckoned there was enough light for Pegasus to see the whip as she pointed it for him to follow. William held the loose reins and the horse walked around, his hooves sending up granules of silver sparkling from the sandy ground.

'Are you all right?' Lottie called. 'We can keep him as slow as you like. He won't mind.'

William did not reply but kept riding. Lottie could not quite tell how much he had to concentrate to keep his seat. He sat awkwardly, too tense. It must be so hard to balance without sight. Wasn't balance connected to the ears? Would being deaf be worse? She did not think so. She brought the horse to a gradual halt herself, using the rope and clicking her teeth and telling Pegasus to slow. Then she turned him and resumed circling clockwise.

After Lottie had changed direction two or three more times, she could see William's posture relaxing. He squeezed the horse with his legs. Either Pegasus did not wish to respond to an unfamiliar rider or the horse was too big and strong for subtle persuasion so William kicked him with his heels and this time Pegasus broke into a trot.

Horse and rider circled the woman in the middle of the paddock. Then Lottie slowed Pegasus and walked towards him casually, looping the rope in a coil hanging from her left wrist. When she reached them she saw how heavily William was breathing. She asked him if he was all right. When he smiled she could see his teeth white in the moonlight.

'As good as I've felt in a long time,' he said. 'A long, long time.'

'Have you had enough?' she asked.

'Not nearly,' he said.

They resumed. William kicked the horse to a trot and after one circumference kicked him again and the horse eased into a gentle canter. Though the speed was greater, it was easier to ride a canter than a trot and William looked so comfortable that Lottie was tempted to let him ride off the rope. It was a fanciful notion. She did not see how it could work. A horse required instruction. It demanded it. And if a rider could not see where he was going how could he give direction to the horse?

They rode counter-clockwise then stopped and turned. Lottie approached the horse, coiling the rope loosely, and unclipped it from the ring on the chinstrap of the head collar. Perhaps Pegasus would not need direction. 'He's yours,' she said. 'He can see where the fence is and he won't want to bash into it. Just give him a loose rein and go at the speed you wish.'

William nodded, said 'Hup' to the horse and kicked him. Pegasus took off. He carried his mount at a canter in similar circuits to those he had performed constrained by the rope. Somewhat eccentric, perhaps. Lottie turned where she stood, watching them canter around her. Was it possible that the horse knew his rider was blind? When they came close by she saw William grinning.

Then she heard a yell behind her.

Lottie turned. At first she could see nothing. Then a figure emerged from the trees in the spinney and Helena came marching towards them. 'Stop!' she yelled. 'What are you doing? Stop at once!'

William slowed the horse. Lottie walked over and clipped the rope back to the head collar. Helena came into the paddock and rushed over to the horse and grabbed her brother's leg and body. 'William,' she said. She turned to Lottie. 'Help me get him down,' she said.

'Helena, I'm fine,' he gasped.

'You don't sound it,' she said. 'Nor look it.'

Lottie held the rope and asked William if he was all right to dismount. He said he was. He kicked clear of the stirrups and leaned forward and swung his right leg over the back of the horse and slid down. Helena stepped forward and held on to her brother as he did so, making the manoeuvre more awkward than it would have been, and making the gentle solid horse a little jittery so that it stepped this way and that as William gained the ground and recovered his standing balance. Helena staggered with him, away from Pegasus. Lottie did not doubt that Helena imagined that if she were not there her brother would topple over. William's sister turned him away from the horse and hurried him out of the paddock.

Lottie led Pegasus back to the yard. She removed his saddle and his bridle. He'd worked up a little sweat and she brushed him down and watered him, and before she put him back in the field she told him he was a good horse, a noble beast, and she thanked him. It was a gamble but she believed it had paid off, despite Helena's interruption. Not all horses would have had Pegasus's patience. But with such horses, what could not be done?

In the morning at breakfast Helena announced that they were leaving today, and would appreciate a ride to the station. She rose from the table and went back upstairs to pack their suitcases. William sipped coffee. Otherwise he sat in silence, impassive. Lottie could not tell what he was thinking. Perhaps his eyes would have told her.

Then he cleared his throat. 'I'm sorry, Lottie,' he said, quietly. 'My sister needs me as much as I need her. I have to go with her.'

'Of course.'

'She can't understand what you did last night, but be assured that cantering on your Pegasus, I felt human again.'

Lottie reached over and put her hand upon his on the table.

At Wiveliscombe Station the porter unloaded the luggage from the buggy and stacked it on his trolley. Lottie accompanied the Carews. Helena said that there was no need for her to wait, she must have many things to do with her estate management and her veterinary practice requiring her attention. Lottie said that of course she would stay and see them safely onto the train.

They stood and watched other passengers arrive. After the clear moonlit night, the morning was cool. People wore more coats and hats than they had done in months. In due course the Exeter train pulled in. Lottie kissed William goodbye. Helena helped him up the steps of their carriage and told him she would be along shortly. 'Wave your cane,' she said. 'People love to help a blind man.'

William walked on into the carriage.

'I knew we should not have come,' Helena said. 'I had established some calm, a certain order, in my poor brother's life.' She spoke in a fierce whisper. 'I have only this to say to you. Many women felt some obligation to marry their sweethearts who'd been wounded.' There was hatred in her eyes, as if all the tension her body could muster was concentrated there. 'Who'd made such a sacrifice. I knew there were women who felt no such obligation, no such sense of duty, I might say even love. But I had not met one face to face before.'

The shock of Helena's words thumped the air from Lottie's lungs. She could hardly breathe. 'We,' she gasped. 'We were not sweethearts.'

'My brother certainly thought you were.'

Lottie shook her head. 'I don't see how.'

Helena held her arms out to either side and pulled a mocking expression at Lottie's obtuseness, or insincerity. 'Letters exchanged?' she said. 'Keepsakes sent, between this slice of West Country heaven and the hell of the trenches?'

'We were friends,' Lottie said.

'Friends?' Helena spat.

'But,' Lottie said, 'William never said anything. All these years. Never asked anything of me.'

Helena smiled. 'We may have no money, Miss Prideaux,' she said. 'But my brother remains a gentleman.'

She turned and climbed up into the carriage. Lottie stood trembling on the platform. She waited, as if to wave away her guests, but was not sure if she could move anyhow. The porter trotted along the platform, shutting the heavy doors, which closed with a resounding clang. The guard waved his flag, the coal-shoveller fed the oven of the locomotive, the driver engaged the gears. The big steam engine hissed, smoke rose from the chimney with the smell of cinders and burning coal, and the wheels began turning slowly. The solid weight of train pulled out of the station. Lottie watched it leave, motionless. She waited until it was out of sight and when she turned she saw that she was the last person on the platform. The whole station appeared deserted. The young porter had disappeared. The stationmaster had retreated to his office.

Lottie walked unsteadily out to the buggy and released the brake and climbed up. She took the reins and clicked her chattering teeth, and Pegasus pulled the buggy in a broad half-circle out of the station yard and back towards his home.

5

There was a weeping silver birch in the hedge of Leo's field. Its green leaves turned autumnal and fell first from the crown of the tree so that it gave the impression of a man with long yellow hair balding on top. There was an old oak with tufts of twigs sprouting from the trunk like an old woman's bristles.

At night his small hut was like a cave, so quiet that at times Leo could hear his heartbeat, and other rumblings from within his own body. It was unsettling. He rose and went outside and rolled a cigarette, and smoked it surrounded by the cool dark.

One evening, the thrum of rain upon the roof sounded so much like horses approaching that he stepped outside to greet them but there were no animals there. It happened again, and he told himself that it was only rain drumming as before but he could not quite convince himself, yearning so for the sight of a rag of half-wild horses.

One morning towards the end of the year he was disturbed by a fluttering about him. There was a sudden diminution of the dour winter light. Leo raised his head. Birds flocked and swooped. Starlings, making no noise except for the faint swooshing of their wings. How many were there? He tried to count them but could not. A flock of thousands, perhaps the coming together of the twelve tribes of West Country starlings in some avian exodus, flying headlong together. The flock all but disappeared over a stand of elm then veered south and flew around and came back not far away. Heading now for a sycamore, only to wheel around and pass above him. He could see no reason nor pattern to their flight yet they flew together, each so close to those all around, as if they knew what they were doing, as if they were following some crazed choreography of flight. He decided that the only possible explanation for their display was that they performed it for a witness, a spectator. Who else but him?

Leo had constructed his hut around a brick fireplace which he now used. He gathered wood that had broken off but been caught in other branches of a tree, without ever touching the ground, and he cut ash, for it burned well when still green. He cut hawthorn and piled it up for a second winter, for he remembered his father saying that he'd as soon have hawthorn logs as coal. Elm he knew was good too. Perhaps the nocturnal visitor who showed up one night had been waiting for smoke. He could not tell in the dark which of the girls it was who took off her dressing gown and nightdress, who lowered herself to the straw mattress and slipped in beneath his blanket. He asked her what she was doing and she laughed, soft and low, and he knew it was Ethel. Leo said he was sorry, he could not love her, his heart was pledged elsewhere, that was his fate and he could not help it.

Ethel said she did not demand his heart. She lay beside him on the mattress and snuggled up to him.

Her skin was cold and she was shivering and he put his arm around her and pulled her strong ample body close to his hard bony frame, and slowly she warmed. Her breath smelled sweet and milky. When she moved upon him he knew he could not escape nor did he wish to.

Afterwards, they lay in the dark. Leo listened. He could hear her breathing and he could hear wood burning. 'It's so quiet out here,' he whispered.

Ethel did not reply at first. Perhaps she too listened, to verify the truth of his statement, or perhaps she slept. But then she said, 'They call us the heathens. I suppose you know it already.'

Leo said that he did not. How could he?

'When Mother died,' she whispered, 'Father asked God why He'd took her. Leaving him all alone with three young maids to care for. God didn't say nothing. Father said if He couldn't even be bothered to reply then Father couldn't be bothered to visit Him and he took us out a church. Father said it proved that God was an illusion, and he did not have time to waste on what did not exist. It would be like trying to run the farm with our toy animals. There was only flesh and blood, he said, and that was all there was. We none of us been back since.'

They lay in the dark. Somewhere outside an owl hooted in the distance, and after that the night seemed even more silent than before. Ethel's meaty body smelled faintly like the cattle she tended, her sweat gave a beefy odour that was not unpleasant. It made Leo hungry for her. They each whispered as if someone might be listening. Some person or animal or other entity. Perhaps God Himself.

'I believe Father was wrong,' Ethel whispered.

'You want to go to church again?'

Ethel chuckled. Her laughter was soft and deep and murmurous, and he could feel it in her body against him. 'Not particularly, Leo. It ain't that. It's more that I don't reckon the fact that God did not speak to Father proves He don't exist.'

'Perhaps He spake but your father did not listen?'

'I'm sure He never spoke,' the girl said. 'People talk about the silence of God but that's where He is, I reckon.'

They lay in the warm quiet dark, nestled one into the other, the embers of the fire still glowing.

'That's why you can feel Him this time a night,' Ethel whispered. 'The quiet is His clue for us, Leo. The hint of His great silence, see?'

Leo squeezed Ethel's ribs where he held her. He felt her turn to him. She kissed him on the cheek then she disentangled her limbs from his and rose from the mattress and pulled on her nightdress and gown, and her boots, and slipped out of the hut.

On some winter nights Leo left his fire and his warm cabin and went outside and lay on the cold hard earth and gazed at the star fields in the black sky above. The world was empty and if in the distance a vixen squealed, a dog fox barked, it did not make the world seem less empty but more so. He was alone in this great silence. He lay shivering on the ground. He was nothing. As if the times he should have died had wiped his name out anyhow from the unwrit annals of time. He was no man or perhaps he was every man. Leo lay watching stars that hung as they had for a hundred thousand years until it came to him that he could slip into numb sleep and freeze there, an icy corpse, so he rose stiffly and returned to the cabin.

Pigeons roosted on the branches of leafless trees. Crows guarded the evergreens. When the pigeons rose into flight, their wings smacked with a sound that brought back to him his mother flapping wet crumpled linen before she hung it on the line. One day he heard what his brain told him was the horn of a bike or motorcycle parp in that empty landscape and he gazed around. Then he looked up and saw five, six, seven geese flying in lopsided formation, an irregular chevron, south across the grey sky. Later that day and on the days following he saw other geese leaning forward, hurrying, in their annual airborne trek along paths wired into their blood. Once he saw a flock of twenty-five or thirty. Usually they pilgrimed in smaller scrums, with even the odd solo goose, left behind or lost or perhaps just cussed birds preferring their own sullen company to that of their kin.

Ethel came to him that winter, dead of night, unannounced, a few times more. She assured him she knew what she was doing. She understood enough of women's cycles to be sure when it was safe. Once he heard her footsteps crunching on hardened snow as she approached the cabin. She always gazed at the fire when they lay together. Leo told her that he'd heard that the stems of Brussels sprouts, left to dry and harden, burned well. She said that some folk on the hills were said to bank their fires up with pomace, the apple husks from the cider press, which dried like peat and gave a good slow burn. They spoke in low whispers, until she rose and pulled on her clothes and left.

One morning the ground was covered in frost. In the low winter sun a pair of magpies flew across Leo's line of sight, bothering each other all the way, whether in combat or play he could not tell.

Made frisky by what the weather had done to their world, the Luscombes' dogs rolled like horses in the white frosty grass. Leo carted manure to the fields, dug over Agnes's kitchen garden, helped Ethel turn out her stock. Then it came time to turn the soil.

They moved amongst the horses by the light of oil lanterns, feeding them with corn and chaff in the manger and with clover in the rack.

Leo helped Myrtle put harness on Shadow and one of the other horses, Scarlet, for a two-horse team. They put the collars on, that would take the weight and pull of the plough on the horses' shoulders, and their bridles, then led them outside to drink from the stone trough below the pump. Then they hooked the traces to the collars.

Wally said he knew last year he was getting too old for the plough. Myrtle was strong but even a man's thicker wrists and ankles could be ruined by the work.

If he was honest, it was the first thing he'd thought of when Leo turned up. Ploughing.

Leo worked the teams in the Luscombes' arable fields for three weeks. Today was the last field, in a high corner of the farm, and a sharp wind blew. All horses hated the wind. Leo tightened the handkerchief around his neck and pulled his felt hat tight on his head. He passed a coppice in which poplar trees squealed as their trunks and branches rubbed together.

The day was cold and clear, the cool air clean in his lungs.

He urged the horses up the hill, and turned them on the headland, and brought them back down. A plough wheel squeaked. The odd snort issued from Shadow's steaming nostrils. The soil up here was light and stony and fell in soft almost crumbling furrows. In wet muddy patches it stuck to the share or to the board, and Leo stopped the horses and cleaned the mud off with a thin spade Myrtle had given him. At a click of his tongue, the team plodded on.

Peewits foraged behind them in the soil they turned over, dark brown until it reacted with the air and paled. Seagulls squawked and bullied the smaller birds. Leo's hands had blistered from holding the wooden handles, and chapped in the cold wind, then hardened. His feet inside his socks and boots had chilblains. His frame had accustomed itself to the work, bent to the plough. The sharp coulter cut into the vegetation ahead of the ploughshare and the share negotiated its passage through the stony soil, and turned it over. Leo could feel himself walking with a rolling gait, shoulders swaying with the plough. It was how his father had come to walk always. The gait of a ploughman.

Though it must have happened by degrees and he'd not really noticed, by late morning Leo was no longer cold but sweating in his shirt and jacket, his corduroy trousers, Wally's leather leggings strapped below the knees. When he glanced around he glimpsed a weak watery sun behind the clouds.

The two horses had different temperaments, and aptitude for work. Scarlet had a tendency to laziness and slowed down, to let her partner in the traces take the strain. Leo told her to gee up and she would do so for a while, then lapse again. His father had explained to him that all his horses had names with two syllables. When you urged one on you stressed the second syllable. Here on the Luscombes' farm likewise. 'Scar*let*. Gee *up*.' Occasionally Leo took up the long thin whip, not to strike the mare but for the sound. He swung it towards her and with a flick of his wrist the whip cracked the air beside her head. The loud report had a more durable impact upon her exertions than his voice.

Shadow, the hair thick on his rounded rump, was steadfast. He kept a regular pace. Leo did not need to hurry nor to urge the black gelding faster. Whether he walked at the same speed as Wally Luscombe or the horse somehow adapted his clip to that of the man behind him, Leo did not know. Shadow slowed as soon as Leo whoa-ed them, and when he made a sound with his tongue and teeth the carthorse resumed without hesitation. It seemed that Shadow knew what Leo wanted at precisely the moment he himself thought it. He understood all of a sudden that this was what it meant to be a horseman. Not what a man or a woman did or how they acted but the alliance between human and animal. The affinity between them.

Leo finished this last field early in the afternoon. He looked across the ploughed furrows and knew a satisfaction all ploughmen must feel. He rode side-saddle on Shadow back to the yard. Scarlet followed. Their harness jingled. Sweat marks on the big black horse dried white in the wind.

Myrtle told Leo that he needed a pig. She said that Ethel haggled for one each spring from an old farmer by the name of James Sparke on the Prideaux estate, over beyond the far side of the village, itself two miles away. They would get him one as well. Leo asked Myrtle to tell him more of this estate, but she admitted ignorance of anything else. 'A pig would like it here. You could give it the run of your orchard.' She said its meat would have a subtle taste of the fruit. 'If you eat pork from an orchard pig,' Myrtle said, 'you can save yourself the bother of making apple sauce.'

One Sunday lunchtime Myrtle asked Leo why he had no friends. She thought it sad. None came to visit and he never went anywhere, not ever. Agnes bought his tobacco for him when she went shopping. Myrtle's eldest sister reproved her. Agnes said Myrtle took advantage of being the youngest to say what should not be said. Wally Luscombe apologised to Leo and poured him another glass of rhubarb wine.

Leo told them he once knew a man in Cornwall whose best friend was a mule. Wally nodded and said that during the European War many mules were shipped from parts of the Empire to the West Country. They were unloaded at Avonmouth Docks and distributed around the counties. Train loads were brought to Wiveliscombe, and sent to local farms.

'We had half a dozen here,' he said. 'Not that these girls will remember.'

'Of course I remember, Father,' Agnes said. 'I wanted to keep one, but you wouldn't let me.'

Wally Luscombe laughed. "Twas the army wouldn't let you,' he said. 'Once the mules had recuperated they were rounded up again and sent out to France.'

There was a photograph on a wall in the dining room of Wally Luscombe and a blonde-haired, round-faced woman who had to be his wife, and the mother of the three very young girls in the picture. Leo had seen it every time he came to lunch and waited for it to come up in conversation, but it never had. Today he felt bold enough to ask after Mrs Luscombe.

'It was a canker that did for her,' Wally Luscombe told him. 'It grew inside and ate her all up, all we could do was watch her waste away.'

'I reckon 'tis your ma you girls take after,' Leo said. 'Which with all due respect, Wally, is a good thing.'

Agnes said that a photographer had come riding along their lane and offered to take a family portrait for a reasonable fee, and though her mother declined the offer as too expensive Agnes and her little sisters managed to persuade her otherwise. They fetched

their father in from the fields while the photographer prepared his equipment in this very room. And now they had this image to remember her by.

'We have our memories,' Wally Luscombe said. 'But what happens to them? They fade. They grow confused inside our heads. This gradual erasure must have tormented mankind from the very beginning, I reckon. That we cannot hold onto our memories of those who've died, and then we die ourselves besides. So man learned to draw, and over hundreds – indeed hundreds of thousands – of years, improved until he was able to produce a likeness. But it was not quite good enough. Not ever. Still men strove. No longer with oil and lead and chalk but optics. Chemicals.' Wally gestured to the photograph with a grand sweep of his arm, that all might look upon it once again, but this time see it not merely as the portrait of this family but as the summit of man's development. Of civilisation.

Wally tapped his skull. 'No,' he said, 'there is no museum in which to exhibit our memories. No gallery but that inside our heads ... vague, faded. Ha! But now we have photographs. And look here, Leo, we are only one West Country farming family. We have one photo-graph, taken by an itinerant photographer who set up a tripod over there in that corner and hid beneath a black blanket. Will man stop there? No. Men never stop. Not if there's money to be made. This be our brack. Our flaw. We cannot help ourselves.'

The girls sat placidly watching him. 'How long will I remember my Louise?' he asked. 'But I look at the photograph, her likeness, and summon her up anew.'

The girls sat, listening, or dozed with their eyes open, as snakes do.

'One day, Leo,' the farmer said, 'every man will have his own camera. He will have a hundred images. A hundred thousand. On every inch of every wall. Our memories will become meaningless. And will men become less tormented?'

Wally Luscombe took up his glass and swallowed a draught of rhubarb wine.

'Thus spake the godless prophet,' Agnes muttered under her breath.

'Perhaps', Wally continued, 'the reproductions will themselves be reproduced, ad infinitum. The world will drown in images of itself.' He chuckled at the prospect.

'No, I do not believe so,' Leo said. 'Man will turn to dust, and everything man-made likewise. The earth will be restored to how it was before.'

Agnes raised her eyebrows and lifted her head, while rising from the table and grasping crockery, as if to say that men might utter nonsense but women had the work of the world to do, as always. She carried the plates to the kitchen.

'I do not remember our mother,' Myrtle said. She nodded towards the photograph. 'Except for this one image. Thus she lives on.'

'Yes,' her father concurred. 'It do confer upon the sitters a certain immortality.'

Myrtle said that now she thought about it, she did not know whether any posterity belonged more to those in front of or behind the camera.

'The photographer?' Wally said. 'Why, I bain't never thought of that.'

Agnes came in and out of the dining room, gathering cutlery and crockery with increasing abruptness. Betrayed by her youngest sister who'd left her sorority to join with the philosophers. Ethel still sat impassive.

'Like my father,' Wally said. 'He painted that picture of some Highland cattle, an' 'tis that daub by which we remember him.'

'We do not remember him, Pa,' Myrtle said. 'Us three. Grandpa died before any of us was born. But you could say we honour him.'

'I do wonder,' Leo said, 'if graven images be idolatrous, are memories likewise, in the eyes of God?'

Wally nodded sagely. 'In the eyes of godly men, at least.'

'You mean that both images and memories are forms of hubris?' Myrtle asked Leo. 'Of man's arrogance?'

Leo frowned. 'Perhaps it is a flaw less in man than in God's craftsmanship. We were fashioned to inhabit the present moment, but we carry with us the past and so can never live in true innocence.'

Wally and Myrtle considered this proposition. Agnes carried out teacups rattling in their saucers. Ethel blinked, and said, 'My stock live in the present and I must tend them.' So saying, she rose from the table and walked out of the room.

'What about our game of rummy?' Agnes called after her.

The more he saw of them, the more easily could Leo discern the physical differences between the sisters. All three wore old-fashioned bonnets outside to keep even the low April sun from their white skins. Agnes, ashen, blue-eyed, had the broadest, flattest features. Ethel's were finer, but she was slightly cross-eyed. Myrtle was almost pretty. Agnes, on the other hand, struck him as the sharpest card-player of the three, while Myrtle was surely the least bothered. It occurred to Leo that he'd stumbled upon some genetic pattern, that in female human siblings intelligence declines as beauty increases. Perhaps in males it was the opposite. Then he laughed. What ridiculous notions the brain conjured, with the help of rhubarb wine.

Myrtle asked if he was laughing at her. Not only was it rude, it was also dim, for the conversation had moved on, in case he had not noticed.

Leo said no, he was not laughing at anyone, only at the memory of his old friend's mule, who used to listen to them talking with an expression that suggested the animal understood and was hanging on every word.

'Perhaps he was,' Myrtle said. 'No one knows how horses reason.'

Leo nodded. 'I have heard that said,' he agreed.

6

There was a barrow or sett of badgers in a bank under the hedge on one side of Leo's field. Each day at dusk they emerged, and set off along their paths. He recalled his brother Sid telling him how these trails could be hundreds of years old, badgers using the paths and the burrows of their ancestors. He watched them trek in search of food.

He observed a badger excavate and consume an entire wasps' nest, ignoring the stings of the desperate insects that swarmed around. Badgers scratched out bulbs, they ate berries. Their chief diet appeared to be earthworms, of which Leo reckoned they consumed hundreds each night. They could smell insects in the soil. If they found a rabbits' nest they'd take the young. One night he saw a sow kill and eat a hedgehog.

Some way from the sett the badgers dug shallow pits or latrines, and there they went to defecate. The boars were calm beasts. They lounged around and removed fleas and ticks from each other with their teeth and claws. But as winter turned to spring, with the breeding season upon them, the males began to fight.

The first green shoots emerged from the soil of Leo's allotment.

There was much to see, for one who had eyes. One morning he saw two hares in his field stand up on their hind legs and strike at each other with their forelegs. He had heard of hares boxing, males fighting each other, yet he now knew this was wrong. What he saw was a female fighting off a male.

One afternoon at the beginning of May Leo heard the sound of a combustion engine in the distance. He stopped and stood and listened as it grew louder, throbbing and insistent, coming towards the farm.

When Leo reached the yard, Wally Luscombe stood before a tractor. The body of it was painted bright red. It had two front wheels with rubber tyres like those of a car and two enormous back wheels as large as the wooden wheels of a waggon. From these uncovered steel wheels metal lugs protruded, for purchase in the earth. They had left the mark of their passing across the yard. The engine was all enclosed. Wally must have climbed down from the seat and left it running. The machine clanked and vibrated and chugged as it stood there like some beast getting its breath back from some great exertion. The three Luscombe daughters beheld it.

'Take a closer look,' Wally yelled. ''Twon't bite. It might run you over, it might run away with you, but 'twon't bite.'

Myrtle took hesitant steps towards the machine. Agnes was shaking her head.

Wally climbed back up onto the seat and shouted something at Myrtle that Leo could not hear. Wally pressed buttons, pulled levers, kicked pedals, smoke belched out of a slim metal chimney and the machine churned into motion. Wally took hold of the steering wheel with both hands and wrenched it to one side. The two front wheels turned, and the tractor proceeded to chug around the yard in wide circles that grazed the stone barns, its driver laughing with delight.

Agnes turned on her heel and disappeared. Leo followed her to her vegetable garden. She told him that they could not afford the exorbitant cost of this vehicle, and she did not believe they could recover that cost by hiring the tractor and its driver, Myrtle, to farmers round about. Her father liked to give the impression he was frugal, sensible, but when he was set on something he flittered their money.

Later, Agnes brought tea and biscuits to the yard, for her father declined to leave his glorious new acquisition and come inside. He could not shift his eyes from its beauty, though he had switched the engine off now, and was showing Ethel how to start it with the crank handle.

Myrtle sat on the driver's metal seat, which was perforated with circular holes and resembled precisely that of a haymaker. Leo looked around and saw that one of the horses was not with its fellows out grazing but in the stable. Curiosity had overcome its fear, and it had come to the half-door and was looking upon the strange beast now at rest in its yard.

'We shall have a tank installed to house fuel,' Wally proclaimed. He told Myrtle that she would have her first driving lesson tomorrow. Leo ate a ginger biscuit.

Ethel told him quietly that her father had been reading up about tractors and their use, extolling their virtues to his daughters, for some time, but none had thought to take him seriously.

'I'm a modern man, you see, Leo,' Wally said. 'I give my daughters the credit. They keep me thinking on the future. Where things are going. How.' He did not stand still as he spoke but kept shifting beside the tractor and touching it, caressing its cooling metal parts or its rubber tyres like a horseman assessing the conformation of a horse. 'A tractor can plough a ten-acre field in a tenth of the time it'll take a team of horses. In the morning you need not feed and groom and harness your tractor, you just hitch what you want to that tow bar there and crank the engine and off you go.'

'Our father gave up religion,' Agnes told Leo. 'He's become an evangelist for the machine age.'

Wally Luscombe ignored his daughter. 'And at night,' he said, 'when you're tired from a long day's work, you don't have to wipe 'em down and brush off their fetlocks, all dobbed up with mud. You drive into the yard, switch off the engine and go on indoors.'

'What of our horses?' Myrtle asked, looking towards the stables, where the one carthorse still gazed out.

Her father dismissed them with a wave of his arm. 'We'll sell 'em,' he said. 'The knacker's yard'll take 'em if no one else will.'

Leo walked into the village for the second time since his return. He stood outside the shop. The shelves in the window to the left of the door were lined with jars of sweets just as they had been when he was a child. Acid drops, pear drops, barley sugar, some fused together by the heat of the sun. His sister Kizzie would order four ounces of one or another and Missis Prowse would break them apart with her wooden spoon, then after weighing them in her scales she folded a square of paper into a funnel and poured the sweets in.

Leo pushed open the stiff, sprung door. The bell rang and a man behind the counter and two customers turned and gazed at him as he stepped inside and let the door close behind him. He nodded to them, then they turned back and resumed their business. The shop-keeper in his stained white apron cut rashers of bacon. Leo walked through the shop. There was a door at the end that led to the bakery, but the door was closed and there was no aroma of yeast in ferment or bread baking. Leo smelled instead cheese, and tea, and paraffin from the forty-gallon iron drum.

Unlike the other reliquaries of Leo's childhood, the shop seemed larger. Then he identified his reflection in a vast, mahogany-framed mirror on one wall, an adver-tisement for soap scrawled in ornate lettering upon the glass, in which the room appeared to extend its length again.

The first customer paid and the second, an elderly man, handed the shopkeeper an old beer bottle and requested it be filled with vinegar. The shopkeeper held the bottle beneath the wooden tap of the vinegar barrel. A feeble woman's voice called out, 'Make sure he don't get no more'n a pint.'

Leo saw as he had not before that an old woman sat on a low stool behind the counter. It was Missis Prowse. The left side of her face had collapsed, her left shoulder leaned down, her left arm hung loose by her side. Leo turned away. There were long bars of soap, candles, cotton reels. Packets of dried peas. Tins of corned beef, which Leo had never touched, for he'd heard that it contained as much horsemeat as beef.

The aged customer left the shop with his vinegar. Leo stepped to the counter and said, 'Give me a twist or two a tobacco, Gilbert, and some papers and a box a matches.'

Gilbert Prowse did not move but frowned and stared at Leo. He wiped his hands on his apron. 'Do I know you?' he asked.

Leo smiled and introduced himself. 'Leo Sercombe.' He asked what had happened to the bakery.

Gilbert blinked at Leo. 'They in Bampton come round the village in a bloody van,' he said. 'All kinds a bread. Rolls. Buns. And cheap. People stopped buyin off us. Father closed the bakery. Do you know what he does now?'

Leo said that he did not.

'He drives their bloody van.' Gilbert grunted a mirthless laugh. 'Loves it. The only thing he misses is bein warm on cold days. Mind you, he don't miss bein hot on hot days. Used to sweat like a porker in there.'

Gilbert asked what Leo was doing back home. Leo told him he was visiting, he did not know for how long. He'd been in the war and stayed on in the Navy and then worked up North.

Gilbert nodded. He told Leo he'd lost a lot of his accent. He hardly sounded like a man who came from the West Country. But then he said maybe Leo hadn't lost it, maybe he'd never had it, because come to think of it Gilbert could not remember ever hearing him speak. Perhaps Leo had only learned to talk as an adult, somewhere in the North Country.

Missis Prowse in the corner chuckled out of the side of her slack mouth at her son's wit. Leo recalled his sister Kizzie striking Gilbert when he'd made fun of the younger boy. Perhaps he still held a grudge against the Sercombes. Leo paid for the tobacco and left the shop.

Leo walked past the vicarage. A man had climbed a poplar tree in the garden and was fixing an aerial. Another dug a hole. He stopped digging and laid the shovel aside and lifted an old bucket. He sank this in the hole he'd dug. Then he looked up and saw Leo watching.

'Do it amuse you to ogle a labourin man?' the digger said. 'You can join in if you want, I got a spare shovel.'

'I wondered why you'd dug a hole to bury a rusty bucket, that's all,' Leo said.

The man frowned. 'For an earth wire, a course.'

A man came out of the vicarage front door and marched across the lawn. He wore a dog collar but he was many years younger than the old vicar, Reverend Doddridge. He spoke to the man up in the branches of the poplar tree. Leo walked on. This new vicar was quite likely the first person in the village to install a wireless. The man of God could listen to voices coming through the ether, and know that these were real.

The countrymen sat in the bar. They drank from mugs of beer or cider. Some emptied their mug in one or two draughts, possessed of a great thirst that the ale slaked briefly, and they gasped after each long swallow, a sound of satisfaction.

Others sipped their beer, savouring the taste of the hops, or perhaps not in fact enjoying the alcohol, or its effect upon them, but drinking only because it was the price of being there, in the taciturn company of men. Leo was one such. None knew him. None addressed him. Most if not all would have known or known of his father, but had no way to connect them.

Leo rolled a cigarette. He drank a mug of beer then went to the bar and asked the landlord to refill it. If a world was coming without horses, he sought no place in it.

The sound of wooden skittles came from the alley. In one corner of the bar two men played cribbage. Another thumbed shag into his clay pipe. Occasionally someone spoke, then there was silence once more for a while. A toast was raised to some woman in a neighbouring village who'd recently passed away.

'I ain't afeared a death,' said an old man. 'My only dread's of bein buried alive. They think I'm gone but I ain't, I's only sleepin, and then I wakes up in a box, under the mud.'

'Don't worry, I should say,' a fellow codger told him. 'Not much you can do about it.'

'Oh, yes, there is. I put instruction in my will to have a vein cut.'

This provoked laughter. 'You's got a will? What else you stipulated? Left your jacket to a scarecrow? You bain't got no will.'

'Maybe not, but if I did, that's what I'd put in it.'

Leo drank much beer. The privy was a bare dim shed with a gully on the floor along one wall, running into a drain. He returned to the bar.

One man said, to no one in particular, 'You seen that maid up Berry Lane? 'Er's in the family way and no mistake.' He took a slow gulp of beer, reward perhaps for this contribution to the conversation.

Another man took a pipe from his pocket, placed its stem between his teeth, closed his lips and puffed. He inhaled and exhaled, in brief rapid bursts of air. He looked at the bowl, or tried to, cross-eyed, then took matches from a different pocket and lit the pipe, pursing his lips and opening them a little periodically to get some kind of suction or airflow going. Once he had done so he removed the pipe from his mouth and said, 'And we all know who takes the credit for that, don't we? Marriage ain't put a stop to Gilbert Prowse's philanderin.'

A third man took a sip of cider and said, 'He's a sinner. But it's hard to blame a man who finds his self with a frigid wife from seekin warmth elsewhere.'

One or two men nodded in agreement. The second man puffed his pipe, pondering this a while, then he said, 'A frigid wife must be worse than one what's on heat permanent, like.'

More men nodded. Then the first man took another slow draught of beer and burped, and said, 'That's what they says the matter with his poor old lordship's daughter, why 'er's alone on the estate. Goin about the place in men's breeches, on that damned motorcycle. Her don't want a man.'

'My old girl reckons her wants a woman,' the pipe-puffing second man said.

Leo raised his mug and swilled the beer around. The mug was less than half full. He left it on the table where he'd sat and rose and walked to the bar and asked the landlord for another pint.

The landlord said, 'You sure you ain't had enough for one night, young fellow?'

Leo considered this proposition, swaying a little on his feet. Then he nodded. 'Yes, I'm sure,' he said. 'I need just one more.'

He watched the landlord pull the beer, and place the new mug on the bar, and with a section of cut wood draw off the foam atop the mug. The landlord shook the wood and put it back in its place beneath the bar.

Leo paid for the beer and carried it towards the man who had spoken of his old lordship's daughter. Leo reached the man and raised the mug and poured its contents carefully over the man's head. At first the man did not appear to realise what was happening. The beer fell upon him, drenching his hair and sliding down over his face and shoulders. Then he began to splutter and wave his arms and twist his body. He moved like someone underwater. When he'd emptied the mug, Leo walked back to where he'd been seated before and placed the empty mug beside the one he'd drunk from, and stumbled out of the pub and all the way back to his cabin on the Luscombes' farm.

7

When he heard the tin bowl clang against the metal bin, the horse raised his head and turned. Presently the woman appeared and poured the oats and chaff into his feeding tray, and the large grey gelding fed. When she had done the same for the small pony in the box adjoining, she climbed the ladder to the loft and pulled hay loose and dropped it into the horses' wooden mangers below.

There was not enough work for the last stable lad so Lottie had to lay him off. He found employment in the lace shop at the Heathcoat factory in Tiverton. There were only the two horses left. Pegasus, her big grey gelding, and the rotund old pony. He was well over twenty years old and had once worked in a mine. Now he could no longer pull even an empty cart. His heart was weak and he had arthritis in the hips and shoulders. Lottie exercised him, on a long lead, but lately he'd begun wheezing, which she feared meant a collapse of his windpipe and did not bode well. Yet the Shetland pony had not grown crotchety in his ageing decrepitude, as some horses did, but was a grave and easy-going beast. He was a grass or field companion for the big grey. Pegasus preferred his unobtrusive company to solitude.

Lottie descended from the hayloft by the stone steps outside and crossed to the bothy. It retained the scent still of Herb Shattock's pipe tobacco. She'd brought her horse's saddle and his bridle and reins there earlier after she'd taken Pegasus for a ride, and cleaned them with a cloth and warm water. They were now dry. Lottie unstrapped the reins and undid the bit from the bridle. She got down the glycerine saddle soap and the neat's-foot oil from the cupboard and picked a cloth from a pile in the basket and set to rubbing soap into the old leather. She had never cleaned her own tack throughout her childhood. The mundane task was not enjoyable, exactly, but one could lose oneself in the routine, in the smell of lanolin in the soap and the slow shine of leather.

When she heard footsteps approaching, Lottie stopped what she was doing and stepped outside. A man came trotting into the yard, leading a pony. He held the end of the leading rope with his left hand and with his right held it tight beside the head collar. He came to a halt, leaning backwards. 'Whoa there, easy,' he said to the horse. 'Hold up.'

The pony came to a stop and the man said, 'Good afternoon, miss.'

'I'd say it was closer to evening myself,' Lottie replied.

'I'll not argue with you, no, I won't, miss, honest to God. I could but I'll not, don't you worry about that now.'

The man wore patched trousers, a once white cotton shirt and a faded waistcoat beneath a frayed tweed jacket. On his head he wore a trilby, at a jaunty angle that may have been due to being bumped out of skew as he trotted but Lottie suspected was not. The hat sported a red feather in the band.

'What can I do for you?' she asked him.

'It's what I can do for you, miss, is more to the point. Will you look at this sweet mare, miss? I've clipped her neat but she'll grow feather on her elegant fetlocks if that's what you prefer. Will you take a good look at her and tell me she's not a beautiful little beast?'

Lottie regarded the bay mare before her.

'Here's a cracking little hoss, miss. She's a temperament of gold, she just wants to please. She moves to the squeeze of a leg and stops to the squeeze a the reins.' As he spoke, the gypsy turned the horse for his witness. 'She's beautiful balanced paces … here, I'll show you. And her canter is so comfortable now you'll believe you're a Chinese empress, miss, being carried in a cushioned litter.'

'Wait a moment,' Lottie said.

But the horse dealer would not pause. He continued. 'She'll hack out alone and in company, perfectly calm, miss, if that's what you want. But if you want to hunt her she's bold with water and ditches, with drops and jumps. She'll jump a hedge twice her height, brave as a lion she is. She just enjoys everything she's asked to do, and you can't say that about every hoss.'

Lottie smiled. 'What makes you think I'm in the market for a horse?' she asked.

'This mare deserves the best possible home,' he said. He looked around the stables. 'And a refined woman like yourself to look after her. She loves people. She's excellent to bathe, to box. To catch, to clip. To stable, to shoe.'

The man ran the bay mare away through the stable yard and turned her and brought her back. She looked sound, certainly.

'Happy with dogs and farm animals,' the dealer gasped. 'She's not fazed by traffic, miss. I can see you smiling there and I can tell what you're thinking.' He looked around. 'Where's the traffic? Here we are in the heart a the country and we've not a lot more than a little farm machinery. That's what you're thinking, is it now? But mark my words, we'll have a lot more traffic around the narrow lanes in days to come.'

The man told Lottie that his bay mare was four years six months old almost to the day. She stood at fourteen point three hands unshod.

'I take it you're selling her,' Lottie said.

The man's shoulders slumped. He looked sad. 'That I am, though I'd rather not. But if you want her badly, I'll let you have her for twenty-five pounds. Though it pains me. Look. See. She's no lumps or bumps or vices.'

'There are two reasons', Lottie said, 'why I cannot pay you. Do you know who I am?'

The man nodded. 'I do, miss.'

'I'm afraid we are no longer wealthy. You may imagine that I am, but it is not so.'

The man frowned, momentarily flummoxed. Then he said, 'You can have her for fifteen pounds, miss. She's the last a my string, I've had a good day, haven't I, and I've a place to get back to before nightfall, that's the truth of it.'

'The second reason', Lottie said, 'is that I cannot bear being taken advantage of.'

'Honest to God, you're a hard woman. You're trying to break my heart and take her off me but I know when I'm beat. All right, I give in. She's yours for ten. If you'll not give me that then I'll take her up on the moor and let her loose, that I will.'

'What is wrong with her?'

The gypsy was aghast. 'Wrong with her, miss? Wrong with her? Are you wondering if she's any good on the gallops, is that it? Yes, she's a jumper, but she's nice paces on the flat, too. She's potential to be good. Very good, to be fair.'

Lottie shook her head. 'If you'll sell her for ten pounds she must be worth less. But I like the look of her. Listen to me. If you tell me what is wrong with her, and she's not a bad one, if whatever it is I can cure her of it, I'll take her off you.'

The horse dealer stood there in a state of agitation, wrestling with his self-respect. Then he came to a conclusion. 'Do you know what, miss? I once had a hoss, a young hunter what had taken to bolting. I had him along with a bunch of others I was selling, see? I was always honest with the groom here, Mister Shattock it was, and he took a shine to this hunter. I warned him that once a hoss had bolted it would do so again, for a beast finds intense pleasure in bolting, see? Mister Shattock nodded in agreement with me, but he took the bad hoss and none of the other good ones. He gave it laudanum and the hoss calmed. He calmed the bolting clean out of him, would you believe it? And that animal became your father's favourite hunter.'

Lottie could indeed believe that Herb Shattock had done as the gypsy claimed.

'My name is Levi Hicks,' the man said. 'Ask anyone, I'm a hossman to the ends a me fingers. I'll tell you what's wrong with this dear hoss. Everything I've said to you is true, miss. She's a good doer who lives on fresh air. I mean, she's a clever girl, she makes you smile, miss, doesn't she?'

'She does.'

'She's not a bad 'un, honest to God. You'll cure her if you have the time. I would but I've not got the time, do you see? I've got to turn my money over, have I not?'

Lottie went into the bothy and found her purse. She took a ten-pound note and went back outside and handed it to the horse dealer. He took the note between the fingers of his left hand and in a single dextrous action folded it and put it in a pocket. Then he handed the rope to Lottie.

'You've got a beauty there, miss, truly.' He began to walk away.

'Wait, Mr Hicks,' Lottie said. 'Are you going to tell me what's wrong with her?'

Levi Hicks stopped and faced Lottie once more. 'Someone treated her bad,' he said. 'Real rough. She's lovely outdoors but pardon my language, miss, she's a bitch in a loose box. You watch her, 'cos she's lightning quick.'

The gypsy horse dealer bent obsequiously forward and tipped his hat, then turned and trotted out of the yard.

8

On the day following his excess of alcohol in the inn, Leo Sercombe rose early and walked once again to the village, and through it, and on to the estate. The sky was grey, heavy, overcast.

Leo made straight for the gamekeeper's cottage. He knocked on the door. This time he could hear commotion from inside. Yelled instruction. 'Answer it, Stan.'

The door opened. A boy stood in the doorway. He was perhaps ten years old, but he could not be, for there stood Leo's brother Sid. He stared up at Leo, with his black Sercombe eyes. Leo gazed back. He could not move. The joints and the bones of his legs turned soft and would not support him, and he reached a hand out to the frame. Had he plunged through some trapdoor into the past? Or Sid risen, a revenant child, from the past into this present moment? Which must mean that Leo himself was dead. He could not breathe.

The boy broke the spell. He turned and called softly, 'Father.'

Another, smaller child came to the door. A girl. In duplication or doubling of the uncanny, she resembled Leo's sister, Kizzie.

Then a man came up from behind them and placed his hand on a shoulder of each child and studied Leo, until from his lips there grew a smile that bloomed as a grin transfiguring the whole of his face. He stepped forward between his children.

Leo hugged his brother's solid flesh. He rested his chin on Sid's head and inhaled the smell of him. When Sid let go and grasped him by the elbows with two meaty hands, Leo felt the strength of the man.

'Let me look at you,' Sid said, taking a step back, still with a grip on Leo's arms. 'You'm grown tall as the old man.'

Leo nodded. 'I spec one of us had to.' He looked down then, and saw the children still staring up at him. They each had those blackcurrant Sercombe eyes.

'This be our kids right here,' Sid said. 'This boy's my Stanley and this maid's our Elsie. You two, this here's your uncle Leo, what as I've told you of many a time. Elsie, tell your mother we've got another mouth for breakfast, and us is comin right in.'

The girl turned and ran into the kitchen. The boy followed. Sid ushered Leo inside, and on after the children.

'Come on and meet the missis,' Sid said. 'Gracie, here's my long-gone brother, Leo. Leo, this be my better half, Gracie.'

Sid's wife had a round and pleasant face, blue eyes. Sid stood beside her facing Leo, and put his arm around her shoulders. Stanley stood beside him, Elsie by her mother. 'This is it,' Sid said. 'What you see's the whole of us. Take a seat, young brother, if yon long legs will fit under the table.'

They ate porridge sweetened with sugar. 'So this is where you live,' Leo said. 'Head gamekeeper.'

'Aye,' Sid confirmed. 'Head, but there bain't no other.'

'Aaron Budgell gone?'

'Gone down, boy. We buried him, along with his proudest possession, the bump on that bald head of his.'

'I recall it.'

'Few forget it.'

Gracie cut slices of bread, on which they spread plum jam. She poured mugs of tea. She was short and plump and moved slowly, performing actions with efficient elegance, giving the impression that what she did was practised, choreographed.

'Is that silly wife a his still about?' Leo asked.

'Went to her sister,' Sid said. 'Over Wellington way.'

When the children had eaten, Gracie told them to hurry along for school. The girl rose from the table and carried her mug and plate to the sink but the boy stayed where he was. Gracie said his name: 'Stanley.'

'Oh, they can be a little late for school today, can't they, me lover?' Sid said.

'Don't blame me if her gives 'em a dap with the cane,' Gracie said.

'They'll go dreckly,' Sid told her. ''Tisn't often they meets an uncle for the first time.'

Leo asked how the work was.

'What work?' Sid replied. ''Tis a different blimmin game now. The shoots is nothin like they was.

'Tis business folk come out from Exeter, a few from Taunton, they pays for the privilege and brings their important clients. To show off, I s'pose. Most of 'em can't shoot straight. I tell this lot here, 'tis not like 'twas for Mister Budgell, with his lordship. You mind how he used to go potterin along the hedgerows with his gun and his two Labs and me?'

Sid shook his head, then grinned. 'You know that old larch plantation up yonder? Four or five year ago I had six- to seven-week-old pheasants in there and one day about a million blimmin starlins decides to come and set up residence. You can imagine, boy. Ruined that wood, they did, with their droppins. But you know how brittle larch is? They all flies down and stands on the branches, I watched 'em, thousands of 'em, and then ...' Sid clapped his hands '... the branch snaps, just like that. Laugh? That'd make you chuckle, Leo. The ground they'm stood on gone beneath 'em, and they all squawkin and fussin like they wants someone to complain to but it's their own fault.'

One thing Leo had already discovered. Sid was as garrulous a man as he'd been a youth.

''Twas no good for my pheasants, I had to move 'em. I tried everythin to be rid of them starlins. Hawk kites. Sulphur fires. I shot a lot but not enough to make no difference. Eventually in the spring they up and left a their own accord and they never come back. But then about ten million elder trees come up from under where they'd roosted. From seeds in the berries they ate, see? Oh, they ruined that wood, boy.'

Leo asked Sid what trouble he had with poachers. 'Can't be easy when you're single-handed.'

"'Tis not too bad,' Sid said. 'I've got me a handy ash plant, I've knocked one or two about with it.'

The boy Stanley rose from his chair and left the kitchen.

'So long as they ain't greedy, I don't mind the odd local helpin his self to a rabbit or two.'

The boy returned holding a thick stick, which he handed to Leo. The end to be held was the circumference of a cricket-bat handle. The plant thickened towards its other end, which bulged with some kind of growth or tumour in the wood. Leo smacked this into his palm. 'No, I shouldn't like to be struck with this.'

'My lad here's keen to keep. I've told him there's likely no future in it but he won't listen. Will you, Stan? You could walk about with this boy and he'll show you where a fox has made his spring upon a rabbit. A pheasant without its head, what's done that, Stan?'

The boy had been watching the men intently as they spoke. Now, required to speak himself, he looked away. 'An owl,' he said quietly.

'That's it, an owl gone bad. And how's about if just the brains is gone?'

Again Stanley looked elsewhere. 'Jackdaw, more an likely.'

Sid nodded, and turned to Leo. 'See? Knows his stuff already. Only just turned eleven. I swear he's better an me with his imitations. If I'm after a stoat or a weasel, Stan here can imitate the shrieks of a dyin rabbit someit lovely, bring the vermin out for me to

337

shoot. I've took im out at night, though Gracie don't like it, do you, me lover?'

Gracie said, 'I do not.' She said to Leo, 'What if he meets a bad 'un?'

'I'd run along, don't worry. Us'd hide and run along, Stan, right? And you and your sister better run along now. Go on.'

Stanley whispered, 'Can I show Uncle my ferret?'

'You heard right, Leo,' Sid said. 'He's got his own ferret. No, boy, show him later. You git on to school now.'

The children rose obediently and their mother too rose from the table and tended to them.

'That's when I like it best,' Sid said. 'At night. It gets a hold over you, so I'll allow it's got a hold over our Stan.'

'What's got a hold?' Leo asked.

'The land,' Sid said. 'The creatures.' He looked out through the window. 'The whistling flight a plovers. Or hedgehogs fightin, makin sounds like the moans a children. Night walkers, I call 'em. They gets to you.'

Gracie returned to the kitchen. She brewed the men more tea and ushered them into the front room, then left them to their conversation or reminiscence. Each man sank into an armchair. There were glass ornaments on the whatnot. An embroidery sampler, framed and hung upon the wall, held an array of birds and leafy decoration, and was signed in stitchwork: *By Gracie Crump, aged ten.*

'Mother,' Leo said, once they were alone. 'Kizzie. Where are they? Do you know?'

'I was waitin for you to ask that,' Sid said. 'They went over into the Somerset Levels. Old man got a job on a farm there. Still there far's I know. Mother writes me Christmas time.'

'And our sister?'

'You'll not believe it, Leo. Her's a teacher.'

'I do believe it.'

'And not just with little tykes, in a local school. Her's up in Bristol now, teachin older ones. Her's done real good.'

Sid took a cake of plug tobacco from his pouch and with his penknife he cut it. The larger part he returned in the pouch to the pocket of his jacket. The smaller part he rubbed in the palm of his left hand with the palm of his right as he spoke more of their family. Leo rolled a cigarette. He asked how things were on the estate. Where were the Prideauxs?

'Remember the Wombwell lads?' Sid asked.

Leo nodded.

'Their ma, Florence? Had the ducks?'

'I do.'

'Miss Charlotte lives in their old cottage.'

Leo was not sure he understood. 'Why?'

Sid lit his pipe. 'Don't ask me,' he said. 'The big house is empty most a the year.'

'I need to see her,' Leo said. 'I have to tell her somethin.'

'She might not be in,' Sid said. 'Her's always vettin on one farm or another, racin round on her motorcycle. It's her who rents out the shoots. Estate manager, she is.'

Leo nodded. He stubbed his cigarette out in the ashtray and said, 'Well, I better be lettin you get to work.' He rose from his chair.

Sid stood too. 'You stayin?'

'I intend to,' Leo told him. 'Hereabouts a while.'

9

Lottie Prideaux rode her motorcycle to the farm of Percy Giffard in the Quantocks. His father had been a friend of her father's. She remembered the bumbling old man from shoots. He was a gun of notorious inaccuracy. Those placed on either side of him begged to change position.

The colonel had died. His son Percy inherited the farm and came home reluctantly from London. He had no instinct for farming and left it to his foreman, but fell in love with horses and spent his time hunting with others or hacking on his own, without learning very much about either the art of equitation, it seemed to Lottie, or the animals themselves. His three children had a pony each. His wife languished in the role of a country squire's wife, and her maids ran the house as they wished.

Percy had a big chestnut mare of which he was particularly fond. She was presently in foal. He escorted Lottie to the stables.

'We've been giving her bran and linseed mashes,' he assured her. 'Three or four times a day.' He paused Lottie with a hand on her arm and pointed to their right. 'And we let her exercise in that field now. Removed her from the small paddock, as you advised, where the ground could get soiled and stale.'

As they came into the yard they saw the Giffards' groom lead an old pony out of the small barn. 'That's the quiet old girl we put in with her,' Percy said. 'Retter there says she's due any day. Her udders are swollen.'

The groom saw them and hitched the pony to a gate and trotted over. 'Sir,' he said. 'Miss. Foaling's started.'

'Righto,' said Percy Giffard. 'Good timing, Retter. Well done.'

They strolled to the door of the barn and looked in. Percy Giffard gasped. 'Good God,' he said. There, well bedded down with straw, the chestnut mare was heaving herself up from the ground, with part of the foal clearly emerging from her.

'For God's sake,' Percy said. 'Do something, man.'

The chestnut mare lay down again in the straw.

'Help her,' Percy ordered.

The groom unbolted the lower door and began to pull it open. Lottie shifted her foot and blocked the door.

'What do you plan to do?' she asked the groom. 'As far as I can see from here, the foal's forefeet are under its chin, as they should be.'

'I'll grab a hold of it, miss,' the groom said. 'Give 'em forelegs a good pull.'

'You are more likely to tear the ligaments or dislocate the bones of the foal than help the mare.'

The chestnut mare once more staggered to her feet. Perhaps the foal was a little further on in the process of its birthing, but not much.

'We can't just do nothing, Charlotte,' Percy said.

'We watch,' Lottie told him. 'She might appear to be in distress but she's almost certainly not, really, and neither is the foal. Not yet anyhow.' She nodded to the groom, Retter. He let go of the door and Lottie closed it and slid the bolt back into place.

When the chestnut mare lay back down, the upper parts of the foal fell awkwardly on the straw.

'She'll crush it or smother it,' Percy said, but they could see this was not happening.

The mare lay, breathing hard. Then she once more rose, and stood, and, as they watched, the foal shifted a little further down and out of the mother. Then all of a sudden it came slithering loose and free, with an audible suck and then a plop, and it flopped upon the straw.

'Thank God,' Percy Giffard said.

They watched as the mare bent and licked the newborn foal. Lottie asked the groom if he had string. He reached into a pocket and pulled out a coil of brown twine and handed it to her. Lottie took a knife from her own pocket and opened it and cut two lengths of string, each some inches long. She gave the coil back to Retter, then let herself into the barn, holding the door open for the groom to follow.

'Mind her for me, will you?' Lottie asked.

The umbilicus still connected the foal to the mare. While the groom made soothing noises to the horse, Lottie tied the pieces of string tight around the birth cord, an inch apart, some six inches from the foal. Then with her knife she cut the cord in between the ties.

The groom told the chestnut mare what a clever beast she was, and what a handsome colt she had brought forth into the world. The mare seemed to display a certain quiet pride in her achievement, or so it seemed to Lottie. She had noted this often. Perhaps it was an illusion that human admirers ascribed to the animal's accomplished labour. She knelt on the straw and studied the foal to make sure that his nostrils were clear, not blocked by birth matter, his breathing unimpeded. Having done so, she rose and stepped back, for the foal was already attempting to struggle to its feet.

Lottie let herself out of the barn and stood beside Percy Giffard, watching the foal climb to its feet and stagger then fall back on the straw. He lay there with a look of surprise on his small face, as if things out here were not as he'd expected them to be. Then he attempted to rise once more.

'Determined little chap, isn't he?' Percy said.

Lottie left him watching the newest member of his stable, with his groom, and went to have a look at the others. The ponies were in a field, grazing. Lottie walked among them and studied them and judged them to be sound. Then the groom's lad came riding Percy Giffard's chief hunter, a big black horse. Lottie walked across to block his way and the lad slowed the horse.

'Been exercising him?' Lottie asked.

'Yes, miss,' the lad said.

Lottie stroked the horse as she studied him. 'He's a fine animal,' she said. Then she stopped and said, 'What's this blood here at his lips?' She wiped the horse's mouth and the blood on her fingers was fresh.

The lad slipped his boots out of the stirrups and lifted the reins and dismounted, carrying the reins to the front of the horse. 'Mister Retter put the prick-pad on 'im,' he said. 'He's been leanin to the left, see?'

'What prick-pad?' Lottie asked, but she knew. They walked the big hunter back to the stable yard. The lad replaced the bridle with a head collar. Lottie found the home-made device that the groom had placed inside the ring of the snaffle on the left-hand side of the bridle. She studied it. The device consisted of tin-tacks stuck into a small round wad of leather, their points projecting through the leather and pressing against the lips of the horse.

Lottie walked to the barn. Percy Giffard and the groom turned in her direction. She carried the bloodied piece of leather in her palm and held it out to them.

'Aye, the prick-pad. What I told you, sir,' Retter said to his employer, 'to cure his inclination.'

'That's right,' Percy said. He turned to Lottie. 'The damned animal is leaning to one side every time I ride him.'

'This is a cruelty, not a cure,' Lottie said. 'If your hunter is leaning to the left, Percy, there must be a cause. Possibly in his right foreleg. More likely in his mouth.'

'Aye, miss,' Retter said. 'I've studied his leg, like you say. Can't find nothin wrong.'

'And his mouth?'

Retter grinned. He held up his left hand. The top of the index finger was curtailed, just above the knuckle. 'I'm not as keen as I once were on stickin my fingers in a horse's mouth,' he said. 'Them molars can get razor sharp.'

Lottie frowned. 'That sounds extremely unusual,' she said. 'You were unfortunate.' She turned and walked away. She glanced back once and saw the two men bent towards each other, sharing some wordless communication about her wider knowledge or abrupt manner. Well, to hell with them. From her motorcycle pannier she took certain implements, and walked back to the yard. When she reached the two men, who still stood watching the newborn foal, she held up a metallic contraption and said, 'This is a mouth-opening bridle.' To Retter she said, 'Come and watch, see how it is used.'

The lad had tied the black hunter's head-collar rope to a ring and removed the saddle, and was rubbing the sweat off him. Lottie said that she would rather study the horse after he had been fed, but she did not have time, they would have to do it now. She asked the lad to fetch salt, and also to light the brightest lantern they possessed.

The mouth-opening bridle consisted of two steel platforms, which fitted round the hunter's front teeth. She dipped this bridle in the bowl of salt. When she introduced it, the horse licked the salt, and allowed the strange implement into his mouth.

'The salt will soothe him,' Lottie explained, 'and also numb his gums a little.' She told Percy that unlike humans', a horse's teeth do not stop growing. Fortunately, the grinding of their upper and lower jaws in mastication wears the teeth down and keeps them at a

346

correct level. If a tooth is damaged, however, its opposite number may keep growing.

The horse licked the salt. Then Lottie inserted a ratchet between the platforms and, by turning it, pushed the upper and lower front teeth apart. She asked the lad for the lantern, which he had lit. In the open air its light was negligible, but when she held it close to the horse's mouth it added a little illumination. She handed it to the lad. Retter stroked the horse. Lottie invited him to step closer and see what she saw.

The groom peered into the hunter's mouth.

'Do you see there?' Lottie asked. 'On the right-hand side. The upper molar there has grown too long. No doubt the corresponding lower molar has been broken. By a stone in the grass or suchlike.'

The groom nodded, frowning.

'I don't doubt the overgrown molar has caused a cut or sore on the inside of the cheek. That is what's causing his inclination.' Lottie had laid her instruments in their cloth upon the cobbles of the yard. Now she bent and unrolled the cloth and selected a rasp. This she dipped in salt as she had the bit, and introduced into the horse's mouth from the side, and let it lie there, holding it by its handle. Again the horse licked the salt, and bit the rasp, and lost his fear of it. Then Lottie filed the tooth down. She told Percy that a horse's teeth were not hard and could be filed like bone. It took her less than five minutes. When she had finished she asked the groom if he had rasps.

He said, 'One or two.'

Lottie suggested that Percy let Retter buy a mouth-opening bridle like this one. 'Care of a horse's mouth is as important as care of his feet. Something like this,' Lottie said, taking the prick-pad from her pocket, 'is more likely to create a fresh vice than cure one.' She asked the groom if she could trust him to remove the mouth-opening bridle, if he had watched her and was capable of reversing the operation.

Retter tightened his lips and said, 'A course.'

While he proceeded, Lottie crouched and put her rasp back in the cloth and rolled it up. Percy Giffard invited her to the house for a drink, saying his wife would wish to see her, but Lottie said that she could not. She took the bridle from the groom and walked back to her motorcycle.

I O

When Lottie Prideaux had first ridden the motor-cycle across the estate, every animal was spooked, but she fancied that they were growing used to it. Other vehicles with internal combustion engines, with all their snarling racket and sudden loud reports, had appeared. James Sparke at Wood Farm had recently bought the first tractor.

Light showers of rain had settled the dust on the lanes, and now the grey clouds were breaking up, blue sky revealed here and there above them.

Leo Sercombe sat on a bench outside the Wombwells' old cottage. When he heard the petulant whine of the bike, he stood. Soon motorcycle and rider appeared. He watched the rider dismount, yank the bike onto its stand, take off her goggles.

Lottie unstrapped the panniers and lifted them off the bike and carried them up the path. When she glanced up and saw the man outside her home she slowed, and came to a halt some three or four yards away. They stood looking at each other in silence. Lottie studied the man for a long time. Then she said, 'It's you, isn't it?'

Leo nodded. 'It is.'

Lottie shook her head. 'I knew it was.' She smiled. 'I did know you would come back. One day. And so you have.'

Leo saw her turn pale, the blood fading from her face. She stepped past him and sat upon the bench. She leaned back and closed her eyes. Leo waited. After some time Lottie opened her eyes and sat up.

'For a moment it struck me that you were not real,' she said. 'That you were some kind of visitation. Forgive me.'

'Perhaps I am,' he said. 'And you was right. I mean, I'm alive, but I sometimes wonder if I really is. How I survived. If I am all here.'

Lottie patted the seat beside her and said, 'Won't you sit down?'

'Thank you,' Leo said. 'But I must tell you something first. I have decided. If you wish it, I shall work for you and your husband.'

Lottie frowned. 'I have no husband.'

Leo looked away. Then back. 'I shall work for you and your children.'

Lottie smiled. 'I have no children, Leo.'

He looked at the ground. His hands were clasped together. 'I am might sorry,' he said, 'for your loss.'

'What loss?'

'You had a child.'

'I did not.' Lottie put her hands out to the sides. 'I do not.'

'I saw you,' Leo said. 'I came here on leave from the Navy. Ten year ago. I saw you playin with your child on the lawn.'

'With my father's child,' Lottie said. 'It must have been one of my brothers. My half-brothers.'

Now it was Leo's turn to feel unsteady and so he took up the invitation to sit. Lottie told him how her father had married Alice Grenvil, and with her produced three sons. How he had died, thrown from a horse. How Alice and the boys had moved to London and came down here infrequently, their summer residence a brief visit.

'I imagine she would like to be shot of it,' Lottie said. 'But she has to wait until James is of age. So I manage the estate. I don't do a great deal. The farms pretty much look after themselves, although we had to sell your old one, Manor Farm, to pay death duties after Papa died.'

She asked what Leo was doing. He told her he was living for the moment on the farm of a man called Wally Luscombe. Lottie pondered this information.

'On the far side of Maundown?' she said. 'With three daughters?'

'That's the one,' Leo agreed. 'I've dug me a little smallholding. I thought that might be what I wanted, but it ain't.'

'What do you want?'

Leo looked away. 'I want to work with horses.' He smiled, and turned back to face her. 'Just as tractors is takin over.'

Lottie nodded. 'I fear the days of the heavy horse are numbered.'

'And not just them,' Leo said. 'I've been considerin the fate a sparrows.'

'Sparrows?' Lottie asked.

'Have you noticed,' Leo said, 'how they peck oats from out of horses' dung? Undigested oats. With fewer horses there'll be fewer sparrows, for sure. All things is connected.'

Lottie said that he was surely right about that. Then she apologised, saying how rude she was, she must offer him something to drink. And food. It must be lunchtime.

'No, no,' he said. 'I should get back. I should let you get on.'

'Will you come again tomorrow?' Lottie asked. 'In the morning. Please. I want you to see something.'

'I shall, then,' Leo said. He got to his feet. 'Once upon a time,' he said, 'I told you I would work for you. I made a promise.'

'We were children,' Lottie said.

Leo made a gesture with his right hand, tilting and holding it upraised and palm open towards her. 'I came back, like I said, but when I saw you with the child, and assumed he was yours, and that you was married, I turned around. I had ideas, and I was too proud. It's took me these years to swallow my pride. Now I don't know what to think.'

Lottie smiled and reached out and took Leo's hand in both of hers. 'Don't think,' she said. 'I'm glad you are here. So glad. Come back tomorrow morning.'

Leo nodded. He withdrew his hand from Lottie's grip and turned and walked away from the cottage.

I I

On the day following Leo rose early. After feeding his pig and his chickens he walked back to the estate. He strode fast, but it took an hour and a half. He thought that he had probably walked more miles than was good for a man. A man should have a horse. Or failing that a bicycle.

He walked past the stables and a little further on he heard a horse nicker. He stepped from the lane and walked through a coppice of beech trees and came out on a path. To his right were the stables. He knew where he was. On almost exactly this spot he had once held on to Herb Shattock's rifle against its attempted seizure by his cousin, the maid Gladys, when Lottie refused to let the groom destroy her blue roan. He turned left and walked down through the spinney to the paddock where he'd first observed Lottie suppling the same animal. Now he saw a man leaning on the outside of the fence poles, watching.

Inside the paddock were three horses. A big grey, a bay mare, and a tubby little beast that resembled a moorland pony but was shorter and rounder. It had a long tail and a thick mane, whose forelock half-covered its eyes. Lottie was leading this diminutive animal by a short rope. A boy walked beside her. Lottie stopped and offered the rope to the boy. He did not look at her but at the ground. The pony stood still and made no fuss while the boy tried to make up his mind. The big grey remained on the far side of the paddock, grazing but watching between his legs what was going on. The bay mare had been following the little pony and the two humans at some dozen yards' distance. The boy made up his mind. He took the rope from Lottie and resumed walking. The pony obediently accompanied him, Lottie walking beside them. The bay mare followed.

Leo stood beside the man watching and after a while he said, 'Is you involved in this?'

The man glanced at him, then back at the proceedings in the paddock. 'That's my boy,' he said. 'Miss Charlotte reckoned the horse might help him.'

'What ails the boy?' Leo asked.

The man glanced at Leo again. His mouth and lips moved, as if he had just discovered some morsels of food, seeds or pips, between his teeth, and was chewing them. 'He don't say nothin, really.'

Leo nodded. 'I was desperate shy at his age myself. Didn't say boo to a goose.'

'He bain't shy,' the man said. 'He don't say nothin. He grunts and growls. He's angry. Don't ask me why. If I could find out what angers him so I'd cast it out and be done.'

Leo asked how often the boy had come here and the man said this was their second visit. He nodded towards the people in the field. They had stopped walking. The boy stroked the pony.

'If you'd wagered me', the man said, 'that our boy would be gentle with that horse, I'd a bet every penny I had against you. 'Twill mean nothin to you, fellow, but to me it's …' The man frowned and shook his head. ''Tis odd. 'Tis incredible, is what it is, really.'

After the man had taken his boy off, Lottie joined Leo at the fence. She drank from a flask of water and together they watched the three horses. Leo said that the big grey was a beauty. Lottie said his name was Pegasus and he was the most confident horse she had known, with a rare authority, and such was his confidence in himself that he was obedient to her. 'If that makes sense,' she added.

Leo said he thought that it did. He asked what she had been doing with the boy. She said she had an idea that horses, or at least certain horses, gentle beasts, might be more patient with people who were crippled or troubled than other people were. The idea came to her after a blind man she knew had ridden Pegasus. She wasn't sure. It was early days.

'It is an interestin notion,' Leo said. 'Appealin.'

'I wanted you to see,' Lottie said. 'And I wondered too if you might help me with the mare.'

'That bay there?' Leo asked. 'Her looks sound to me.'

'She has a vice,' Lottie said. 'An affliction. I don't understand it.'

Lottie put a halter on the bay pony and led her out of the paddock. Walking up towards the stables, she explained to Leo that the mare was a smooth and comfortable ride. Her mouth was delightfully soft. She broke promptly into a gallop. 'She has a fire inside her, but she's gentle too.'

Leo asked what was wrong with her.

'She attacked me,' Lottie said. 'And I'm not sure why. Perhaps you might work it out.'

Lottie went back to the paddock for her gelding. They saddled up the horses and rode across the estate, Leo on the big grey, Lottie on the smaller mare. On the old gallops they let their mounts have their heads until the mare was wearied. They walked them back to the stables.

In the yard Lottie took her Pegasus. Leo unsaddled the mare and rubbed her down. As he slipped a rope halter on her she nuzzled his arm. He led her into the largest loose box, and held her with his right hand as he began to pull shut the bottom half of the door, which he did by feel, not taking his eyes off her for a moment. Then he felt the door being closed by someone else.

Lottie bolted the lower door. 'How does she seem?'

'Content,' Leo told her. The mare stood quiet. He patted and stroked her, and spoke to her, and rubbed her withers.

'Be careful,' Lottie said.

'I shall,' Leo told her. 'But I can't feel no violence in her.'

'Neither could I,' Lottie said. 'My hope is it was because I'm a woman.' She told him that she would climb to the hayloft and watch from up there. She hung a short, stout riding crop on the door, and told Leo he should keep it handy.

He frowned. 'I seem to recall you do not believe in such chastisement.'

Lottie smiled. 'For self-preservation I'll allow it,' she said.

Leo spoke to the mare, as he spoke to all horses, in his calm, gritty voice. He heard Lottie on the boards above his head. After a while he said, 'I reckon 'tis about time to turn her loose.' He left the halter on the mare, and simply loosened the rope and pulled it through its own loop and free. He stepped back and grasped the riding crop, and held it behind him, and waited. The bay mare watched him.

'I've seen plenty a horses,' Leo said, 'with everything from mischief to madness, and you can see it in their eyes. Their eyes change. Hers ain't changed.'

'Not yet,' Lottie said. 'Keep on your guard.'

'Maybe you're right, a woman was cruel to her.'

'She does seem content with you.'

Leo looked around the loose box. 'If she do go berserk, she might try to leap over the top half a the door.'

He stepped back and closed it. The morning sun was shut out, light dwindling in the windowless box. Leo could no longer see the mare's eyes, only the dark shape of her form as she walked to the far wall. She whinnied once, quietly. Leo moved towards her. And then it happened.

The bay mare spun away from the wall to face the man. It took Leo a moment of disbelief and hesitation before he began to react, but the horse's turn towards him gave him that moment. He lunged away to the right as the mare, her ears flattened, threw herself at him. He smelled the hot, herby smell of her breath as he twisted away. Her teeth missed his face and sank into his left shoulder.

Leo cried out as he felt the point of his shoulder, the flesh and the bone, crushed in the animal's jaws. The riding crop was held in the hand of that arm and it dropped from his fingers. He felt the mare's teeth slide off his shoulder and down his arm, the sleeve of his jacket tearing apart. Then her teeth got a grip. Before they could rip his flesh Leo regained his balance and, with the fingers of his free, right hand bunched into a fist, brought it down as hard as he could on the side of her nose.

The mare let go her teeth on Leo's arm and swung her head up towards his face again. He side-stepped and punched her a second time. She spun around, and Leo found himself facing her flexing hind legs. A kick would be a bone-breaker for sure, and there was no escape. He darted in towards her flank, and punched her as hard as he could in the belly. The mare recoiled. The man leaped back and away. Just as he reached the door it opened and Lottie pulled him out, then pushed the door shut and bolted both halves.

Leo leaned back against the stone wall, his eyes closed against the brightness of the sun, sweating, gasping, his chest heaving for breath. Lottie pulled his jacket off and led him to the stable bothy, Herb Shattock's old office, and sat him down. The left sleeve and whole side of his shirt was soaked with blood. She unbuttoned the shirt and took this off too, then she washed the blood from his arm and shoulder. Leo gritted his teeth and stared at a particular brick in the wall opposite and kept his gaze upon it. Lottie said she did not think anything was broken. Maybe the shoulder was torn somewhat, but the pain he must be feeling was mostly from the muscles.

'The bruising's already coming through,' she said.

Leo closed his eyes. 'I can feel it comin.'

'She's cut you, but it's not deep,' Lottie said. 'I don't think you need stitches.' She bathed Leo's arm in antiseptic, and bandaged the wounds.

Leo rolled himself a cigarette with his right hand. Though the fingers of his left hand were not numb, exactly, they felt oddly unwieldy. He rolled the cigarette as tight as he could. It was somewhat misshapen. He licked the paper, and lit it, and smoked with his eyes once more closed. When he opened them he saw that Lottie was watching him. Studying his face, or waiting for his verdict, he was not sure which. He shook his head, and said, 'She did that to you?'

'No. She was still tied up when she went for me, thank God, or I'm not sure I'd be here.'

Leo took a long drag on his cigarette and blew out the smoke and said, 'Well, I think we can rule out her fury bein towards women only.'

Lottie smiled. 'A savage equine demon. I suppose I'll have to sell her. For horse meat.'

Leo frowned. 'Please do not do that. Give me a little time, at least.'

'You'd go back in there with her?' Lottie asked.

Leo considered this proposition. Perhaps it was indeed insane. 'If I might wish to call myself a horseman,' he said, 'time's one thing I should give her. Let me think on it some, and her and me can have another go together.'

They sat in the bothy. Leo finished his cigarette. Lottie waited patiently for him to say more. Did he mean that he was thinking now? Or that he would go away and think about the problem another time, elsewhere, and now was simply recovering?

Leo opened his eyes and stood, wincing, and then he walked back across the stable yard. He opened the upper half of the door and looked in. The mare stood agitated in the far corner of the loose box. Lottie joined him and they stood together, watching the bay mare.

'If either of us went in there now, do you not think she'd go for us?' Lottie asked.

Leo watched the mare. Her breathing was becoming less febrile. 'I do not,' he said. He spoke further and Lottie realised he was speaking not to her but to the horse, telling her there was no need for her to be afeared, no one here planned to hurt her. The mare turned and walked across to the door. Lottie took a step back. The horse put her head over the top of the door, and nuzzled Leo's right arm. He raised his hand and rubbed her neck. Then he unbolted the lower half of the door and opened it.

'Leo,' Lottie said.

The man stepped through the doorway, and resumed stroking the bay mare, and speaking to her. She continued to nuzzle him, and rubbed away an itch on her ear against his undamaged shoulder.

'How can you be sure it's safe?' Lottie said. 'Please be careful.'

Leo turned to Lottie and said, 'It's safe. But if I close the top half a the door and cut out the light again, she'll rip me to pieces, I reckon.' He patted the mare's shoulder. 'I do suspect that someone mistreated her in the dark. In secret, I shouldn't doubt. Knowin in their heart a hearts it was wrong.' He scratched the mare's ear. 'This old girl here is afraid a the dark,' he said.

12

Most days were wet, with warm summer rain. Leo walked to the estate each day and rode the bay mare and turned her out in the paddock. After one week he rode the mare to the stable yard as usual where he unsaddled her and rubbed her down, but this day he took her back to the loose box. Inside he hitched her to the wall and gave her a good armful of hay. Then he left her, shutting both sections of the door behind him. He stood outside listening. The mare stopped eating. Leo made no noise. After a minute or two he could hear that the horse accepted that she was alone in the box, and resumed chewing her food.

'Tomorrow I shall do the same,' Leo told Lottie, when she returned from her veterinary visits. 'And the next day. And the next.'

'You don't need to,' she assured him. 'It's too much trouble. It doesn't make sense. I can buy another.'

Leo did not say anything.

'At least take Pegasus with you,' Lottie said. 'If you're going to go to and fro. It'll be good for him. Can he graze in your field?'

For a week Leo rode the big grey to the estate and exercised the bay mare and let her feed in the dark, then

rode the grey back to his smallholding. One evening
Myrtle Luscombe came to gaze upon the handsome
horse. Leo let him loose then came and stood beside
Myrtle.

'You're going to leave soon, aren't you?' she said.

Leo said that he probably was.

Myrtle said, 'Will you take me with you?'

Leo looked at her and his expression must have
betrayed his surprise, for she continued. 'I can't stay
any longer. All three of us clogged up here.'

'You want to skedaddle?'

'Do not tease me.'

'You're the youngest,' Leo said.

'I come eighteen in a month or two.'

'Or ten.' Leo sat on one of the sawn logs overlooking
his field. 'Wouldn't one of the others wish to push on
first?'

'Agnes won't.'

Leo nodded. He rolled himself a cigarette. 'I suppose
your father relies upon her most of all.'

Myrtle laughed. 'You could say.'

'I don't mean he don't rely on you, Myrtle, nor
on Ethel.' Leo lit his cigarette. 'Just that Agnes does
everythin in the house.'

'She's like a wife to him,' Myrtle said. 'You do know
that, don't you?'

'That's what I'm tryin to say. She cooks, cleans.
Grows vegetables. Tends poultry.'

'No,' Myrtle said. 'She is like a wife.'

'Do you mean …?' Leo asked.

Myrtle nodded.

Leo smoked and thought about this. 'I can't rightly believe that,' he said at length. 'Agnes don't seem abused.'

'No. Pa don't beat her. They bicker like some long-married couple, more like. Look, they're welcome to each other. The thing is, I don't want to drive no tractor.'

Leo turned and looked the girl in the eyes. 'You could get work anywhere,' he said.

The rain stopped. The weather grew warm. After a week of leaving the bay mare alone in the dark box, tied by a rope, munching hay, Leo did exactly the same except this time he closed the door from the inside and stood motionless, silent, in the gloom. The mare resumed eating. After a minute or two Leo began to speak, softly. The mare abruptly lost interest in the hay and turned towards the man. Leo stepped slowly towards her. The mare gave a whinny that became a drawn-out grunt of a sound, from deep in her belly. Then she jerked towards him.

The rope brought her head back with a jolt.

Leo continued to talk to the horse, telling her she was safe, he was no threat to her, there was no danger, but it did not mollify her. She exploded with a wild frenzy at the end of the rope. She lunged forward with a force that Leo feared would rip the tendons of her neck or break the thick rope, one or the other. He doubted the knots he'd tied. Then she changed her mind and swivelled around. Leo stepped back all the way to the door, just out of reach of the stabbing hind hooves that slashed towards him. He opened the door, and let himself out, leaving the upper half of the door open.

For three days Leo shut the horse in and stood in the box with her, and spoke to her, but he did not take a single step towards her before letting himself out.

On the fourth day Lottie lay on the boards above as Leo had once done, looking down upon Lottie and her tortured blue roan. Leo repeated the procedure with the mare then once more took steps in the dimness towards her. Again she lurched and lunged, and strained against the rope in her efforts to attack him, making noises he had never heard before from a horse. Screams and shrieks that faded into tremulous whispers then suddenly resumed as high-pitched wails of terror and aggression combined, before falling again, low and broken. Then the screams swelled once more.

Leo stood and spoke to the horse. The words were drowned out by her cries. Once, in the contortions of her violent struggle, the mare got her leg over the rope. Leo made a move to free her, but Lottie yelled down, 'No,' and he held back. Eventually, when she reared again, the horse freed the limb herself. The smell of her hot sweating body began to smoulder through the stables, overwhelming that of the sweet dry grass. The old chaff dust rose under her hooves in the loose box. Gradually her shrieks began to subside. Either she was tiring or she was losing heart in her wild exertions, for some of the violence ebbed out of them.

Lottie lay on the wooden boards, peering over the edge, her eyes adjusting to the gloom. How insane this was. How foolish she had been. To buy a horse she didn't need with a vice she couldn't cure. Even if the mare was put right, would she ever be able to use her for the plan she had in mind? And now Leo Sercombe, returned after all these years, was spending his time trying to cure her. Lottie gazed down into the ill-lit box, at the brooding horse, the still man. A tense and compelling spectacle. It occurred to Lottie that she'd never seen such patience. In partnership with such a man, perhaps they might achieve what she was dreaming of.

Leo soothed the horse, and waited. After a long while she finally stood motionless. Only a spasmodic tremor rippled beneath her dusty, sweaty skin. Leo took a step closer. The mare made no move. Scrutinising every twitch of her, the man eased closer, holding his right arm high on her neck as a protection should she swing her head at him. He reached out a hand and touched her withers, and felt her tremble. He smoothed her body and rubbed his hands along her neck and back. Still she did not move. He could feel the muscles beneath her skin soften, as she held herself less rigidly, and after some minutes she turned towards him. But she did not bite him.

Leo continued to talk to the mare and to handle her, and he only left her when she bent her head to resume her meal with the man standing there beside her. He looked up, and said into the space above, 'I don't believe her's cured yet, quite, but her's on the way now, for sure.'

There was no answer. Lottie must have grown bored and left. Leo could not blame her but he was amazed by the disappointment that bloomed like some malignant yeast in his gut. He walked to the door and opened it and stepped outside, eyes downcast from the glare of the sun. He turned and closed and bolted the lower door, and opened wide the upper door, clipping the hook to the wall. The bay mare munched her hay in the light-filled stable.

Leo watched the horse. He did not notice Lottie appear, but there she was, standing beside him.

'I thought you'd gone off,' he said.

'I just climbed down,' Lottie told him. 'I saw it all.'

Leo turned to find her looking at him.

'It is incredible,' she said. 'Your forbearance. After what she did to you.'

Leo did not shift his eyes from hers. Thus they stood. All his life when he'd felt another's gaze see too deep into him, it was unsettling, he had to look away. Yet he did not need or wish to avert his eyes from Lottie's. Did he want her to see into him? It was not explicable. 'Just took a bit a time,' he said.

Lottie shook her head. 'No,' she said. 'No. You really are a horseman, Leo Sercombe.'

They stood looking at each other. Then Lottie reached forward her right hand to Leo's left arm and leaned into him. With his right hand he pulled her towards him, and they kissed.

In Lottie's cottage they ate sausages, mashed potato and carrots. She apologised for the plainness of the fare. Leo said that he was used to finer food in her presence, recalling the trays brought to the stables as she tended her blue roan when it lay dying.

So, Lottie said, Leo Sercombe had become an epicurean now, had he? A gourmet? He smiled. 'No man', he said, 'who's done a whole stint in the Royal Navy can call himself a judge of fine food.'

They ate, and made love again. Lottie said, 'I knew it was you. Your eyes are still the colour of blackberries.'

'And you', Leo said, 'still have some freckles there, across the bridge a your nose.' He kissed them.

They spoke more then and in the days to come. Of what they had done, of what had happened to them. In time they reached things that were hard to describe. Leo wanted to tell Lottie how his blood had been frozen, and now she was sending fire through the veins and arteries of his existence.

Was that it?

Or that he had once been thrown into the future. Catapulted. But he did not wish to live there. He wanted to live in the present.

No, that was not it.

He had been away, he had been wandering, now he was home. But to his surprise home was not a field in the West Country. It was not even the estate. It was her.

'I remember the first time I saw you,' Lottie said. 'We must have been no more than five or six. Do you know what you were doing?'

Leo shook his head.

'You were climbing up the tail of a carthorse.'

Lottie said that when she looked into the eyes of a horse, she acknowledged that it does not see as much as humans do, nor understand much of what it sees. 'But I have the feeling that I glimpse what is behind the horse,' she said. 'What made her.'

'God?'

'I don't know. Is there a need to name it?'

Leo shook his head in agreement. 'I remember in Sunday School, Reverend Doddridge, he once said to us, "The eye that sees God is the same eye by which God sees me."'

Lottie nodded. 'Perhaps that is what I mean.'

Leo softened the bay mare. At his last Sunday lunch with the Luscombes he told them that he could not buy the field. He was leaving. Ethel said she might take over his cabin and his plot, it was time she had some distance from her sisters. Agnes said she was the eldest, if she fancied the cabin it was her right. Leo understood that the two girls were already consigning him to the past even as he sat beside them. Then Wally Luscombe spoke.

'I'll decide it,' he said. 'The cabin is Myrtle's. You two's needed here.'

Lottie began to let it be known that troubled people could visit her and her horses. She met doctors. Some were curious. Intrigued. She visited hospitals in Taunton and Exeter. Their first patients began to come to the estate.

If there was gossip, a local scandal, Lottie and Leo ignored it.

One evening in the early summer of 1929 they sat outside Lottie's cottage. Leo rolled a cigarette. They drank red French wine. Lottie watched the evening sky. Leo rested a hand on her belly.

'It may just be late,' she said.

'It may,' Leo agreed. 'I hope not.'

Lottie stroked the scar on his hand. She asked him how he'd got it. 'I was bitten by a conger eel,' he said, and told her of diving among the German wrecks.

Leo smoked, then said, 'Three times I might a died. Drowned each time. You may just recall the first a them.' He paused. Lottie waited. 'Perhaps one a them times I did,' he resumed. 'And this is some kind a dream, of what might have been.'

Lottie put her hand over his. 'Then I must be dead too,' she said, 'for I find myself in the same dream.'

Leo frowned. 'Was there a time you could have died?' he asked.

'I considered it,' Lottie said. She told him of her time as a vet's assistant and, as she had never told anyone else, of what Patrick Jago did to her.

After she had finished, Leo squeezed Lottie's hand. 'I am glad you did not go through with it.' He smiled. 'And what I said just now? 'Twas bull. Drivel. This is no dream. It is life, my love, our life, and now we shall live it.'

The old man took up his stick and went out of the back door of the house. He turned and put his mug of tea on the windowsill (whose slope brought the hot tea up to the lip of the mug on its lower side) and closed the door. He took the mug and walked around the side of the house and opened the door of his shed, placed the mug on the bench and switched on the electric light. Without this the shed was dim for, though one side had a long window, spiders' webs hung there all engorged with sawdust. Leo studied blocks of wood up on the high shelf while sipping his tea. Some he took down and examined. Each had a date inscribed. He chose a piece not much larger than six inches square.

The old man put the block of wood in the vice, and sawed a section off the side. He loosened the vice, shifted the wood and took off another slice. When he was content with the overall shape he eyeballed the block of ash and, using a bradawl, made a hole in the centre of what he had decreed should be its hollowed top. He placed a screw chuck on the lathe. He then drilled the hole in the middle of the ash deeper, using a bit the same size as the shank on the screw chuck, and screwed the wood onto the lathe.

He set the lathe turning and swung the rest across and used a spear-point chisel to take off the corner. The wood came off in ribbons towards him and in moments amassed like a head of hair or a wig of light brown shavings. He took the chisel off the wood and tossed the trimmings off to the side then resumed, flattening the base with the same chisel.

His tools were hand-forged carbon steel and he had recently ground them. He removed the block from the lathe and replaced the chuck with jaws, into which he placed the base of the wood and clamped the jaws tight.

Now he would hollow out the bowl. He used a half-inch bowl gouge, lining up the bevel of the gouge towards the centre. The lathe turning the wood created the power. All he had to do was to place his hand on the rest and ease the blade of the tool into the wood. He had done this many hundreds of times in his retirement yet still the pliancy of wood engrossed him. The power of the turning lathe. The subtlety of his handiwork. The sharp sweet scent of sawdust.

Oak was good, if somewhat hard to handle. Cherry was stable. Plum could have odd, appealing green and maroon patches. Laburnum held black wood and white wood in the same tree. Acacia was yellow, and possessed elegant rings. This piece of ash was nicely variegated in both the rings and the colour.

The old man turned the wooden bowl. He'd been born in the previous century. He would not make it to the next. His life had been eventful. His children and his grandchildren had heard one or two of his stories but there were more. They had their own lives to discover.

He had seen and done many things, especially in his early years. All would pass with him.

The base had not been carved true. When the bowl spun, it did so in an eccentric manner. He switched the bowl around again and measured and marked the base with callipers. He used a spindle gouge to rough out the base then the half-inch bowl gouge to shape the profile of the bowl, working up away from the base to the rim. What really determined how pleasing to the eye the bowl ended up, was the curve of the wood. Soon he was happy with the smoothness of the surface but he wished to improve it, so he used a one-inch sheer scraper. Then he rolled a spindle gouge over the outer lip of the base to give it a slightly rounded rim. The bottom of the bowl would be rarely seen, but it brought satisfaction to him to render it attractive.

His name was Leo Jonas Sercombe, son of Albert and Ruth, brother of Fred, Sid and Kizzie. He was the son of a horseman, and a horseman himself. He had lived as the slave of a tribe of gypsies, worked on a cruel farm, resided with an old tramp in a Cornish wood. He had served on a battleship in the Great War, and as a sailor and a diver in the Royal Navy for twelve years. Then a further year he had spent as a diver, resurrecting German ships from the deep of Scapa Flow. It was not understood back then that years of diving could affect a man's heart. He was lucky to have got out when he did.

He had known a few horsemen. The best of them was the master's groom when he was a boy, Herb Shattock.

Leo folded over a sheet of one hundred-and-eighty-grit sandpaper and smoothed the bowl further, then did so again with a two-hundred-and-forty-grit paper, finely abrading the wood still more.

The old man had loved but one woman, a meagre portion perhaps but enough for him. She once was beautiful and still was, though he allowed that others might not see it as he did, for when he beheld her he saw Lottie now and as she had always been, since they were children. His father had worked horses into the ground, as had others for hundreds, thousands, of years. Leo had assumed he would do the same. Man's technological ingenuity brought an end to such work, but Lottie saw how man and horse might work together in an entirely new way.

Only now, envisioning Lottie in the sawdusty shed, did he remember that she was two years gone under the ground. She had gone before him. He missed her so much. Death was final yet there was more to it than that, a mystery no man could fathom. And it would be his turn soon enough.

The wooden bowl turned on the lathe, under the light of the bare electric bulb. Outside, the afternoon dimmed into evening. Leo held a lump of beeswax against the bowl. He rubbed it into the wood with a rag. The surplus he wiped off with a clean cloth. This bowl was for their granddaughter, soon to be thirteen years old. She could keep her hairbands, rings, other trinkets in it. The old man could not recall in truth whether or not he had given her one much the same the year before. He suspected that his family had all been inundated with his wooden bowls. Well, he would turn them while he could. He would turn them on the turning lathe. Time proceeds along its ever-onward spiral. We join it for a moment.

We are like horses, turning in the dust of a river bed on a clear morning, turning in the sand as the mist rolls over the water, hooves prancing, bodies steaming in the morning light, their muscled flanks rippling, revelling in their freedom.

ACKNOWLEDGEMENTS

Thanks to my editor, Alexandra Pringle, and to Allegra Le Fanu, Marigold Atkey, Philippa Cotton, Amber Mears-Brown, Angelique Tran Van Sang, Lynn Curtis and all at Bloomsbury, and to Anton Mueller, Lauren Hill and Grace McNamee at Bloomsbury USA.

And thanks to my agent, Victoria Hobbs, and to Jennifer Custer, at A.M. Heath.

Special thanks to: Simon Jackson, Acting Deputy Chief Operating Officer, the Royal Veterinary College; Tom Mercer, wood turner; David Charles-Edwards, ornithologist; Richard Stanley, for the James Baldwin quote; Rick Stroud for such helpful notes and horse knowledge; Doug and Tinker Stoddart for suggesting a list of Principal Characters; Hania Porucznik for her sharp red pen.

Paul Evans's nature notes in the *Guardian* have been a regular nudge to scrutinise the natural world through which one moves. The books of Fred Archer likewise, a continual inspiration.

Helpful equine books include:
Elementary Lectures on Veterinary Science by Henry Thompson

Memoirs of a Veterinary Surgeon by Reginald Hancock
Healers on Horseback by R.H. Smythe
Fifty Years a Veterinary Surgeon by Sir Frederick
  Hobday
Handling Horses by Colonel P. D. Stewart
Equitation by Henry Wynmalen
Bracken Horse by Gareth Dale provided the story of the
  bay mare frightened of the dark.

Leo's encounter with a grey seal quotes from Ted
Hughes's encounter with a roedeer as described in a
footnote in *Moortown Diary*, while two horses in a field
are borrowed from Melissa Harrison's *At Hawthorn
Time*.

The starting point of the Battle of Jutland chapter
was my grandfather's experience. Steuart Arnold Pears
was a young gunnery lieutenant on the light cruiser
HMS *Falmouth*, which was caught up at the centre of
the maelstrom. His naval record includes: *Showed great
aptitude in Gunnery controlled fire in Jutland Battle with
coolness and in other ways, showed marked zeal & ability,
good manner with men.*

HMS *Queen Mary* set off from the Firth of Forth
with a crew of 1,286. 1,266 were lost. Of the twenty
survivors, eighteen were hauled out of the North Sea
by British destroyers, two by German boats.

The passage on the Battle is threaded through with
excerpts from *Jutland 1916, Death in the Grey Wastes*
by Nigel Steel and Peter Hart, a masterly telling of the
monumental naval battle through memoirs, letters and
recollections of those who were there.

Further detail was given by Alexander Fullerton's fine novel *The Blooding of the Guns.*

Able Seamen by Brian Lavery illuminated life on the lower deck of the Navy.

The True Glory by Max Arthur and *Gone a Long Journey* by Leonard Charles Williams were also helpful.

There are many books on Scapa Flow, on the scuttle and subsequent salvage of the German Imperial Fleet. Especially helpful were:

Scapa Flow by Malcolm Brown and Patricia Meehan, another brilliant history book composed largely of the memories of those who were there
The Grand Scuttle by Dan van der Vat
The Wrecks of Scapa Flow by David M. Ferguson
Jutland to Junkyard by S. C. George
Cox's Navy by Tony Booth was particularly rich and extensive.

Salvage of the scuttled ships continued long after the events described in this novel. In the 1930s Metal Industries, a company which had taken over from Ernest Cox, sold much scrap metal from salvaged ships to Krupp of Essen, in Germany. Krupp had constructed most of the ships, and their armour and guns, in the first place. They now bought back this same metal, and began to use it in their building of Hitler's navy.

Later, in 1945, at the moment of the explosion of the world's first atomic bomb, at Hiroshima, the earth's atmosphere was polluted by nuclear radiation. In the process of steel manufacture, enormous quantities of air are sucked in. All steel forged since 1945 therefore contains traces of radiation. Untainted steel is essential for extremely delicate scientific instruments, such as those used in nuclear medicine. The still unsalvaged scuttled ships of Scapa Flow remain the greatest resource of such high-grade, untainted steel to this day. Some of the Scapa Flow steel was used in the Voyager II spacecraft. Salvage continues ...

The wrecks have had other effects. www.scapaflow-wrecks.com was fascinating and helpful:

The underwater wildlife is one of the quiet marvels of Scapa Flow. On a seabed comprising mainly of silt and sand, the wrecks have become rich artificial reefs. Each wreck is now a thriving ecosystem – benthic (ocean bottom) animals such as starfish and urchins cover the wrecks and inject vibrancy and colour. The multitude of nooks and crannies provide the perfect hiding spot for crabs and lobsters, while the wrecks teem with fish.

Tim Pears is the author of ten novels, including *In the Place of Fallen Leaves* (winner of the Hawthornden Prize and the Ruth Hadden Memorial Award), *In a Land of Plenty* (made into a ten part BBC series), *Landed* (short-listed for the IMPAC Dublin Literary Award 2012 and the Royal Society of Literature Ondaatje Prize 2011, winner of the MJA Open Book Awards 2011) and, most recently, *The Horseman* and *The Wanderers*, the first two books in The West Country Trilogy. He is the winner of the Lannan Award and Writer in Residence at Cheltenham Festival of Literature and Royal Literary Fund Fellow at Oxford Brookes University. He lives in Oxford with his wife and children.

timpears.com

A NOTE ON THE TYPE

The text of this book is set in Fournier. Fournier is derived from the *romain du roi*, which was created towards the end of the seventeenth century from designs made by a committee of the Académie des Sciences for the exclusive use of the Imprimerie Royale. The original Fournier types were cut by the famous Paris founder Pierre Simon Fournier in about 1742. These types were some of the most influential designs of the eight and are counted among the earliest examples of the 'transitional' style of typeface. This Monotype version dates from 1924. Fournier is a light, clear face whose distinctive features are capital letters that are quite tall and bold in relation to the lower-case letters, and *decorative italics, which show the influence of the calligraphy of Fournier's time.*